ATONEMENT

for

Emily Adams

To God be the glory!
Susan R Lawrence

By Susan Lawrence

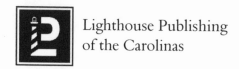

Lighthouse Publishing
of the Carolinas

PRAISE FOR *ATONEMENT FOR EMILY ADAMS*

Emily Adams loves her husband, her job, and her rosy future, but in one irretrievable instant, her world turns upside down. One tragedy touches the lives of many, and anguish spreads like a stain—but a far greater grace stands ready to heal. In a gentle, straightforward style, the author touches sensitive places with tender compassion. This story will wring your heart, but the satisfying resolution will leave you smiling.

~ Yvonne Anderson
Author of *The Story in the Stars*
2012 ACFW Carol Award Finalist

A devastating accident leaves one family grappling with tragedy, while another family deals with guilt and its consequences. Susan Lawrence's debut novel gives readers much to like: interesting characters, a well-crafted plot, and a heart-rending scenario that offers plenty of conflict and ponders deep faith issues. Susan's deft hand with characters and interpersonal conflicts reveals a story that is profound in its meaning. You don't want to miss this one. I'm looking forward to her next novel.

~ Adam Blumer
Author of *Fatal Illusions* and *The Tenth Plague*

Susan R. Lawrence is an accomplished storyteller who weaves realistic characters into this engaging tale of guilt and grace. *Atonement for Emily Adams* shows how the ability to forgive ourselves and others comes only through true atonement.

~ Glenda Mathes
Speaker and author of *Little One Lost: Living with Early Infant Loss* and *A Month of Sundays: 31 Meditations on Resting in God*

ATONEMENT FOR EMILY ADAMS BY SUSAN LAWRENCE
Published by Lighthouse Publishing of the Carolinas
2333 Barton Oaks Dr., Raleigh, NC, 27614

ISBN 978-1-941103-01-2
Copyright © 2014 by Susan Lawrence
Cover design by Ted Ruybal, www.wisdomhousebooks.com
Book design by Reality Info Systems, www.realityinfo.com

Available in print from your local bookstore, online, or from the publisher at:
www.lighthousepublishingofthecarolinas.com

For more information on this book and the author contact: srlauthor@mchsi.com

Brought to you by the creative team at LighthousePublishingoftheCarolinas.com:
Eddie Jones, Rowena Kuo, and Andrea Merrell.

Library of Congress Cataloging-in-Publication Data
Lawrence, Susan
Atonement for Emily Adams/ Susan Lawrence 1st ed.

Printed in the United States of America

Acknowledgments

Writing a novel is a journey of many steps, uphill and down, over and under obstacles, with a destination that sometimes seems remote. Thankfully, there are those who accompany us, coming alongside for a portion or the entire journey. They show direction when we think we are lost, encouragement when the path is difficult, and a hand up when we've fallen. "Thank you" does not seem adequate for those who have walked the journey with me.

To the medical personnel who gave advice: Jeff Doolittle, Craig Wood, and Lois Nelson, thank you. To my nephew Curt Wolfe, thank you for your legal expertise. To the policemen I consulted, Jeff Robinson and Eric Hoffman, thank you. Thank you to Linsey Hoppestad for her advice on funeral homes. To the doctors at Indianola Veterinary Clinic, thank you for your knowledge on ailing kittens. Jean Flaws, your input on school business managers was invaluable. Thank you to Dave Logemann for his input on engineering firms. To my critique groups, Sharpened Pencils and The Three Amigos, I cannot imagine taking this journey without you. Andrea Merrell, you were wonderful—not only your excellent editing, but your positive and encouraging words and attitude lifted my writing to a new level. To my publisher, Eddie Jones, and Lighthouse Publishing of the Carolinas, thank you for taking a chance on me. And last but not least, thanks to my dear husband, my first listener to the jagged rough draft and in all ways the foundation I lean upon.

You each have been God's blessing to me on this journey. To God be the glory.

CHAPTER 1

Children skipped and darted past the office window and spilled onto the playground like showers of confetti. An unusually warm Missouri afternoon in mid-February had freed them from the confines of inside recess, and their laughter pulled Emily Adams away from her work. As she gazed out the window, one pony-tailed girl looked up and lifted a tiny hand in greeting. Emily smiled and waved back. A new, sweet longing twisted its way into her heart and the spreadsheet full of numbers on her computer was momentarily forgotten.

Emily loved the position of business manager at Maple Valley Community Schools. A little perk of the job was her office that overlooked the playground. Watching the children scamper outside the window brightened her days. Emily's gaze shifted to the oak desk, where, amid the stacks of papers, stood a picture of her dark-haired husband with his constant, award-winning grin. She and Nate discussed children frequently—how many, what they would name them, even who would read the bedtime story. Her hand briefly touched her belly. Just last week they had made the decision for her to discontinue taking the pill. Emily sighed in contentment as she pivoted in her chair and pulled herself back to the computer.

She'd always liked working with numbers. Making them add up correctly was like solving a puzzle—although lately, the puzzles seemed to be piling up while she painstakingly tried to solve them.

Two hours later, Emily logged off her computer and fished car keys out of her bag. Long purple shadows covered the empty playground as she slipped into a red peacoat and tugged on matching gloves. Her Camry was the only car left in the parking lot.

Emily pulled out of the parking lot, humming softly to the soothing music from a classical station. She wondered if Nate had already put the chicken on the grill and began to mentally inventory her refrigerator shelves. *Lettuce, check. Dressing, check. Milk …*

Abruptly, she turned the Camry west, squinting into the last rays of the setting sun. She'd promised to bring home a gallon of milk. She'd turn and circle back to the Super Valu. You'd think Nate was a teenager the way he drank the white stuff.

Emily slowed as she approached an intersection on an unfamiliar side street. The maples that gave the town its name spread their branches over the road like an embrace. By May, the trees would form a leafy canopy, but tonight the bare limbs only pointed bony fingers.

A lone bicycle rider, head bent as he pedaled hard, hugged the edge of the pavement. *Probably trying to get home before dark,* she thought.

She checked the oncoming traffic and pulled over, giving the rider plenty of room. Carefully watching the rearview mirror, she pulled back into her lane when the rider was safely behind her.

Movement to the right caught her eye. Her foot automatically stomped on the brake, but not fast enough. A boy, eyes wide with fear, mouth open, suddenly appeared in front of her. Her brakes squealed in protest as she desperately willed the car to stop. After one horrifying thump, the windshield crackled into a spider's web and the child disappeared from sight. Tires screeched and then there was a deafening silence.

Emily turned the car off. A scream broke the silence, but it took a moment to realize the sound came from her own mouth. She forced it to close and somehow stumbled from the car.

The bicyclist, a wiry middle-aged man, dropped his bike and sprinted to the front of the Camry.

A boy who looked to be about ten years of age lay draped over the curb. His eyes were open, staring. One arm circled his head as if to protect it. On the opposite side of the street, the skateboard that had projected him into her path rested quietly, one wheel still spinning.

The bicyclist fumbled in his pocket, produced a cell phone, and punched in numbers. His voice seemed loud and harsh. "We need an ambulance on Eighth Street. A child's been hit by a car. Please come quickly."

Emily pointed at the number posted on the house, but couldn't make her voice work.

"Twenty-two-seventeen." The bicyclist gave the address, his own name and cell number, then dropped the phone back into his pocket. He knelt by the boy and glanced briefly at Emily. "Do you know CPR?"

She shook her head as numbness spread through her body. Why didn't the boy move? Why didn't he look at them?

Bending his head, the man blew into the boy's mouth and gently pressed on his chest. Emily watched helplessly.

"Isaiah! Isaiah! Time to come in now." The shout drifted across the yard, probably a mother calling her child in for supper.

"Isaiah!" When the voice called a third time, Emily knew. The blue eyes, the thatch of blond hair, the sturdy little body ... he had to be Isaiah. A small, pony-tailed woman walked around the side of a two-story Colonial house.

"Nooooo!" The woman raced across the yard and dropped to the grass beside the still form. "Is ... is ... he breathing?" she gasped.

The man shook his head as he continued CPR. The woman shot a look at Emily.

"I'm so sorry," Emily whispered.

In the distance, sirens wailed. The police car arrived first. The driver angled behind Emily's car, blocking the street from the east. Lights continued to blink red and blue as the officer leaped out and strode toward the group gathered by the curb. With a quick glance, he took in the boy, the bicyclist who never paused in the CPR, the woman on the grass, and Emily.

"Are you his mother?" He gently touched the weeping woman's shoulder.

Her head bobbed, sobs punctuating her sentences. "I was fixing supper. He was riding his skateboard ... we told him never to be without his helmet ... never to go in the street." Her hand reached out to stroke the boy's pale cheek.

The shrill siren of the ambulance smothered her voice. It approached from the west, lights flashing, and stopped near the curb. Two people in green coveralls jumped from the cab and immediately took charge. The young female EMT placed a bag valve mask over the boy's face and took over chest compressions, never pausing in the rhythm. The bicyclist backed away, looking relieved, and sank to the ground. The other EMT, an older man with a gray mustache, appeared to have come from a construction job. Work boots peeped out from under the coveralls, and the arm that held the clipboard was streaked with sawdust.

"Name? Birth date?" He quickly jotted down information on the form and then jogged to the back of the ambulance. Within seconds, he yanked out a stretcher and, with his partner's help, maneuvered the boy onto it.

Emily watched silently. She had never felt so helpless or afraid.

A car skidded to a stop behind the ambulance, and a tall, broad-shouldered man in a business suit stepped out. A moment passed as he stared at the group circled on the street. Then with a cry that Emily could not understand, he bolted across the yard.

"Isaiah!" He leaned over the stretcher, then raised his head and looked around. "What happened to my son? What's going on?"

The policeman held him back, speaking softly and gesturing with his free hand. The mother moved closer and leaned into him. The man put a protective arm around her, but continued shouting his questions. "Who did this? Who hit him?"

The two EMTs lifted the stretcher into the ambulance, and the mother stepped away, following the stretcher inside. With a hard look in Emily's direction, the man mouthed something unintelligible, returned to his car, and sped off.

★★★★★★★

Josh Nelson clutched the steering wheel, spinning it right, then left, trying to keep the ambulance in his line of vision. The joy of his life lay on a stretcher inside and he couldn't go fast enough to change the events. The image of his son, pale and still, flashed in his mind without his willing it. Where had the skateboard helmet been?

A flash of memory—holding his newborn son, red, tiny, and wrinkled—tenderly cupping his hands around the fragile head, and promising God he would protect this precious gift forever. A blond toddler racing to meet him, the baby-bird voice chirping, "Daddy, Daddy, you're home." And the warm, sweet smell as he swooped him up, nuzzling his son's neck while his wife looked on.

Where had Stephani been tonight? How had she let this happen? And who was responsible—the woman standing by the white car? He had to know, but that would have to wait. Right now he had to make sure his son was okay.

Vivid memories continued to fill his mind. Christmas last year with the joyous clutter of tree and gifts and shiny piles of crumpled paper came back to him. Isaiah's face had shone with delight as he tore open the box. "I got it! I got my skateboard—finally." He had clutched it to him like a two-year-old with a teddy bear. Josh's mom stood beaming at her grandson.

His mom! He needed to let her know about the accident. She would pray, and they needed prayer. He shifted a hip and groped for his phone. He followed the ambulance through an intersection on yellow, quickly glanced down to find his mom's listing, and pushed SEND.

"Mom?" His voice croaked and he tried to clear it so he could leave a somewhat coherent message on her voicemail. "There's been an accident. Isaiah was hit by a car. They're taking him by ambulance … Memorial Hospital … please pray." He pushed the button to end the call and laid the phone on the seat beside him.

His mom would call the rest of the family, mobilizing the troops—Sara, his take-charge big sister and Carrie Ann, his twin sister and best friend. They would pray and Isaiah would be fine. He would open his incredible blue eyes and laugh about his adventure of riding in the ambulance.

The wail of the siren faded and the ambulance turned into the driveway of Memorial Hospital. Josh followed closely, swinging the car wildly into a parking spot. He slammed the car door and raced into the emergency room entrance.

"My son," he gasped out, "… in an ambulance." Surely they wouldn't make him stop and show his insurance card now.

"I'll take you to him," someone said. The woman led the way to a room where Stephani hovered as they moved his son's still, pale form to a bed. His eyes were closed and he didn't laugh. Relentlessly, they continued CPR.

And Josh wept.

CHAPTER 2

As the scream of the ambulance faded into the distance, Emily had the eerie feeling she was watching the scene from somewhere other than her own body, maybe like those near-death experiences when people hover above themselves. She saw her car, the driver's door still hanging open. Numbly, she moved to shut it.

"Ma'am?" The policeman strode toward her. "Are you the driver of this car?"

She nodded. "My door …" She couldn't formulate complete sentences or coherent thoughts.

"I'm Police Chief Steve Geiken. Do you have your registration and driver's license?"

Emily nodded again and pointed. "In the car."

"Please get them and we'll talk."

With thick steps, Emily plodded to the car, fished her registration out of the glove compartment, and grabbed her driver's license out of her purse. She slammed the car door, the noise loud and metallic.

A second police car pulled up where the ambulance had been and the driver maneuvered his vehicle so it blocked the street from the west. Chief Geiken walked over and the two officers talked briefly, while Emily reminded herself to breathe.

The second policeman approached the bicyclist, who talked fast, gesturing with his hands and occasionally glancing at Emily while the officer wrote furiously on a clipboard.

When the chief approached her, she handed over her license and registration. One of the large maple trees stood near the curb and Emily leaned her back against it, her legs wobbly and threatening to give way. She whispered, "Is he, is the little boy going to be okay?"

Chief Geiken glanced up from the papers, a frown hardening his face. "I don't know, ma'am. The EMTs are doing all they can."

The second policeman approached and waited. The chief handed her documents over to him and asked him to run a check. He turned back to Emily.

"Let's have your version of what happened." He opened a folder and stood with pen poised.

Emily tried to wipe the cobwebs from her brain. She couldn't remember. She was driving home, but why was she on this street? Milk. She needed milk.

"I needed a gallon of milk …" Emily choked back the stream of tears. In halting sentences, she chronicled everything from the time she left the school parking lot until Isaiah's eyes met hers. The chief wrote as she spoke, occasionally asking a question or prompting her to continue.

"I heard … a thump. He was right there." Her finger pointed to the image that still hung in front of her—so different from the face of the pony-tailed girl at her window earlier that afternoon. The images assaulted her and she let the flood loose. Tears streamed down her cheeks as she frantically searched her jacket pockets for a tissue. Giving up the search, she sniffed like a child and wiped her cheek with the back of her hand. The deputy returned and handed Chief Geiken the registration and license. A small knot of people had gathered on the other side of the street. Neighbors, maybe, or just curious onlookers. Emily felt as if she were on display.

Overhead, a streetlight blinked once, twice, and then glowed steadily. Emily stared at the circle of light it cast.

Time for all the children to go inside.

The chief snapped the folder shut. "We need to take some pictures and measurements. We'll be impounding your car for a few days until the investigation is complete. Is there someone you can call?"

Call? Of course, she would call Nate and he would take care of her. She breathed a sigh of relief. He would make things right again.

"My husband. I need to call my husband." Where was her phone?

"Where's my purse? I need my purse." Emily glanced wildly about.

"Is that what you're looking for?" The chief pointed to her shoulder, where her purse dangled by its strap.

"Phone. In here … somewhere." She groped among the contents of the leather bag. When she retrieved the phone, she saw five missed calls. Nate must be frantic with worry. She punched in his number and waited.

★★★★★★★

Nate Adams stepped into the kitchen and opened the refrigerator. Tipping the jug of milk to his mouth, he drained the last drops. He rinsed the jug at the sink and dropped it in the recycling bin.

He used the remote to switch on the TV in the family room. A pass-through window allowed him to keep one eye on the news while he was in the kitchen. He pulled vegetables out of the refrigerator and tossed them on the counter. As he chopped and filled the salad bowls, he glanced out the window at the setting sun. Where was Emily? It wasn't unusual for her to stay late at work, especially the third week of the month when she was busy with the payroll. But this was the first week, and she hadn't mentioned any projects that would keep her. Maybe she remembered they needed milk, but it didn't take that long to go by the Super Valu and pick up a gallon. And why wasn't she answering her phone?

Nate slid the salads into the refrigerator, made a pass over the counter with the towel, and retreated to the family room. He tried to reach Emily one more time. Still no answer. He laid his phone on the end table and switched the TV to the sports channel before he kicked back in the recliner. Thirty minutes later, the phone jolted him awake.

"Emily?" Nate flipped the chair upright as he grabbed the phone.

Her voice sounded tiny and far away. He only heard terse words and short phrases. "Accident … little boy … police. Please come. I … I need you."

"Where are you, Em?" Nate reached in his pocket for his keys.

There was a pause and he could hear her, sounding even more remote, evidently asking someone, "Where am I?"

"Twenty-two-seventeen …" She broke off again. "What street?"

"Eighth Street. I'm on Eighth Street," she repeated.

Nate wondered why his wife, who had a memory like a calculator, was having trouble remembering a simple address.

"Twenty-two-seventeen Eighth Street, right?" Nate asked, but she had already ended the call.

It took less than ten minutes to drive across town. Two sets of blinking lights were visible as soon as he turned off the main road. Nate pulled over and parked.

He didn't see her at first. There were little groups of people standing everywhere. Yellow and black police tape sectioned off an entire area of the street. Emily's car squatted directly in the middle. A tall, broad-shouldered policeman strode past, carrying a clipboard. A camera dangled from a strap around his neck. Where was Emily? Apprehension turned to dread and twisted through him, knotting his insides.

Then, with a rush of relief, he saw her. She sat on the curb, knees drawn up and head down, her strawberry blonde hair spread like a curtain on each side of her face. The lights from the police cars cast strange red and blue shadows on her back.

"Emily!" Nate raced down the sidewalk. She looked up, but her eyes were dull. He dropped to the curb beside her and pulled her close.

"Are you okay?" He brushed the hair off her face, looking for bumps or bruises.

The policeman he had seen earlier strode toward him. "You her husband?"

Nate stood up, but Emily remained on the curb. He took her hand and pulled her to her feet before he answered. "Yeah. Is my wife in trouble? I couldn't hear her very well when she called."

"She hit a boy, a little guy on a skateboard."

"Hit a boy? Didn't you see him?" Nate stared down at Emily.

Her hair flew across her cheeks as she shook her head. "No … didn't see …"

"Is she … can I take her home?"

"Not yet. We want her to wait until we finish here, in case we have more questions."

"The car?" Nate glanced at the Camry, as if the vehicle were the culprit.

The policeman shook his head. "We'll impound the car until our investigation is complete."

Nate looked at the car again. They couldn't have driven it home anyway, not with a crumpled hood and shattered windshield.

Emily sank to the curb again. Nate folded his lanky form beside her, curving a protective arm around her shoulders. For what seemed like hours, they watched the two policemen take notes, measurements, and pictures from every angle. Occasionally, Chief Geiken would stride over with another question. Finally, he gave permission for them to leave.

"Mrs. Adams?"

Emily rose to her feet, clutching Nate's forearm for support.

"We're finished for now, but I'll be calling in our state patrol collision investigators. They'll want to question you. It'll be a few days before we know if you'll be charged with anything."

Charged? Nate's mind spun out of control. *With what? Reckless Driving? Hitting a pedestrian? What if the boy dies? Maybe even ... murder? Could that be possible?* Nate had a brief image of visiting Emily in prison. A chilling finger of fear shuddered through him. He shifted his weight as Emily pressed herself against him, nodding her head at the chief.

The chief turned to Nate. "You might want to take her to the emergency room. She's in shock and may need something to help her sleep tonight."

"Thanks, I will." Nate picked up the purse lying on the grass and, with Emily trailing behind him, led the way to his Explorer. She climbed into the passenger seat and he laid the bag carefully in her lap. Her hands covered her face, but as Nate climbed in the driver's seat, he could hear her soft sobs.

CHAPTER 3

Donna Nelson hurried through the wide automatic doors into the emergency room. An information desk stood to her right.

"My grandson was brought here by ambulance. He was hit by a car." She tried to keep her voice from trembling. "Isaiah Nelson. He's ten."

A stout, middle-aged woman with white-blonde hair looked at her over the top of her glasses. "I'll check on him, honey. Just a minute." One red manicured fingernail traced down the computer screen. "Nelson … Nelson … Isaiah." The eyes peered over the glasses again. "Yes, the doctor is with him now. You're his grandmother?"

"Yes, I'm Grandma Nelson." Donna shifted her weight nervously. She resisted the urge to rush through the hospital looking for her grandson on her own.

"I'll let them know you're here." The glasses now dangled on a sparkly chain across her ample chest. High heels tapped down the hall and through swinging doors.

Donna continued what she had been doing since she got the call from her son. *God, please spare our Isaiah. He's such a special child. Please don't take him yet. He's so young. Let him be okay. Let me see him laugh and run and play again.*

The swinging doors swooshed open and a red fingernail beckoned her. "You may come back, Mrs. Nelson."

The room where the receptionist led her was crowded with medical personnel. Crisp orders were being given as they bustled about the much-too-still form on the bed. Isaiah's body, almost as tall as hers, seemed small again. A bag covered his face and a tall man pressed rhythmically on his bare chest. An IV was attached to one slender arm.

Huddled in a corner, arms wrapped tightly around each other, stood her daughter-in-law and son. Josh was a taller version of Isaiah. Same intense blue eyes, same unruly shock of blond hair. His eyes lifted briefly to hers, and the anguish she read in them made her long to hold and comfort him as she had when he was a child.

Suddenly, the doctor stepped away from Isaiah.

"No, no, please don't stop," Stephani pleaded as she broke from her husband's arms.

The doctor shook his head and looked uncomfortable. "I'm sorry; we've done all we can. Your son is not responding. Technically, his life ended when the car hit him. CPR was given at the scene, in the ambulance, and here. We couldn't get his heart started again. You may stay here with him as long as you like. We'll get the equipment out of the way." With a look at one of the nurses, he said quietly, "Time of death, seven thirty-three."

The nurse gently removed the bag from Isaiah's face and the IV from his arm, then handed the doctor a soft white blanket. Donna watched him tuck it around Isaiah as carefully as if her grandson could feel the warmth of it. With gentle movements, he wiped the blood from Isaiah's face. After a quick nod at Donna, he slipped from the room.

Stephani's sobs sounded harsh and loud in the tiny space. As the room emptied, Stephani flung herself across the bed. Donna watched, heartbroken, as her daughter-in-law stroked Isaiah's hair and called his name over and over. Josh stood behind her, one hand on her shoulder, the other reaching to touch the little body on the bed.

Donna moved to stand beside her son. His face twisted as he looked at her. "Mom, God wouldn't really take him, would He? Last week Isaiah told me he wanted to be a missionary in South America with Aunt Carrie Ann."

Donna nodded. "He told me too."

"Surely God wouldn't take a child who wanted to be a missionary."

Donna couldn't answer. She opened her arms to her son and he wept on her shoulder, sharp, raspy sobs. Donna's own tears trickled down her cheeks and dripped in his hair.

After a few minutes, Josh swallowed his tears and stepped out of her embrace. He made his way to the opposite side of the bed from Stephani and took Isaiah's hand.

Donna sat on a cold plastic chair. Outside the room, the clatter of stretchers, equipment, and medical personnel flowed in a steady current, but here, time had stopped. A nurse swished by, paused briefly at the door, then hurried off.

Donna reached in her purse and found the small Bible she carried. It fell open to the twenty-third Psalm. She read the comforting passage. When she came to the words, *Even though I walk through the shadow of the valley of death,* she paused. *No, God. Not Isaiah.* But next came, *I will fear no evil, for you are with me.* How comforting to be reminded of God's continual presence.

She stood again and went to Stephani, who glanced up, eyes red and swollen.

"Thanks for coming," Stephani mumbled.

Donna gave her a long hug before she turned to the body of her grandson. She patted the still hand lying on the blanket. It was so cold. She'd held his hand for countless walks and adventures. When he'd gotten older, he no longer held her hand, but ran ahead, leading the way for their explorations in the woods. Now, she would never again walk with him on this earth. A small sob escaped her and she covered her mouth with her hand. She had to be strong for Josh and Stephani.

Two nurses entered, their white shoes whispering across the floor. The younger nurse hung back slightly and let the tall, older woman with gray hair approach the bed. Sympathetic eyes gazed through round silver glasses. "Mr. and Mrs. Nelson?"

Josh raised his eyes and nodded.

"We're sorry for your loss. We know you're grieving, but we need to ask you a couple of questions. We're part of the organ donation team here at Memorial. We'd like you to consider donating Isaiah's organs. Some parents who lose a child find this is a way they can honor his or her memory."

"Can we think about it?" Stephani's voice was low and muffled as she stared down at the blanket.

"Absolutely." The nurse's gray curls bobbed emphatically. "We want to give you some time to discuss this privately. We'll check back later."

Stephani sniffled and reached across Isaiah's midsection for Josh's hand. "If there's no way we can have him back ..." Her voice broke.

Josh finished the sentence for her. "We should help. That's what Isaiah would want." He looked over at Donna. "Mom?"

"Honey, that's your decision, and Stephani's. I support whatever will bring you healing."

"Healing?" Josh's voice had a grim undertone. "I'll never be healed of this."

★★★★★★★

The dark shadows of night were lifting as Josh and Stephani drove home from the hospital. But Josh knew the darkness would never lift from his heart. Everything bright and joyful and sweet had been swept from his life.

When they reached the house, he parked outside the garage. Someone, perhaps the police, had placed Isaiah's skateboard beside the driveway. Josh helped Stephani from the car. With his arm securely around his wife, he walked her inside where she sank down on the couch.

Josh stroked the hair off her face. "Can I get you anything? Water? Blanket?"

"No. I'm going to lie here on the couch for a bit."

Stephani looked lost and confused.

"Call me if you need me. I'm going to put the car in the garage."

Josh moved the skateboard, drove the car inside, and parked. He took all of Isaiah's skateboarding paraphernalia to the rear of the garage and stacked it carefully where Stephani wouldn't have to see it.

The doctor at the hospital had given Stephani some pills to take so she would sleep. When Josh went back in the house, she was curled on the couch, her head resting on the pillowed arm. Clutched to her chest was the stuffed rabbit Isaiah had always carried with him when he was small. One long, fuzzy ear drooped across her arm. Josh touched the plush animal with his finger and wondered where she'd found it. After a moment, he unfolded the afghan lying across the back of the couch and covered Stephani.

Since Josh had refused a sleep-aid, he knew it would be useless to try to sleep. He needed something physical to do, something to numb both his body and brain. In the three-season room off the kitchen, there was a treadmill he and Stephani used when they couldn't make it to the gym. He turned on the machine and stepped up. His entire body was tensed for action.

When he finally switched it off, he was gasping, muscles limp with exhaustion. Tears mingled with the sweat and he brushed a towel across his face.

He wandered into the office where he often spent hours working on projects. With a sharp twist of new pain, he regretted every minute spent there, every minute away from Isaiah.

This day had been spent working on plans for a Memorial Hospital addition. It had seemed so large, so significant, only a few hours before. Now, all he could think was if he had left work ten minutes earlier, he would have been home and Isaiah would have followed him into the house. And he would be alive.

They never should have allowed the skateboard. Isaiah had begged for at least two years and, finally, for Christmas, they relented and purchased a top-of-the-line model. Isaiah had been thrilled. In January, when snow and ice covered the driveway, he practiced in the unfinished part of the basement. But the last few weeks, in the unseasonably warm weather, he spent every possible daylight hour riding in the driveway. Josh and Stephani always insisted he wear his helmet. Why had he disobeyed?

Josh thought about the next few days and his heart clinched. They would pick out a casket, decide what would be said at the funeral, and choose a final resting place for the little body that for ten years had been so full of life. He wished he had the courage to end his own life, because he saw no way he could live without his son.

He went to the family room and settled into the recliner. He watched Stephani sleep as he willed his own body and mind to go numb. But sleep would not come. For hours, Josh kept watch and the pain intensified. As the sky pinked in the east, he finally drifted off. From somewhere in his dreams, Josh heard Stephani calling to him.

He pulled himself awake, moved to the couch, and held his wife as she cried. If only there was some action to take, something he could do to lessen the pain, for Stephani and for himself.

CHAPTER 4

They hadn't gone far, maybe a block, when Emily's stomach rolled. "Stop the car!" she shouted hoarsely.

Nate eased the car to the curb and she opened the door, leaned out, and emptied the contents of her stomach on the grass.

"I'm sorry." Her voice quivered as she looked for something to wipe her mouth on.

Nate handed her a wrinkled napkin he'd found in the cup holder. "Honey, it's okay. You're in shock. I'm taking you to the hospital."

"No. I'll be all right. Just go home, please."

Nate leaned his forehead against the steering wheel. "Trust me, Emily. You need to see a doctor, be checked out. Even the police chief suggested I take you to the emergency room. They'll make sure you're okay and give you something to help you sleep tonight."

Sleep? That would be impossible. Her mind replayed the images of the accident—the boy's frightened face, his mouth opened wide. If she closed her eyes, she saw him, over and over. She could hear the thump against the car and it drowned out Nate's voice. She covered her ears with her hands and moaned.

"We'll go to the urgent care clinic," Nate said as he steered the car into the stream of traffic. Maybe he'd guessed her fear of seeing the ambulance at the hospital, the small still body on the stretcher, and the distraught parents.

At the clinic, Emily stiffened as Nate opened the door, but she allowed him to put an arm around her waist and guide her in. She watched as he gave her name to the receptionist, handed over the insurance card, and took a clipboard to fill out required information. She sat slumped in a chair, feeling completely detached. Emily was vaguely aware of people as they entered and left the clinic in front of her, but she didn't really see them.

Nate stood to hand the clipboard back to the receptionist. When he sat back down, he reached over and took her hand, holding it gently and stroking with his thumb.

"Emily Adams."

Nate tugged on her hand. "Come on, Em, the nurse is calling for you."

Emily eased out of the chair, pulled her hand away from Nate, and followed the figure in the lavender scrubs to a room.

"You were in an accident?" the nurse asked as she wrapped the blood pressure cuff around Emily's arm.

When Emily didn't answer, Nate spoke up. "Yes, she was. She's kind of in shock."

"Accidents can do that." The nurse tightened the cuff and watched the readout of her blood pressure. She put a digital thermometer in Emily's ear and recorded the results in her chart.

"The doctor will be here shortly. You just relax." She hurried out and closed the door behind her.

A few minutes later there was a slight knock on the door and a man entered. He was older, with white bushy eyebrows that wiggled when he talked, like two fuzzy caterpillars. Emily tried to focus on his questions, but she couldn't make sense of what he was saying. Nate took over, telling him about the accident.

The doctor examined her pupils, looked for bumps and bruises, and checked her reflexes. Emily felt as though she were watching from a distance as someone who looked very much like her was poked and prodded. Even the voices sounded very far away.

"Medically, your wife seems fine," the doctor said, addressing Nate. "But she has suffered an emotional trauma. I'm writing a prescription for a sleep aid. Keep her quiet, bring her back in if either one of you notices anything unusual—double vision, pain, swelling, or extreme confusion." He scribbled something on a pad and handed it to Nate.

"Thank you, Doctor. I will."

Nate's hand reached to help Emily down from the exam table. She slid limply off and followed him out.

At home, Nate helped her into some pajamas, shook a blue and white pill into her hand and handed her a glass of water. She swallowed the pill and lay down on the bed. Just when she thought the pill would never take effect, sleep rolled over her, clouding the images and muffling the sounds that tormented her mind.

★★★★★★★

Saturday morning, Nate eased out of bed, taking care not to bump his sleeping wife. He tucked the blanket around her. His feet fumbled for the slippers he knew were somewhere beside the bed, and he tugged a worn gray sweatshirt over his white tee. Sweats and slippers were Saturday clothes. He moved to the kitchen to start the coffee, the horror of last night's nightmare settling about him like the cold fog that frosted the windows.

When the coffee pot's gurgle signaled the brewing was finished, he filled a large mug and carried it to the table where the folded paper waited. He was halfway through the sports section when he saw an article about spring-training and remembered.

A few weeks ago, an old friend and teammate on their high school championship baseball team had asked him to help with a pitching clinic for Little League boys, kind of a warm-up for the try-outs which would be held in March. Nate had agreed. It would give him a chance to participate in a sport he loved and to be around kids too. But the clinic was today. Did he dare leave Emily? Would the police come by and arrest her? He glanced at the clock. He had less than an hour before he was to be at the high school gym.

Nate stepped into the guest bathroom, the one he used so Emily could have their master bathroom for all her cosmetics and female stuff. He took a quick shower, rubbed his stubbly chin, but decided against shaving. Wrapped in a towel, he stepped back into the bedroom.

Emily's ragged breathing indicated wakefulness, so he moved to her side of the bed. Her hair wound in a wild nest over her face.

"Emily? You awake, honey?" Nate touched the bare arm curled around her chin.

She sniffed and moved her arm, but didn't answer.

"I'm supposed to help Rich with the pitching clinic today. I can cancel if you need me here. What do you want me to do?"

"Go." The one word was low and growly.

"But what if you need something?"

"I can take care of myself."

"Will you be okay? I'll be gone most of the day."

"Just go."

"Can I get you anything? There's coffee in the kitchen."

"Just go," Emily repeated, turning her back to him.

"I have my cell phone. Call if you need me and I'll come right home."

There was no answer.

Nate dressed quickly, kissed the portion of Emily's head not covered by the pillow, and left. He tried not to feel guilty.

Maple Valley High School's gym reverberated with the high-pitched voices of young boys. They scurried everywhere, tossing balls and punching fists into well-oiled gloves. The accident pushed to the back of Nate's mind as he moved into the familiar world of baseball.

The gym, new when he had entered high school, looked pretty much the same. Windows high above let in natural light that flooded the polished wood floor. Banners which proudly proclaimed champions of various sports embellished the walls. The bleachers, where moms, dads, and students sat, could be folded into themselves or pulled out for seating. Today, in order to make all the space possible, they were pushed against the walls.

Shortly after Nate arrived, his friend Rich blew a whistle and lined the boys up in two rows facing each other. Warm-ups began as the boys tossed balls back and forth, stepping backwards each time the whistle blew and increasing the speed of the balls. The gym was filled with the smacking sound of balls hitting leather gloves and an occasional high-pitched shriek from one of the boys as he reached for an errant ball or missed an easy one.

Nate walked behind the boys and called out to them: "Good catch—that's the way—oh, you'll get it next time." He immersed himself in the moment and concentrated on teaching techniques, individual style, and safety.

At noon they stopped for a catered lunch from Jen's, a small deli in town. Everyone got a sandwich, small bag of chips, an apple, and a snickerdoodle cookie. Nate set his lunch down and stepped outside to call Emily. The phone rang several times before she answered.

"H'lo." Her voice sounded groggy and sleep-laden.

"Are you okay, honey? Have you heard from the police?"

Emily made a noise indicating disgust. "No, I haven't heard from the police. I'm okay. I was sleeping."

"It's lunchtime. Can I bring you something?"

"No, I'll make a sandwich if I get hungry."

"Do you need anything? I could come home."

"I'm okay. I just want to sleep."

"I'll let you go, then. Love you."

Nate dropped the phone in his pocket and shook off worry for his wife as he returned to the gym. Rich was organizing the boys into groups to work on specific skills. Nate focused his attention on the clinic.

As the day ended, a curly-headed boy came up to him. His nametag identified him as Danny.

"Hi, Danny. What can I do for you?" Nate asked, scooping up baseballs and dropping them into an equipment bag.

"Thanks for teaching us, Mr. Adams. I learned a lot. You'd be a good coach … or just a good dad." Looking slightly embarrassed, he ran off to join a huddle of boys who were obviously waiting for him.

Nate watched the boy and let the words warm him all the way through. He could picture a wiry, dark-haired boy and himself playing baseball in their backyard. The boy would look up at him and laugh, calling him, "Dad." His dreamy image faded as he remembered Emily, and he was overcome with an urgency to get home to her.

The house was quiet and dark. Nate threw his keys and phone on the table and hurried down the hall to the bedroom. Emily lay in bed, looking like she hadn't moved the entire day.

Her calm, even breathing made him sigh with relief until he saw the prescription bottle on the nightstand. His heart lurched as he grabbed the bottle and counted the pills. There were only two missing. As his breathing returned to normal, he replaced the cap and tiptoed from the room. He would fix something, then wake her and see if he could get her to eat.

They needed to start getting their life back to normal.

CHAPTER 5

Donna slipped into the sanctuary as the music began and sank into the soft cushions of the pew. She tried to avert her eyes from the sympathetic glances of friends and neighbors. News travels so quickly in a small town. The music washed over her, but did little to soothe the pain. Even the words of the pastor's sermon drifted in and out of her mind. And when she shut her eyes to pray, tears overflowed.

The path of grief was sadly familiar. Six years ago she had lost the love of her life to cancer, her husband of thirty-nine years. She was just beginning to feel she could breathe without David, even laugh and smile again. And now Isaiah had left them too.

Not that she would wish either of them back. She knew where they were, and their joy far exceeded any earthly pleasures. But the pain of loss, the emptiness, overwhelmed her. The heartache was multiplied as she watched her son and daughter-in-law mourn. How could any of them live without Isaiah?

Donna fiddled with the buttons on her jacket. The magenta flowers splashed across the bodice usually made her cheerful. Today, she wished she had picked a more somber wardrobe.

As the notes of the last song drifted away, people stood and scooped up purses, Bibles, and kids with their sippy-cups and uneaten Cheerios.

Her friend, Sandy Johnson, appeared at her elbow. "What can I do to help?"

Donna gave her a look of relief. "Hi, Sandy. Just get me to my car. I can't stand to see one more sad face. I don't feel like talking to anyone yet."

With Sandy expertly running interference, they escaped down the back stairway, out through a little-used side door, and into the parking lot.

Donna used her remote to unlock the car door and Sandy opened it. After a long hug for her friend, Donna slid into the driver's seat.

"Want some company this afternoon?" Sandy asked.

Donna shook her head. "I need to walk and spend some time alone. Sara and the girls will be here tonight. She couldn't come until today because she works on Saturday."

"What about Carrie Ann?"

Donna could no longer hold back the tears. She wiped at them as they trickled down her cheeks, knowing she was leaving a clownish smear of mascara.

"I got in touch with her Saturday and she can't make it home. Josh wanted to wait to make funeral arrangements. He really wanted her here."

"Oh, Donna, I'm sorry."

Donna's youngest daughter, Carrie Ann, served as a missionary in Bogotá, Columbia, and was the inspiration for Isaiah's desire to serve. She and her twin brother had been inseparable when they were young, and when Josh's son was born, her nephew was her little buddy. Isaiah and his aunt seemed to connect in a way that was special. But since she lived entirely on a donation-funded salary, Carrie Ann could not afford to come for the funeral.

"Let me know when you need to talk, even if it's three in the morning." Sandy gave her another awkward hug through the open car window. Donna drove away, hoping she could see the traffic signs through the tears.

At home, Donna put on a pair of jeans, a worn sweatshirt, and her walking shoes. She slipped on a coat and headed out the door. Meaningful prayer time always came easier when she walked along the trail through the wooded area near her home. And her family needed prayer. Besides grieving for Isaiah, Donna ached for Carrie Ann. She was so far away. Her oldest, Sara, would be arriving this evening, along with her two children. But as the family gathered, there would be three missing spots—David's, Carrie Ann's, and Isaiah's.

The trail wound behind the houses, paralleling a small creek to the outskirts of town. The warm weather had melted any remnants of snow. The trail was clear and dry, but few people were out on this Sunday afternoon. Grateful for the solitude, Donna moved briskly, her words and tears pouring out in a jumble. She prayed for Josh and Stephani, for Carrie Ann, even Sara and her two girls, who would miss their cousin. She asked for strength and comfort for herself.

When she came to the first in a series of small wooden bridges, Donna paused in her conversation with God and leaned over the railing to watch the stream flow over the rocks. The sound of the water was soothing and, like a ripple of water, came a thought.

You're forgetting someone.

"Who, God? Who am I forgetting?"

She thought of all the people who knew Isaiah—his classmates, the boys on his Little League team, even the children he met at camp last summer. She prayed for comfort for them, and even that Isaiah's death would lead them closer to God.

You're still forgetting someone.

"Who, God?"

Like a thunderclap it came, so clearly she glanced up at the sky to see if it was still cloudless. "God, you mean the woman that hit Isaiah? You want me to pray for *her*? I don't even know her name or anything about her."

Donna stepped off the bridge and walked on down the path, looking at the green foliage as it pushed its way through the dark earth.

"Please, God, don't ask me to do that. It's too hard," she whispered.

She increased her speed, wanting to move faster so she wouldn't think, wouldn't hear. Her heart and breathing rate increased. Donna knew at some point she would have to pause to catch her breath, but she pressed on.

The path followed a curve in the stream and there was the bench where she often stopped to rest. Donna knew what was required. And she knew she wasn't strong enough to do it.

"God, I can't do this with my own strength. Give me the words."

Donna dropped to her knees beside the bench, and prayed for the peace and consolation of a woman she didn't know. She prayed that, somehow, Isaiah's death would mean something, that God would bring good, even from this horrible tragedy.

Later that evening, Donna scooped homemade chicken and noodles onto plates and handed them to her daughter. Sara passed them around the oak table in the dining room. Josh stood behind his chair, one arm holding Stephani. Sara's two daughters streaked down the hall, long brown ponytails bouncing.

The group took their places at the table, with none of the banter that usually accompanied their family dinners.

"Let's pray." Donna reached out and they obediently took hands with only a minor scuffle between Sara's two girls. Donna asked a blessing on the food, and that God's presence would be very near to them all. "Amen."

For a few minutes, there was only the clinking of silverware. Then Sara's youngest, five-year-old Tessa, piped up. "Is Isaiah having supper with Jesus?" Her face, with the little upturned nose and sprinkle of freckles, wore a somber expression.

After a startled pause, Stephani answered. "Yes, Tessa. That's exactly what he's doing."

Not one to be upstaged, seven-year-old Jocelyn chimed in. "Will he have to take a bath?"

Stephani looked befuddled. She turned to her husband for help. "Josh?"

He put down his fork. "Maybe. Maybe not. We don't know everything about heaven."

Tessa slurped up a noodle before her next question. "Does he miss us like we miss him?"

Donna answered this one. "No, I don't think he misses us. The Bible says there is no sorrow, no sadness in heaven."

Jocelyn added, "He won't even cry."

The children asked more questions and the adults relaxed. Talking about Isaiah in heaven was easier than ignoring the aching fact he wasn't at the table plying them with questions too.

Finally, Sara spoke up. "Eat your chicken and noodles, girls. It's almost bedtime."

"Awww, Mom. We just got here. We haven't even got the Barbies out," Jocelyn protested, but they both picked up their forks.

Donna wiped her mouth with her napkin and sighed. She might as well go ahead and ask him. "Josh, do you know the driver's name?"

"The driver?" His eyes widened and he looked a little confused. "No, I don't. Why?"

Donna twisted the napkin in her lap. "I've been praying for her."

Josh's eyes narrowed and his fork stabbed at a noodle. "I suppose that's the *Christian* thing to do."

Donna opened her mouth to agree, but at that moment Tessa plunked down her fork and asked, "Can I be done?"

"Sure, honey," Sara answered. "You ate more than you ever do at home. Take your plate to the kitchen and then head into the bathroom. I'll get your jammies from the suitcase." Turning to Donna, she added, "Thanks, Mom, for supper. It was great as always. I try and try, but my chicken and noodles never taste like yours."

Donna stood and began stacking the dishes. "I have pumpkin bars for dessert."

"Yummm!" Tessa squealed.

"After baths." Sara shooed the bouncing little girl from the room and Jocelyn followed.

"Do you mind if we don't stay?" Stephani pushed a half-eaten plate of food away.

"Of course not. You go home and try to get some sleep. Can I send anything with you?" Donna moved around the table to put her arm around her daughter-in-law's shoulders.

"No, we have a counter full of brownies and a refrigerator full of casseroles. I'll bring one tomorrow for lunch after ..."

Stephani's voice trailed off. Donna understood. Who could speak of making funeral arrangements for their son?

Donna gave both Josh and Stephani hugs. "We'll meet you at ten tomorrow." She stood at the door and watched them as they climbed into the car and drove away.

★★★★★★

Carrie Ann Nelson tried to concentrate on the meal she was serving at Hope for the Nations Outreach Center. She leaned over the counter to pass out steaming bowls of *ajiaco,* a chicken and vegetable soup. The dark-eyed children stood in a wiggly line, chattering to each other in Spanish. They paused to talk to Carrie Ann before they picked up their bowls. Sometimes they switched to halting English when they spoke to her.

The Outreach Center was situated in downtown Bogotá in an old warehouse that once housed coffee. When the center first opened, Carrie Ann could smell the lingering odor of the fragrant beans which once waited to be shipped all over the world. Overhead, high ceilings crisscrossed with ductwork and pipes. The worn wood flooring had been covered with cheap green linoleum in the kitchen area, but in the main room the rough floor remained. The director and his wife, Jeremiah and Rose Noring, had painted some of the walls in bright colors. One wall was covered with children's handprints, each signed by the owner of the hand.

Many of the children lived on the streets and the meal they got at Hope was their one meal for the day. They were always gracious and polite, and there were never leftovers. Carrie Ann loved her work as a missionary, but tonight she could only think of her family so far away.

Instead of dusky-skinned boys reaching for the bread, she saw blond Isaiah. Instead of the shouts in Spanish, she heard her beloved nephew calling, "Aunt Carrie, Aunt Carrie, look at me. Look what I can do."

After the last child was served, she ladled some of the remaining soup into a bowl and carried it to an empty table. She smiled at the eager offers from some of the children to share their table with her, but chose a place by herself. She put a spoonful in her mouth, but her throat refused to let it slide past. She swallowed hard and stared at the bowl.

A scuffle at the door brought her to her feet. Two policemen shoved a boy about ten years old through the door. He held his right arm, wrapped in a dirty towel, close to his chest.

The policemen's rapid-fire Spanish told Carrie Ann the boy had been sliced by a knife during a fight with another street child. He refused to be taken to the hospital, insisting he be brought to Hope for the Nations.

"Juan, isn't it?" Carrie Ann asked in Spanish.

His head nodded and his chin tilted up in an apparent effort to be brave.

"You take care of me? Fix me up, Miss Carrie?" His brown eyes pleaded.

She patted the thin shoulders. "*Si,* Juan, we'll take care of you." As the policemen backed out of the doorway, Carrie called, "*Gracias,* sirs." She turned her attention to Juan. The jagged cut ran the length of his forearm, but was not spurting blood. Carrie Ann led him to the sink where she washed and disinfected the wound. She knew if he were in the United States his arm would require stitches. Here, however, she would simply clean and bandage it and he would be back on the streets tonight.

She pulled some clean cotton tee shirts from a box of donated items and cut the cloth into strips for bandages. Juan sat quietly as she wound the makeshift bandage snugly around his arm.

"Have you had supper?"

His dark head shook and she watched his eyes dart toward the tables with other children, whose spoons scraped the bottom of their bowls.

"I have a bowl for you too. Let me tape this up and I'll get it." She cut off a length of white tape and secured the bandage.

"You must leave this bandage on. And try to keep it clean. If you come back next week, we'll change it for you." She paused and waited for him to look at her. "Next time you might not be so lucky. Next time they might cut your throat, Juan. Now go, find a seat and I'll bring you something to eat."

Juan scurried to a table with some older boys. He probably wanted to impress them with his knife wound. Carrie Ann sighed, stepped into the kitchen, and scooped the final bits of soup into a bowl. She picked up her own supper and brought both bowls to him.

He mumbled, "*Gracias,*" but did not look up as he shoveled spoonfuls into his mouth with his left hand.

The door opened and Jeremiah Noring entered. Jeremiah would help her with the difficult task of shooing the youngsters out of the mission and into the streets for the night. Some of them would go to apartments. Some had ramshackle shelters, while others slept in alleyways in cardboard boxes.

"I'll take over, Carrie. You need to get going."

She glanced through the row of tall windows in the front of the building and saw the gray shadows of dusk as they slipped over the city streets. Jeremiah didn't like Carrie Ann or his wife, Rose, to be out on the streets after dark.

"Okay. I just patched up the boy at that far table. His name is Juan. He's been here before, but he's not a regular. He got cut in a knife fight." She nodded toward the slender, brown-skinned boy tipping his bowl into his mouth for the last bits of soup. "Do you think he might come during the day for classes?"

Jeremiah scratched his head. "I don't know, Carrie Ann. We're at our limit now. And we're trying to reach kids who'll commit to coming every day. It's hard, but we don't want to waste our resources on those who don't stick with it."

"Just let me ask him. Please, Jeremiah."

He studied her for a moment before he nodded. "Okay, but make it quick and then get out of here. I'll see you tomorrow."

Carrie Ann stepped to Juan's table as he wiggled out of his seat. "Wait," she called. "I want to ask you something."

Juan moved around the table to stand in front of her.

"We have classes during the day. We teach reading and math and English. If you come and study hard, maybe you can get a job and get off the streets."

His dark eyes widened. "You'd teach me?"

"I'm one of the teachers. Jeremiah," she pointed at the director, "teaches some and his wife, Rose, does too. But you have to promise to come every day. You can't come one or two days a week."

"Can I come tomorrow?"

"*Si*, Juan. You come tomorrow."

"Thanks for fixing me up, Miss Carrie." His dark eyes shone up at her before he turned and scampered out the door.

Carrie Anne gathered her bag from the office and followed him out. She had a short, two-block walk to her tiny efficiency apartment. How lonely the one room would seem tonight.

And how far away from her family.

CHAPTER 6

Nate poured his coffee, along with a mug for Emily. He didn't know how, but he was determined to get her out of bed today. She'd refused anything to eat Saturday night, so he ate by himself in front of the TV. She took another pill sometime before he went to bed, but he wasn't sure how much she slept. She woke him up once in the night, moaning, but when he put his arm around her and tried to draw her to him, she pushed him away. Now, she lay diagonally across the bed, his pillow stuffed under her arm and the covers wadded around her.

"Emily." He sat beside her and rubbed her back. "I have coffee made. You want some pancakes?"

She rolled over and opened her eyes in a squint. "No. I don't want anything. Just leave me alone and let me sleep."

Nate raked his hand through his hair. "You can't sleep forever. We need to talk about what we're going to do."

"Have you heard anything?"

He wasn't sure what she meant. Had he heard from the police? The doctor?

"No. I just got up."

She pulled his pillow over her head. "Go away. I'll get up later."

Nate went back to the kitchen, picked up his mug, and sat down at the table with the newspaper and a slightly stale bagel he found in the pantry. A front-page article screamed: *Local Boy Killed While Riding Skateboard*. The coffee soured in his stomach as he read. *Killed?* The boy was *dead?* The article named Emily as the driver, but said no charges had yet been filed. Nate tried to let that fact reassure him, but fear still gripped him.

His wife had killed a child.

He paced the kitchen. He'd never felt so helpless. For most of their marriage, when there had been problems, he'd been able to fix them for Emily. Catching a mouse in the basement, paying off a credit card bill, comforting her when a friend from college committed suicide—those were easy situations to resolve compared to this.

The phone startled him and horror clutched his heart as he grabbed it. A quick check of the caller ID and he sighed with relief. His brother, Darrin.

"Hey." Nate wasn't sure he wanted to tell Darrin what was going on, but he had to talk to someone or he was going to burst.

When Darrin asked, "What's up?" Nate straddled the kitchen chair and unloaded. Nothing like a big brother to calm you down. After listening to the whole story, Darrin suggested that he find out who the good lawyers in the area were, just in case—and to let Emily sleep. "She's been through a lot. Sleeping will help her heal."

Darrin's voice was soothing and made him feel like things could be okay again.

"Thanks, big brother." Nate ended the call. His large, exuberant family always intimidated Emily when they visited. She'd been raised with only one sibling in a rather strict household. But at times like these, he was glad for the support of his parents, three brothers, and three sisters. He wished they lived closer. Nate knew Darrin would inform the family, but he would make a point to call his dad later.

Maybe Emily needed to talk to family too. He could call her sister. Surely she would talk to Andrea. He dialed the number. "Andrea? Something terrible has happened to your sister." He filled her in on the details. "Hold on. Let me see if she'll wake up."

"Em, your sister is on the phone." He shook her shoulder gently.

"I don't want to talk to her. Leave me alone. I want to sleep." She rolled over and her stiff back looked like a wall.

"Sorry, Andrea. She's trying to sleep. Maybe you can call back later." Nate slipped the phone in his pocket and went to the family room to see if there was something on TV, anything to keep the fear at bay.

Emily stayed in bed. Off and on all day Nate tried to get her to respond. He held her, suggested she take a shower, or at least eat something. No matter what he did, she lay there, usually turning her back to him when he entered the room.

When his stomach complained, he scrounged in the refrigerator and decided he'd better do some grocery shopping. He poked his head in the bedroom, but Emily appeared to be sound asleep. He wrote a note saying he was at the grocery store and laid it on the nightstand.

Grocery shopping was Emily's domain—had been since they got married five years ago. Occasionally, Nate picked up a loaf of bread or some ice cream, but he didn't have to decide what they would need for a week's worth of meals.

An hour later, Nate pulled the truck into the garage and hit the remote to close the door. From behind the front seat he lifted several plastic sacks bulging with food, hefted them into the house, and dropped them on the kitchen floor. Now, to decide where they went. Nate did his share of the cooking, but his skills were mostly confined to grilling, fixing salads, or baking premade pizzas from the local pizzeria.

After he stacked cans and boxes haphazardly inside the cupboards, he opened a can of soup, filled two bowls, and placed them in the microwave. While he waited, he removed a fragrant loaf of fresh-baked rosemary bread from the wrapper and sliced it in thick pieces.

He trooped down the hall, determined to roust Emily out of the bedroom and get some food in her.

"Em? Are you hungry? I fixed some soup. And I stopped at the bakery for some of that bread you like. Come on, Em, you need to eat something." His voice began softly, but ended somewhat on the stern side.

Emily didn't move. She was still wearing the tee shirt she'd worn to bed Friday night. "I'm not hungry."

Nate felt a twinge of anger. He moved to the side of the bed and knelt down. "Emily, not eating isn't going to help anyone. It won't help the boy. It won't help his parents. And it may hurt you. I'll do what I can, but you've got to take the first step. And right now, that step is to go into the kitchen and have a bowl of chicken noodle soup."

Emily buried her face further into the pillow.

"This isn't doing you or anyone else any good."

"Chicken soup?" Her voice was muffled by the pillow.

"Yeah. My mom always said it would cure anything."

"It won't cure this." Emily swung her feet over the side of the bed. Nate held out his hand but she brushed it away. "I'm not an invalid. I can move on my own."

She followed him to the kitchen. As they ate, Nate tried to get his usually chatty wife to talk, but any conversation was met with a shrug or a noncommittal, "Ummm."

After they finished eating, Nate took the empty bowls to the sink. At least he had gotten some food in her. "Do you want me to call Jim Van Scoy?"

"Why?" Emily sounded baffled.

"You're not going to work tomorrow, are you?" It was Nate's turn to be confused.

"Of course I am. We're working on the budget for next year. I'm not going to shirk my responsibilities. I've done something terrible, but I can't make it go away by hiding."

"I think they'd understand if you needed to take a few days off." Nate put the leftover bread back in the wrapper.

Emily asked in a voice that was almost a whisper, "Have you heard anything?"

At first he thought she was asking if she'd been charged with a crime. Nate had thought of little else all weekend. He jumped when the phone rang and expected to see police at the door any minute.

"The boy ...?" Her eyes pleaded for his reassurance.

Nate tensed. He ached for his wife, but knew she needed the truth, even though the paper containing the article about the accident had been carefully hidden in the recycling bin. He stared at a spot of food on the floor without answering.

"Nate? What are you not telling me?"

He continued to stare at the floor.

"Please don't tell me he ... he *died*."

Nate could hear the panic in her voice and his arms reached out for her. "Emily, it wasn't your fault. You couldn't stop the car."

"If I'd looked at that driveway … if I'd slowed down a little."

"Emily, he came right out in your path. The boy was at fault."

"The *boy* was at fault?" Emily exploded. "How can a little boy be at fault? I drove the car that hit him. I was responsible. I *killed* him." Her voice rose with each syllable until the last three words came out in a shriek.

Then she turned, stumbled back to the bedroom, and slammed the door.

CHAPTER 7

Josh stood in the bedroom in his pajama bottoms. He had to get dressed. Stephani was waiting for him downstairs. They had twenty minutes before they were to be at Johnson's Funeral Home. And Josh didn't think he could do it.

Saturday and Sunday had passed in a blur of visitors. As the news of Isaiah's death spread through the community, friends, church members, and coworkers called or stopped by to offer sympathy and support. Pastor Allen, Josh's friend and pastor, made a visit on both days.

"Josh, are you ready?" Stephani's voice drifted up the stairs.

He grabbed a pair of jeans, something he wore to work in the yard, slipped them on, and pulled on an old Kansas City Royals tee shirt. When he got downstairs, Stephani looked at his clothes, but didn't comment.

His mom and sister would meet them at the funeral home. They would be there to offer support, but it wouldn't help. He had already crumpled and fallen.

Josh parked in front of the large, gabled, white house that had once been the home of the son of Maple Valley's founder. Giant leafless maple trees stood proudly on the lawn, waiting for spring to burst into life again. Josh stared straight ahead. For him, there would be no spring. Stephani made no move to get out either. She just sat, clutching Isaiah's clothes, the clothes they had brought to bury him in.

He reached for her hand. "We'll get through this. Mom and Sara are here. Pastor Allen will be here later."

Stephani took a deep breath and opened the door. Josh came around the car, took her hand, and they walked into the funeral home together.

His mom and Sara were waiting for them in the foyer.

"Where are the girls?" Stephani asked Sara.

"Mom's friend, Sandy, is watching them. I thought it would be easier without them here." Sara hugged Stephani and gently rubbed her back.

Inside, Brian Fisher met them. Josh had gone to high school with Brian, an upper classman when Josh was a freshman. He clasped Josh's hand warmly.

"Josh, I am so sorry. I like to see old Maple Valley High graduates, but not under these circumstances."

When Brian released his hand, Josh turned and took Stephani's elbow. "This is my wife, Stephani, my mom, Donna, and my sister, Sara Franklin."

Brian shook hands with each of them. "Let's go to the conference room where we can be more comfortable. Can I get anyone some coffee? Water?"

"I'd like a water, please," Stephani requested. Brian waited until they were seated in the upholstered chairs before slipping out to get Stephani's water.

He returned with a folder. "Let me verify the information for the death certificate." He slid a paper across the table and Stephani studied it, filling in empty blanks.

"Do you want an obituary? Maple Valley paper only or Kansas City paper too? Did you bring a picture?"

Stephani rummaged in her purse and handed Brian last fall's school picture—a laughing, healthy boy. One glance at it and Josh felt the world had tipped and everything was wrong.

Josh listened as Brian asked questions and Stephani answered. Isaiah loved baseball and skateboarding, he was a member of Maple Valley Fellowship Church, he was in fourth grade at Maple Valley Elementary. How could they sum up his son's life in a paragraph?

"Let's set the day and time for both the viewing and the funeral." Brian tapped the pen he was using on the table.

"Mom, did you talk to Carrie Ann? When is she coming?" Josh looked across the table and knew before she spoke.

"She's not able to come, Josh. I talked to her on Saturday."

Josh felt numb. Maybe it didn't matter that his twin sister couldn't come. Nothing mattered anymore.

"Wednesday night visitation and Thursday for the funeral. Okay, Josh?"

Josh nodded and wondered how he would ever make it through the next few days. "I'll call Pastor Allen and get him to check his schedule."

Josh escaped to the hallway and made the call. "Works for him," he said as he sat back at the table.

"Let's move to our casket room and you can see what we have available."

Brian stood and Stephanie, Sara, and his mom followed obediently into a large room on the opposite side of the building. Josh stood in the entryway. The room was lined with caskets. Large ones made of ornate carved wood, satiny pastel lined ones with shiny surfaces, and one area of little caskets, designed to hold a child.

Josh couldn't do it. He couldn't choose a casket, a box, for his son. Stephani was wandering the perimeter of the room, touching a casket here and there and murmuring something to Sara and his mom. She turned and looked at him. "Josh? Are you coming?"

When he didn't answer, she came out into the foyer. "Are you coming?" she asked again.

"I can't do this," Josh said through clenched teeth.

"We have no choice, Josh. Not choosing a casket won't change anything."

Josh leaned his head against the wall and didn't answer. Stephani returned to the room of caskets. He could hear her speaking and the calm tone of his mother's voice. Brian spoke now and then, a low rumble probably meant to be comforting.

A few moments later, Stephani was at his side again. "I think we've found one that would be okay. Please come see."

Josh trudged into the room. Stephani showed him a pale blue casket, lined in white, with a panel on the lid showing a large hand and a small one with the words, *In God's Hands Forever.* Josh choked back a sob. "Yeah, that one's okay, honey. Whatever you want."

They all returned to the conference room and answered more questions. *Did they want a sign-in book? Did they want printed programs? Would there be a display of pictures? What about a casket spray of flowers? Who would ride in the hearse?*

The decisions went on and on, and Josh sat quietly, letting his wife answer and only nodding his assent when asked.

At last it was over. Josh stood and shook the hand Brian held out to him.

Brian grasped Josh's arm with his free hand in a gesture meant to comfort and support. "We'll get through this, Josh. Just let us know what you need."

What I need is my son, Josh thought. He took Stephani's hand and led her out to the car. They still needed to go to the cemetery and choose a place to bury Isaiah.

CHAPTER 8

The alarm beeped incessantly. From the fog of drug-induced sleep, Emily reached out and shut it off. Could it be Monday? Her body felt weighted with weariness. She sat on the edge of the bed. *What do I do next?*

Her full bladder steered her to the bathroom. She blinked in the harsh glare of the vanity lights. The mirror revealed a face she almost didn't recognize. Dark circles ringed expressionless eyes, and strawberry blonde hair hung in greasy, dull strands.

She clambered into the shower and lathered up, wishing she could scrub away her feelings. Afterward, she would put on makeup and clean clothes to go out and face the world.

How can I do it? It's not possible to make up for what I did. There is nothing that can make things right again.

Sunlight spilled through the bedroom window as she pulled on navy dress pants and a ruffled pale blue top. The warm, tantalizing smell of coffee drifted down the hall. Nate was up. He would be sitting at the kitchen table drinking coffee laced heavily with creamer. The morning paper would be open, probably to the sports section. The world smelled and looked the same, but everything had changed.

On the table sat a cup of coffee Nate had already poured for her. She sipped slowly, thinking maybe he'd been right. Maybe she should call Jim and stay home another day or two. Her bed was so inviting, and another sleeping pill would block out the memories for a while.

"You okay, hon?" Nate watched her over the top of his newspaper.

That irritated her. She wasn't sick or hurt, and she didn't want to be treated like she was. "I'm fine." She poured coffee into a travel cup, set it on the counter, and pulled a carton of yogurt out of the fridge, not missing the fact that Nate's eyes followed her every movement.

"If you're determined to go in this morning, I'll drive you when you're ready."

Emily paused, her yogurt held in midair. She'd forgotten she had no car. She replaced the yogurt, closed the refrigerator door hard, and picked up her coffee.

"Let's go now."

When Nate parked in front of the school, he reached across the console for her hand. "Call me if you need anything today, okay?"

"Yes, Nate. Don't worry about me. I need to go." She gave him a quick kiss, squirmed out of his hug, and walked into the office.

The receptionist, Shirley Addy, glanced up from her computer. Her smile froze for a second and then slid into an expression Emily wanted to believe was sympathetic. "We didn't expect you to come in today."

She was the object of office gossip. Her eyes fell on the newspaper on Shirley's desk. *Local Boy Killed,* and underneath, *Hit by a car while riding skateboard.*

The bitter taste of coffee rose in her mouth as her stomach lurched. The room swayed and she grabbed for the edge of the desk.

"There's too much work right now for me to take off."

Shirley's nails tapped nervously on the desktop.

"Do you know, umm … did they tell you …?"

Emily decided to rescue her. "No, I haven't been charged with anything yet. The investigation isn't over."

Shirley smiled, showing a tiny lipstick smear on one front tooth. "Well, if you need anything … if you need to talk, I'd be glad to help."

"Thanks, Shirley." Emily fled to her office, closed the door, and leaned against it. Her empty stomach still churned and she wondered if she should make a run for the restroom. Amy Lee, the office assistant and her good friend, had been pregnant last year. Every morning for weeks, she'd lost her breakfast at work. No, anything but that. Not now. She took a sip from the travel cup she'd brought. The coffee was warm and soothing, and she felt a little better.

Emily used the calendar on her desk and did some mental

calculations. No, she wasn't late yet. She flipped her computer on and the familiar hums and beeps filled her office. Turning her head, she gazed out over the playground. The swings, slides, and monkey bars stood empty, waiting for laughing children to fill them at recess. Had she ever sat here and watched as Isaiah played a basketball game or slid down the slide? She pulled the cord to lower the shade and swiveled to face her computer.

She'd barely gotten started when there was a quick knock and Jim Van Scoy entered. The tall, nearly bald man's slight stoop didn't detract from his imposing figure. As the superintendant of Maple Valley Schools, he was the undisputed head of the administrative offices as well as the school itself. Emily respected his authority, but was never sure where she stood with him. She sucked in her breath, hoping she hadn't made an error on a report or some other document that had crossed his desk.

He closed the door and cleared his throat. "What can you tell me about Friday night?"

For a moment, Emily couldn't breathe. She forced the words past a tongue and mouth that didn't want to work. "On my way home from work there was an accident … I hit a boy on a skateboard."

"Have charges been filed?"

She shook her head. The words came out in a whisper. "Not yet."

"We will continue your employment for now, but if criminal charges are filed, it will be necessary to bring it before the school board. I'm sorry."

Emily nodded, no longer trusting her voice. She was a criminal— someone who deserved to be in jail.

Jim laid a hand on the doorknob, and then turned back. "Will you be ready to discuss the budget changes this afternoon?"

"Yes," her voice squeaked out. "What time?"

"Why don't you come to my office about three?"

"I'll be there." Emily pressed her lips tightly and gave a slight nod as he exited her office.

It was several minutes before her breathing slowed to a normal rate. She returned to the computer and tried to concentrate. When the phone rang, she assumed it was Nate checking in with her, so she didn't even glance at the caller ID. She answered curtly. "Yes?"

"Emily Adams?" The voice was unfamiliar.

With a touch of embarrassment, she softened her tone. "This is Emily."

"This is Police Chief Geiken. Our collision investigation team will be meeting with the state patrol tomorrow. Can you be at the station at one o'clock?"

Her stomach rolled again and she wished she'd eaten some breakfast. "Yes, I can be there."

"Good. We'll see you tomorrow, Mrs. Adams."

Emily held the phone for a minute, everything on her desk swimming before her.

★★★★★★★

At the real estate office, Nate's friend and coworker, Steven Mathes, glanced up from his desk. "Hey, Nate. I didn't think you'd be in today. I mean, is Emily okay? I thought you'd be with her."

Nate folded into his office chair at the desk next to Steve's and shoved papers around to make room for his coffee cup. "She went to work this morning. I had to drive her, that's why I'm early. I'm not sure if she's okay or not, but she insisted on going in."

"She's a tough gal."

"I guess. I tried to convince her to stay home. I don't know, maybe it's best. Working keeps your mind occupied."

"Is she … did they … is she in trouble?"

Nate swallowed. "She hasn't been charged with anything."

"That's good." Steve swiveled back to his desk.

Nate glanced at the day's schedule he'd already memorized. It was three hours before he was to show houses to a young couple moving out of Kansas City. He mindlessly rearranged the items on his desk. He missed his usual leisurely start to the morning, drinking his coffee at the kitchen table after Emily left for school.

Turning to his computer, he brought up a search engine and began researching *traffic accidents resulting in a death*.

★★★★★★★

Emily powered off her computer. The day had been harder than she expected. Some people avoided her, looking down at the floor when she passed. Others were solicitous, treating her as if she'd been diagnosed with a fatal disease. Even the janitor had come to her office to tell her he was there if she needed anything.

Don't offer to help me, she wanted to scream. *I don't deserve it.*

Emily called Nate to pick her up and straightened her desk. Although she worked the entire day on the budget, the numbers still didn't add up correctly. She grabbed a stack of papers, stuffed them into her bag, and hung it over one shoulder. She could work at home tonight and come in early tomorrow, if necessary. Picking up her purse, she turned off the light and closed the door.

On the way home, Nate quizzed her. "That night, after the accident, you stopped your car right away, didn't you?"

"Of course I stopped," she snapped.

"Did you do what you could to help? You have to render aid if necessary."

"I didn't know what to do. The guy on the bicycle was giving CPR. And then the ambulance came." She turned and stared out the window. "I don't want to talk about it."

"The parents, they could file a lawsuit for wrongful death. You know that, don't you?"

Emily didn't answer, but fear rose inside like a devouring beast.

At home, she followed him inside and he gestured to the table, already set for dinner. "I got some salmon to grill and fixed some fruit. Sound okay?"

Emily rubbed her forehead with one hand. "I brought work home with me. And I'm not hungry. You go ahead and eat."

As Emily settled in the office, she could hear dishes clinking in the kitchen and the patio door opening and closing. A little while later, Nate stood in the doorway with a smile and a plate of food. "Dinner in here?"

Feeling guilty, she took it. "Thanks, Nate."

Several hours later, she carried the empty plate to the kitchen. Nate had cleaned up and put everything away. Emily placed her dishes in the dishwasher, added some detergent, and started it.

When she slid under the sheets on her side of the bed, Nate wiggled close. His arm went around her. The gentle pressure begged her to snuggle into him. Emily stiffened until Nate withdrew his arm and rolled over. She lay awake for what seemed like hours before sleep claimed her again.

CHAPTER 9

Nate pulled up to the school and waited for Emily to emerge. She hadn't mentioned her appointment with the state patrol, but this morning at breakfast, he'd asked, "Have you heard from the investigation team?"

"I have an appointment at the police station this afternoon," Emily mumbled into the refrigerator as she pulled out her yogurt.

Nate felt like he'd been broadsided. "When were you going to tell me? What time is it?"

She shrugged like it was no big deal. "At one. I thought you'd be busy showing houses."

"And how were you planning to get there?"

"I could call a cab."

"You're not calling a cab. I'll pick you up at twelve forty-five." He wasn't going to let his wife face this alone.

From the time they first met, Emily's spunk and independent spirit impressed him. He never wanted the type of woman who could do nothing on her own, but sometimes he wished Emily was just a little less independent. He wanted to at least feel like he could protect her. That was the problem now. He felt she needed protection, but she kept pushing him away.

Fear gripped Nate with icy fingers—fear that Emily would be charged with something. He had a sickening sense their whole life was off balance. That the sweet years they'd shared and their dreams for the future were all somehow altered and their lives would never be the same.

Emily stepped out of the front door of the school, clutching a jacket against the chill wind sweeping across the parking lot. Her dark dress pants made her long legs appear even longer and, under the short jacket, the purple sweater accentuated her shapely figure. Nate marveled. Even after five years, even when their world had been turned upside down, she could still take his breath away.

He resisted the impulse to pull her to him as she slid into the passenger seat.

"You didn't need to take off work. I could have called a cab." Emily's face was stiff.

"I know, but I want to be with you. We're in this together."

Emily watched out the window as he drove. Traffic in Maple Valley was never heavy and during the middle of the day there were only a few cars that whizzed past. Nate wished he could take his wife and keep driving out of Maple Valley to somewhere far, far away. Instead, he turned on Main Street and headed downtown.

The police station was a newer building with small evergreens and shrubbery softening the brick exterior. Nate found a parking spot and pulled in. He glanced at the clock on the dashboard. They were ten minutes early.

"Need anything? There's a convenience store right there."

"No, I'm fine." Emily pushed the door open. Nate followed her in, watching her back, straight and strong.

Once inside, the slick floors, locked doors, and a receptionist behind a glass barrier dissipated any warmth the green landscaping evoked. Emily gave the receptionist her name and she and Nate sat without speaking on the hard plastic chairs.

When one of the doors opened with a loud click and the police chief strode through, Nate stood. But the officer ignored him. "Mrs. Adams? Follow me, please." He held the heavy door for Emily and it slammed and locked behind them.

Nate stared at a poster of the state's most wanted criminals pinned to the wall, but Emily's face kept swimming before him. He tried to imagine the questioning, but could only picture scenes from TV crime shows with small windowless rooms and police detectives that paced around and fired questions like bullets at the suspect. Would

Emily's answers prove her innocence? Or would she claim, like she had repeatedly told him, she should have gone slower, or been watching to the side? Frustrated, he stood and walked to the door where he watched the wind blowing a tattered paper cup down the sidewalk and into the street. A car drove by and the cup disappeared under the wheels.

When the door clicked open again, it startled him. He saw Emily give a brief smile to the police officer, but when she turned to him, the sadness in her eyes tore his heart.

"Let's go." Emily picked up her jacket from the chair where she'd dropped it and led the way to the car.

After Nate eased into the street, he glanced sideways at her. She sat calmly, hands folded in her lap. "How'd it go?" he questioned.

"They asked the same things they asked Friday night." She paused and Nate wondered if she was trying to block the memories. "There was a state patrolman from the collision investigation team. He was the one with the most questions. I told them what I remember."

Nate drove quietly for a minute, questions pushing at him. "Did they say anything else?"

Emily's hands fluttered like tiny birds in her lap. "That I probably wouldn't be charged, unless they come up with new information or incriminating evidence. The investigator will make his report. Oh," she pulled some papers from her bag, "we can pick up our car and get it fixed. They gave me my license back."

"Good news." Nate's sigh puffed out noisily. He guided the car to a spot in front of the office, put it in park, and reached over to cover her hands with his. "You know, you could take off this afternoon. Rest a little."

Emily opened the car door. "No. I don't need to rest. I've got work to do." Her voice was tense and firm. She looked at him with an expression he couldn't read. "I'll be fine."

"Yeah, but will we be fine?" Nate whispered as the car door slammed shut behind her and she hurried into the office.

****

It was quiet at the real estate office. Everyone was either out showing houses or they'd left for the day. Nate checked his calendar. He had an appointment, but not until later that afternoon. He pulled out the papers Emily had given him releasing the Camry and studied them for a minute before picking up his phone.

Thirty minutes later he arrived at Midwest Auto and drove around the lot. They had several rows of used cars. Maybe he could protect Emily from some of the painful memories. He parked his car and entered the sales room.

A smiling, neatly-dressed young man strode across the shiny floor. "May I help you?"

"I have a Camry that was impounded here. I've got the release papers and I want to trade it in as is. I've talked to my insurance agent and they will give you a check for the amount of damages, less my deductible. You can subtract those charges from the purchase price."

The salesman raised his eyebrows for a second. "Sure."

"Bad memories," Nate explained. "I want to trade straight across. I don't need anything new, just something different and reliable. And I'd like to keep my payments about the same."

"Let me take a look at the car you're trading. We'll see what we have on the lot that's comparable."

An hour later, Nate drove away with the keys to a dark blue Ford Taurus in his pocket.

When he picked up Emily that afternoon, he handed her a set of keys.

"What are these?"

"Keys to your new car. A Ford Taurus."

"A Taurus? Where's the Camry? Oh, Nate, you didn't—"

"Yep," he said proudly, but the look on her face caused his enthusiasm to dribble away. "Is that okay? I thought you'd like it."

Emily pulled her bag onto her lap and stared out the window. "I don't know why you traded. It wasn't necessary."

"I did it for you. Do you want to pick it up tonight?"

"I guess so."

Nate steered the car onto the road. Minutes later, he pulled into the car dealership and parked beside a dark blue car. He helped Emily transfer her bag. When she slid behind the wheel and reached up to adjust the rearview mirror, he noticed her trembling hands.

"You want to come back later and get it? We don't have to get it tonight."

Her voice stiffened with determination. "No. I'll be fine. I'll follow you."

Nate shut the driver's door, got in his Explorer, and drove slowly, glancing at Emily through the rearview mirror. It seemed he couldn't do anything to please his wife.

She was slipping away a little more every day.

CHAPTER 10

Memories surged around Donna as she entered the church. At David's funeral, Josh was a rock, constantly at her elbow, literally holding her up physically as well as emotionally. Now she would have to be the strong one.

Sara and the girls followed her inside and scooted off to the restroom, Tessa complaining loudly, "But I don't have to go."

A few early arrivals stood in the entryway. Sandy dropped the brochure she was holding, hurried over, and enveloped Donna in a hug.

"I'm here for you." Sandy's voice was warm in her ear.

Donna's head nodded against her friend's shoulder. She didn't trust her voice.

The little casket stood on a stand at the side of the foyer. Donna choked back a sob when she saw it. Isaiah was dressed in his Kansas City Chiefs jersey and his favorite blue jeans, the pair with the holes in the knees. Donna couldn't bear to see her grandson so quiet, so still, so cold. She turned away and used an old handkerchief of David's to wipe her face.

Sandy gestured toward the sanctuary. "The church looks beautiful."

"Come see it with me." Clutching her friend's arm, Donna pushed open the heavy swinging doors. The air was fragrant with the flowers overflowing the stage area. Isaiah's favorite band, *Go Fish,* played softly over the sound system, the lively children's music sounding slightly incongruous in the quiet room.

The song brought a twitch of a smile to Donna's lips, even as her eyes filled with tears. She laid her head on her friend's shoulder. "How can I be strong for Josh when I'm falling apart myself?"

Sandy patted Donna's hand. "You can't, but God can. Just lean on him."

They made their way back to the entry just as Sara emerged from the bathroom, the girls capering after her.

Brian Fisher, the compassionate young man from the funeral home, hurried over.

"Mrs. Nelson, the family is gathering in the lounge. May I take you there?"

"I know where it is." Donna reluctantly let go of Sandy's arm, took Jocelyn's hand and led the way down a long carpeted hall.

Inside the lounge, Donna felt grief spread over her like thick smog. She took a deep breath and looked for her son. In other circumstances, Josh would be described as dashing in his dark blue suit and white shirt, as he paced back and forth.

When he saw her, he crossed the room, but rather than step into her embrace, he took hold of her arm. "I can't do this, Mom. I can't put my little buddy in the ground."

Donna moved again to hug him, but he kept hold of her arm.

"Ahh, Josh, you know the body they're putting in the ground is not Isaiah. He's not in it anymore. Ask for strength, Son. God will carry you through this."

Without replying, Josh strode away toward the window. Donna followed with her eyes and her heart, but didn't go to him.

Stephani, red-eyed and weepy, sat crumpled in a chair. Donna wished for some comforting words, but speaking seemed somehow superfluous. She touched her daughter-in-law's shoulder gently and Stephani tried to smile.

Sara sank into the cushions of the flowered couch and the girls plunked down, one on each side of her. She tried to gather Tessa's curls into a pony tail holder, but Tessa promptly pulled it out. Sara sighed noisily, but put the holder in her pocket without comment. Jocelyn sat with her back straight and arms folded, probably still pouting because her sister had gotten the side of the car that she wanted on the drive to the church. It had been a long week for them too.

Donna moved to sit with Jocelyn, but Pastor Allen stepped into the room. He went directly to the window and spoke to Josh, his voice soft and low. Then, turning, he addressed the entire room.

"Is there anyone who would like an opportunity to speak during the service, either at the church or the graveside?"

Their heads shook almost simultaneously.

"This is not easy, but everyone is here today because they love you and your son." Pastor Allen looked directly at Josh. "Although it may not seem like it now, God loves you even more."

Josh nodded, but kept his eyes downcast.

"Let's pray." The pastor waited as the family stood and grouped themselves around him. "Dear God, I pray for these dear friends of mine, the Nelsons, as they gather to remember and to celebrate Isaiah's short life. Please give them your strength and your comfort today and in the days to follow. Amen."

Josh led the way into the church sanctuary, his arm curved around Stephani. Sara and the girls followed, Jocelyn and Tessa solemn and quiet. Donna was last, shepherding her loved ones where she did not want to go. Crowded into the pews were church members, coworkers, neighbors, and friends. Many of Isaiah's teachers were there, as well as his Little League coaches. Three whole pews were lined with children and their parents—Isaiah's classmates. It seemed the entire town of Maple Valley had gathered to say goodbye to her grandson.

The family moved stiffly into the front row. Tessa climbed onto her mom's lap and covertly slipped her thumb in her mouth, a habit she'd dropped over a year before. Jocelyn leaned against Donna. Shuffling the program to her other hand, she hugged the little girl close. The words and music of the service flowed about her, but as they filed out, she could not remember much. Only her son's face, staring without expression, like features carved on a rock.

Later, at the brief graveside service, Josh gave one anguished cry as the small casket was lowered into the ground. He pulled Stephani close. Sobbing, they held each other while the pastor prayed. Donna rested her hand on her son's arm, but he seemed not to notice. How would her family survive this? How would they ever heal?

Members of the church served a meal after they returned from the cemetery. Donna tried to swallow small bites of salad and sandwiches, but finally pushed her plate away. Stephani visited with some of the people present, but Josh sat in silence, politely refusing food or comfort. When the sympathetic crowd finally thinned out, Josh and Stephani drove to Donna's house to say goodbye to Sara and the girls.

Donna watched as Jocelyn and Tessa climbed into their car seats, arguing over a handheld video game. Sara loaded two flower arrangements, suitcases, and a container of Donna's famous gingersnap cookies.

"Email Grandma," Donna instructed the girls. She kissed and hugged Tessa, then moved to the other side of the car to get to Jocelyn. She held Sara tightly for several moments. "Call when you get home. Not just a text. I'll need to hear your voice."

"I will, Mom." Sara turned to Josh and Stephani standing in the driveway. "I'm praying for you. I wish I could do something to make it easier."

Stephani stepped forward and hugged her sister-in-law. "Just come see us."

"Love ya, Josh." Sara slid into the car and, with a wave, started her two-hour ride home.

"We're leaving too, Mom. Thanks for everything." Josh's shoulders drooped and pain etched his face into fierce lines.

Donna embraced Stephani, but Josh slipped behind the steering wheel, so she just patted his arm hanging out the window. She watched as the car backed out of the driveway, moved down the street, and turned a corner. A flash of memory came to her—a time when Josh and Sara crashed into each other on their bikes. She cleaned them up, applied Band-aids, and gave them each a Popsicle. If only she could comfort them as easily today.

God, I feel so helpless. Please comfort them in ways I can't. Help them to find some peace in this senselessness.

She picked up two morning papers, left forgotten on the step, and went inside her quiet house. One of the girls had dropped a Barbie doll in the hall. Donna picked it up and stared at the toy for a moment before dropping it on the table to put away later.

With a Diet Coke in hand, she sat down and opened the newspaper. The article about Isaiah, front page news, mocked her pain. She stifled a sob and started to put it down, but remembered the driver. She picked up the paper and read the article. *Emily. Her name is Emily.*

She laid the newspaper down and leaned back.

I need strength to do this.

Donna rubbed her forehead and tried to picture a woman named Emily—a woman who had caused immeasurable pain to her and her family. And God wanted her to pray for this woman. It seemed too much to ask, but she bowed her head in obedience.

God, I don't know how to pray for Emily. You know her needs. This has surely been a tragedy for her as well. Help her to heal. And if she doesn't know you, let Isaiah's death be a way to guide her to you.

CHAPTER 11

Carrie Ann rolled over and pushed the curtains aside to look out her small bedroom window. Still dark outside. Knowing sleep would be impossible, she flipped on the lights and lit the burner under the teakettle. While the water heated, she pulled on a flowered shirt and a long dark skirt. Dressing in a modest style was important, especially in Bogotá.

Columbia's time was an hour ahead of Maple Valley, but Carrie Ann suspected her brother was awake too. How could he sleep on the day they would bury his son? The ache for her family was almost unbearable. Jeremiah and Rose suggested she take the day off. They could cancel her classes at the mission and others would cover the rest of her duties, but being alone in her apartment was no comfort.

She hung a teabag in her Maple Valley High School mug, poured the steaming water over it, and inhaled the fragrance. She couldn't be with her family, but her prayers could. Carrie Ann grabbed her burgundy leather Bible from the nightstand and curled into the pillowed basket chair. She opened to the Psalms. As she sipped the tea, she read and prayed, lifting up each of her family members by name, but beginning and ending with her twin brother and his wife.

The sun was up by the time she walked the two blocks to the mission center. She felt buoyed by her morning quiet time and ready to face her students. She greeted the street vendors, some of them by name.

"How is your wife?" she asked the flower vendor.

"Muy bien, muy bien, gracias." A broad toothless smile creased his face as he offered her a single flower.

"Gracias." She accepted it with a smile, even though he barely eked out a living from the sale of his flowers. But to say no would offend him greatly.

When she reached the mission, her students were huddled outside, eager for class. She unlocked the door and they all trooped inside, the boys jostling each other and the girls giggling as they joked in Spanish.

As the ten boys and two girls found places around the table, Carrie Ann went to the kitchen to put her flower in water. She found a few slices of stale bread and a slightly overripe *higo*. She sliced the prickly pear into pieces, carefully avoiding the tiny thorns on its skin. The mission only served an evening meal, but Carrie Ann couldn't bear to make the children study with no fuel for their brains.

She carried the makeshift breakfast to the table. Dark heads bowed as she spoke a prayer in Spanish, thanking God for the food and asking a blessing on the children as she called each one by name. When she added the *amen,* they eagerly reached for pieces of the bread and fruit. The door banged and a breathless Juan slid into his place. The bandage on his arm looked dirty and tattered, but still intact. Carrie Ann made a mental note to redo it later.

"*Hola,* Juan." She welcomed him with a smile.

Juan brushed the long dark hair out of his face and grinned up at her as he reached for his share of food. "Good morning, Miss Carrie." He spoke the English words perfectly.

When the children had emptied the plate, she returned it to the kitchen and took the opportunity to whisper one final quick prayer for her family. Carrie Ann straightened her back and took a deep breath so she could face the children with a smile.

"Let's begin. Today is Tuesday, February eighth."

The children chorused after her in their sing-song accented voices, "Today is Tuesday, February eighth."

They were eager learners and soaked up English like sponges. Juan was her special blessing, a bright boy, and blossoming even in the short time he had been coming.

"Tell me the words in English," he would say whenever she slipped into Spanish.

After two hours of lessons, including a Bible story Carrie Ann read to them in English, she dismissed them. It often took thirty minutes or more for everyone to get out the door. The children loved to share news with her or tell a joke or a riddle. Sometimes one of the girls would whisper a question about makeup or clothes. She wished she could take every one of them home, clean them up, buy them pretty clothes, and keep them off the streets. Jeremiah worked continually to find foster homes in Bogotá, but there were hundreds of children who lived on the streets and only a handful of homes that would take a child.

"Juan, wait," she called to him as he slipped out the door. "Let's redo your bandage."

"It is okay, Miss Carrie. I can take care of it."

"It's getting kind of raggedy and dirty. It won't take long. Do you have somewhere you need to be?"

"No." His dark eyes studied his bare feet. "Sometimes we get scraps from El Canelazo. The leftovers from the restaurant. But you have to be there early or they're gone."

Carrie Ann strove to hear as his soft voice switched between English and Spanish. "Okay. I'll hurry. Come back here to the kitchen so I can get the bandages." She led the way. Juan hopped up on the stool as she rummaged through the drawers for bandages and scissors.

Carefully, she cut off the old bandage and examined the wound. Healing had begun and there was no sign of infection. *Good.* Just to be sure, she poured on a little hydrogen peroxide and smiled to herself as Juan struggled to be manly and not wince or say ouch. She cut strips off of a clean towel and made a new bandage that covered the wound completely.

"Will you be here for the meal tonight, Juan?" Carrie Ann asked.

A frown darkened his face. "Maybe, *Senorita.* Maybe not. Someone is looking for me."

"Looking for you? Is it your dad?" Juan's alcoholic father drifted in and out of his life.

"No. Not my dad."

Carrie Ann didn't pry further. "Well, I hope you can make it. We're having stew."

A smile brightened Juan's features as he scooted off the stool. "I will try. *Gracias,* Miss Carrie."

After Juan left, she ate a quick lunch of fruit, wondering if she could get a call through to the states. The funeral would be over now. Josh and Stephani would be going back to their empty house. She hoped for a good connection as she pulled out her cell phone and punched in Josh's number.

"Hey, Carrie Ann." His commanding voice could have been coming from the same room.

"Hi, Josh. How are you?"

She could picture him pacing the kitchen floor. "I'm okay, I guess. It isn't easy."

"I wish I could be there for you. I don't know what I could do, but maybe a shoulder to cry on. Did … did the funeral go all right?"

Carrie heard a noise like an animal being strangled.

"No! There is no way a funeral for Isaiah could ever be right."

"I'm sorry, Josh. I know that. You know I'm praying for you and Stephani, that you will be comforted."

Josh's voice had a brittle edge to it she'd never heard before. "There is nothing that can comfort me. Don't waste your breath praying for that."

"I love you, Josh."

His voice softened. "I know, Carrie Ann. Thanks for the call."

"Keep in touch, Big Brother. Bye."

The Big Brother nickname came when Josh found out he was seven minutes older than her. He could never stop boasting about being older. If only she could tease him and make him laugh again.

Sorrow washed over her like tidal waves. Laying her head on her arms, she gave in to the flood of tears that had threatened all morning. Her sobs echoed in the empty warehouse. When she regained control, she wiped her face and pushed the cell phone back into her bag, wishing she could push the thoughts of home out of her mind too.

Jeremiah bustled in the door, carrying, as always, an armful of papers, donated items, and his laptop. In a few minutes, several older children would arrive. Many of them were being trained for specific jobs or skill support so they could continue their education. A few dated computers were used to teach technology. That was Jeremiah's job.

Obviously noticing her wet, reddened face, he paused. "Are you all right, Carrie? You can go home if you need to."

Carrie Ann sniffed. "It's okay. I don't want to go home. I just talked to my brother and it made me cry." She pulled a notebook out of her bag and jotted down notes over the morning's English lesson. She would teach an afternoon class in writing and reading English, then switch hats and prepare for the evening meal.

The name of the mission was not just a name to Carrie Ann. She held great hope for each of the children, longing for them to continue their schooling, get jobs, and be able to be productive citizens. Even more, she prayed they would know the hope within her—that with every English lesson, every meal, they would get just a little gospel and would someday be brothers and sisters of hers in heaven.

With a little jerk, she remembered. She had a nephew who, at this very moment, was in heaven with Jesus.

Oh, God, why did he have to go home so soon?

CHAPTER 12

Emily tried to concentrate on the spreadsheet filling her computer screen—a report she'd done hundreds of times before. But today, nothing made sense. She thought about closing it out and escaping to the Internet for a few minutes. When her office door opened, she jumped as if she'd actually misused work time, not merely thought about it.

Jim pulled up the chair opposite her desk and sat down. As usual, he didn't waste time with pleasantries. "What's going on with the investigation into your accident?"

Emily's hands knotted in her lap. "I still haven't been charged with anything. The patrolman will compile evidence and make a report. I got my driver's license and car back."

Jim nodded. "Okay, then. That's good news. Keep me posted. Are you ready to look at the new insurance forms this afternoon? We need to have them ready to present at the March faculty meeting."

"I could do that." She glanced toward her computer, thinking she wasn't getting anything accomplished there. "What time?"

"After lunch, say, one o'clock?"

"I'll be there."

Emily turned back to her computer, but two hours later was no closer to finishing the report than when she had first started. When her door creaked open again, she saw with relief that it was Amy Lee.

"Busy?" Amy's cheerful countenance was a welcome interruption.

Emily attempted a smile. "Trying to be, but I'm not getting very far. What's up?"

"We haven't had lunch yet this week. Let me treat you. Shirley's offered to stay and answer the phone."

"Okay. I'm not accomplishing anything here." Emily closed out the reports, grabbed her purse, and followed Amy out the door.

"Want me to drive?" Amy offered.

With a glance at the new Taurus, Emily nodded. "Yes."

Amy unlocked the doors of her red Chrysler Le Baron convertible, and Emily sank into the leather bucket seat.

"Still too cold for the top down." Amy slid into the driver's seat and started the car.

She drove right past Jen's, their usual sandwich place, and pulled into the parking lot of The Roundup, a steakhouse that did more dinner business than lunches. "I thought this might be quieter if we wanted to talk," she explained.

On Monday, Amy had caught her in the hallway. "Emily, I heard about the accident. I'm so sorry. Let me know if there's anything I can do." Emily's throat was so tight she couldn't answer, so she'd just nodded.

They scooted into a booth and ordered drinks and the luncheon special: open-faced steak sandwiches with a salad.

Amy leaned across the table, her brown eyes gentle. "Are you doing okay?" Amy's round face held such an expression of sympathy, Emily nearly burst into tears.

"Sometimes yes, most times no ..." Emily found comfort in the listening ear of a friend, and she told her about meeting with the investigation team. "I'm not charged with anything. I wish I was. What I did was so horrible. I can never fix it, never make it right."

"You weren't at fault, Emily."

"Then why do I feel so guilty?"

At that moment the waiter appeared with their salads. The conversation turned to Amy's six-month-old baby, Rachel, and work-related items.

By the time they finished their salads, Emily was laughing at a story involving Amy's husband Jonathan, Rachel, and a diaper change. It felt good to laugh again. But Amy never did reply to her question.

They returned to the office just in time for Emily to drop her purse and coat in her office and hurry down the hall to the superintendant's office. It was exactly one o'clock when she slid into one of the comfortable chairs around the conference table.

Jim spread out the insurance forms. As they discussed them, Emily's eyes kept falling on a flyer on the edge of the table. A brightly colored brochure announced: Volunteers Wanted! There were several pictures of people doing various construction activities.

Jim started to gather up the papers. "Well, I don't think these will give us much problem. Not too many changes from the old forms. You'll explain these to the faculty at the meeting next Tuesday?"

"Mmm hmm." Emily nodded, still trying to read the brochure without being obvious.

Jim slid it across the table. "Would you and your husband want to join us? Several of us from the school are going to work on a Habitat for Humanity house over on Crocker Street."

Emily picked up the flyer. "I wouldn't be much help. I don't know anything about building a house."

"No problem. Most of us don't either. They have supervisors who know what they're doing. You just follow directions. We've got several teachers, a couple board members, and some of the support staff all volunteering for the day. It's Maple Valley's first Habitat Home. Good PR for the school too."

Emily studied the pictures. "When are you doing this?"

"Saturday the twenty-fourth."

"And you just have to do what they tell you to do?"

Jim nodded. "That's it."

"Well, I can follow directions."

"Then you could volunteer."

Emily folded the brochure and slid it back to Jim. "If you think I would be of help to them, I guess I'll come."

"Great. I'll add your name to the list. Go ahead and take the flyer with you. It has the address of the house. We're starting at eight. Too early for you?"

It was good to hear a hint of teasing in Jim's voice.

"No, I can be there. Should I bring anything?"

"Not unless you have a special hammer to use when you build houses."

"I'll have to borrow one of theirs. I wore mine out." Emily grinned at him, then hurried down the hall. Sitting in her chair, she reread the brochure. Volunteering to help build a house for someone that didn't have one was a good thing to do. And she could do it.

A tiny glimmer of hope lit within her. It was impossible to go back and undo what had already been done, but she could move forward and do all the good that was possible to do. She turned to her computer with a great feeling of determination.

A few minutes before five, there was a tentative knock on the door.

"Come in," Emily called.

Amy stood hesitantly in the doorway. "Want to go with Shirley and me? We're going to The Big Scoop for a shake or something before we go home."

Emily shook her head. "I don't think so, Amy. I've been working on the transportation report and I'm not quite done. But thanks for asking."

"You sure? It won't be as much fun without you."

"I'm sure. You girls go on."

The door started to close, then opened again. "Emily, you know I'm here if you need anything."

"Yes, I know. And thanks for going to lunch with me. It was good to talk to someone." Unexpectedly, her eyes filled with tears in the warmth of Amy's compassion.

The door closed and Emily could hear Amy's footsteps fading down the hall. For a moment she thought about hurrying after her. Emily wanted nothing more than to sit with friends over some ice cream and giggle about something one of their husbands had done over the weekend. But the weight of the job pulled her back.

She thought again of her resolution. Just how much good would she need to do to outweigh the wrong?

CHAPTER 13

The house looked as dark and empty as Emily felt. She'd worked late every night and was still behind. Now it was Thursday and she didn't have much hope of catching up before the weekend. She couldn't focus at the office, and at home she was distracted. Even driving the short distance between work and home was nerve-wracking. She drove slowly, putting on the brake at every little movement to the side. She pulled into the garage and parked the Taurus. The shrill song of her cell phone startled her. Nate.

"Hi, Em. How was your day?"

"I'm still three reports behind."

"You'll catch up."

"I hope so. Oh, and Jim asked if I would help with a Habitat for Humanity house they're building."

Emily heard a chuckle. "You? Swinging a hammer? What is he thinking?"

"Probably not a hammer. He said there are all sorts of jobs. They'll find something I can do, and then I can contribute to a family getting a home. Will you be here for supper?"

"That's why I called. I have a client who wants to look at a property for the second time. Want to meet for pizza or something when I'm done?"

"No, I'm really tired. I'll just grab something out of the fridge."

"Okay. I won't be too late."

Emily wandered through the house, dropping her coat, bag, and keys in a haphazard trail to the bedroom. As she changed to a pair of sweatpants, she had an idea. She would go for a run. Running helped relieve stress, right? The temperature was warm for February, and she could get by with layering on a couple of sweatshirts.

An old pair of running shoes was buried at the back of the closet, leftover from her college days. She laced them tightly and they still fit. Dropping her keys into her pocket, she stepped outside.

Emily stretched and breathed in the cool night air. She jogged in place a few times before heading out. After about a mile, her muscles seemed to remember. She slid into a comfortable rhythm as her legs and feet propelled her into the darkness. She ran through their residential district, an area of mostly small ranch homes with neatly landscaped lawns and swing sets and toys in the backyards. As she passed the houses, lights glowed from kitchen and dining room windows. Families were gathered for an evening meal, talking and sharing about their day.

An hour later, she stood in the driveway and did a few cool-down stretches. She was winded, her muscles were out of shape, and she would be sore tomorrow, but it felt good to run again. Unlocking the front door, she headed to the kitchen and filled a glass with ice and water. The cold drink quenched her thirst. She layered a plate with fruit, crackers, and cheese, cleaned up the mess, and moved to the office.

She'd just started working on the computer when Nate walked in.

"Hey, honey." He bent to kiss her. She turned her head just enough and the kiss landed somewhere in the vicinity of her left ear.

"Did you eat?" Nate glanced at the empty plate.

"Umm hmm. Had some crackers and cheese."

"Care if I fix myself a sandwich?" Nate had already stepped out the door.

"Go ahead." Emily kept working.

Later, Emily stood in the bathroom brushing her teeth. She pulled open her cosmetic drawer. Far at the back was a cardboard packet. Fourteen pills—enough for two weeks. She turned it over. The prescription was renewable five more times. She could be sure of not getting pregnant for five months. She popped one pill into her mouth and washed it down with a swallow of water. She crawled into bed beside Nate, careful not to wake him.

★★★★★★★

"Good morning." Emily poured a cup of coffee into her travel mug.

"Morning." Nate peered at her over the top of the newspaper. "Finish your reports?"

"Signed, sealed, and delivered. Or emailed, to be exact." Emily sipped the coffee. "I ran last night."

"Ran? As in jogging-shorts-and-hitting-the-road ran?"

"Yep. Only I wore sweatpants instead of shorts. It felt good. I think I'm going to get in shape and do some charity runs. You know … community things. I looked on the Internet and there's a Run for SIDS here in Maple Valley the end of March. Just a five-K. I think I can do it."

"SIDS?"

"Sudden Infant Death Syndrome. They do all sorts of research to prevent babies from dying in their cribs."

"Okay. How're you going to train?"

"I'll run at night when I get home."

Nate was shaking his head. "Yeah, when you get home. You've been working some long hours." He put down the newspaper and studied her face. "I don't want you overdoing it, Em."

"I won't, I promise." She glanced at the clock and gave Nate a quick kiss goodbye. "Gotta get going."

At the office, she took time to log on to the website for the Run for SIDs and add her name to the roster of runners. She printed out the pledge sheet and laid it on the table in the break room with a sticky note attached, asking people to support her.

When they didn't go out for lunch, the staff took turns eating in the tiny room tucked to one side of the central office complex. Amy was already eating when Emily stopped for lunch. She looked up from her salad and gestured toward the pledge sheet.

"I didn't know you were into running."

Emily slipped a frozen chicken and rice entrée into the microwave. "I just started. I used to run in college, but haven't for awhile. The Run for SIDs seemed like a good cause."

Amy nodded. "I'm sure it is. I used to worry about Rachel when she was tiny. I'd stand and watch her as she slept and wonder what it would be like …"

As Amy's voice trailed off, Isaiah's face flashed through Emily's mind. His parents were facing the unspeakable. Had they had a funeral yet? Buried their son?

Emily mentally brushed away the questions. "I hope to raise a lot of money for SIDS. I'll get back into shape and maybe run several races for different causes. It's something good I can do." She pulled her meal from the microwave and sat down across the table from Amy.

Amy looked at her with a curious expression, but didn't question her any more on running. They ate their lunches, sharing bits and pieces of life outside work. When Emily stood to clear her plastic dishes from the table, Amy asked, "Do you go down Valley Drive when you go home?"

"Yeah, why?"

"I have a bag of clothes to donate to the Lighthouse."

"The Lighthouse?"

"It's a women's rehab facility. I have some clothes that haven't fit since I got pregnant with Rachel." Amy gave a wry grin. "And I'm not holding out much hope."

"You should come running with me."

"I'd like to, if I could ever find the time."

"So, you want me to drop the clothes off for you?"

"Oh, would you? That would save me going across town. Just go in the front door and hand them to the receptionist. I'll bring the bag down to your office later. Thanks, Emily."

"Sure." Emily swiped across the table with her napkin, wadded it up, and tossed it away before heading back to her office.

Later, as she powered off her computer for the day, Amy tumbled in the door dragging a bulging garbage bag.

"Here are the clothes. Thanks again, Emily. You're terrific. The Lighthouse is right past that big park on Valley Drive. It's a brick building, kind of set back from the street."

Emily poked through the bag and held up a top she'd always admired. "You're giving this one away?"

Amy lifted a shoulder. "You can keep it if you'd like. But most of the women that come to The Lighthouse are homeless, or live in poverty. They use lots of donations."

Somewhat embarrassed, Emily tucked the top back into the bag. "I promise, I'll take it all. I won't remove a thing. Wonder if they'd take some of my things?"

"I'm sure they would." Emily's phone rang and Amy waved and moved toward the door. "See you tomorrow," she mouthed.

The Lighthouse was so easy to find, Emily wondered why she'd never noticed it before. The trim L-shaped brick building could have held offices, a school, or a business. Instead, it sheltered broken women who were working at rebuilding their lives.

The receptionist looked very young, perhaps one of the women in the program.

"I have some clothes to donate." Emily held up the bag. "Actually, the donation is from a friend. I'm just delivering for her."

"Thanks." The girl smiled, revealing a dimple and lighting up her rather plain face. "Does your friend need a receipt?"

"She didn't say. I guess I'll take one just to be safe."

The woman did a quick perusal of the items in the bag, and turned to write the receipt.

Emily gazed at the tidy office. Behind the receptionist, women bustled back and forth, some of them glancing curiously in Emily's direction. Most of the walls were plastered with scenic posters proclaiming messages like: *Courage is only an accumulation of small steps,* and *This is the first day of the rest of your life.*

"Here you go."

Emily took the receipt and tucked it into her bag. "Do you ever need volunteers?"

"Sure. We always need volunteers." She stretched across the desk to reach a clipboard. A pen dangled from a string. "If you're interested, fill this out and someone will contact you."

Emily took the clipboard and filled in the lines, wondering how she would explain to Nate her need to volunteer at a rehabilitation center for women.

The smell of baking bread and melted cheese engulfed her as soon as she stepped into the house. Nate must have stopped for a take-and-bake pizza.

"Ummm, smells good."

"Good timing on your part. I was afraid you were working late. Thought I'd have to eat the whole thing by myself."

Emily leaned in for a quick kiss. "Thanks for fixing it. I stopped at a place called The Lighthouse on the way home. Ever heard of it?"

Nate shook his head. "Nope. We're kinda far from the ocean to have a lighthouse, don't ya think?" He chuckled at his own joke.

Emily tossed her jacket on top of the bag she had dropped and slid into her chair. "It's a rehab center for women."

"And you stopped there because …?"

"Oh. I dropped off some clothes for Amy. I think I have some stuff I could donate too." She took a long drink from the Diet Pepsi Nate had put at her place. "What do you think of me volunteering there?"

Nate carefully pulled the pizza from the oven before he answered. "Don't you think you're overdoing it?"

"No. I think I haven't done enough." Cheese dribbled from the hot pizza onto the plate Nate handed to her. She swiped it up with her finger and popped it into her mouth.

Nate sat down with his plate and leaned toward her, his mouth set and his eyes dark. "Emily, you've had a shock. Give yourself time to recuperate. First you're going to build some house for a needy person. Then you're going to run in a charity race, even though you haven't run since college. Now you're going to help at a rehab center? No, Emily. It's too much."

They ate the rest of the pizza in strained silence.

CHAPTER 14

Josh almost collided with his friend and partner, Adam Griffin, as he rushed into the offices of Delta Engineering.

Adam slapped him good-naturedly on the back. "Hey, man. You shouldn't be here. We're taking care of things for you."

Josh didn't want to say he couldn't take another day of writing thank you notes, accepting casseroles from the neighbors, and wandering through a quiet house that screamed of Isaiah wherever he moved.

"It's time. I need to be back at work. Nothing I can do at home." Josh nodded at Adam and stepped through the inner glass doors.

His assistant, Jaleen, looked up at him. "Welcome back, Mr. Nelson. I'm so sorry for your loss." Her warm brown eyes filled with tears, and she reached for the tissues on her desk.

He felt he should say something to comfort her, but had nothing to give. "Thanks, Jaleen. Let me check my emails and then you can brief me on what's happening with Memorial Hospital. I need to get going on those plans." He stepped into his office and lowered his computer bag to the floor.

Before twelve days ago, his office had always given him a sense of satisfaction. The leather chair felt masculine and comforting. A cherry desk and massive bookshelves spoke of who he was and what he did. But today, the photograph of the Little League team, the framed crayoned drawing of their family, and the candy dish Isaiah loved to empty when he visited, cut to his soul. He removed his computer from the bag, set it on the desk, and powered up. Within a few minutes he accessed his email, and the routine task steadied him. After replying to all the messages that required a response, he pulled out the Memorial Hospital file.

As he studied plans for the new wing, he came across a list of the architects' names and one stood out. Curtis Jay Williamson. Could it be? His roommate, sophomore year of college, CJ Williamson? Skinny, red-headed, and freckled, CJ tried to make up for his lack of physical attributes by being the life of any gathering. He coaxed Josh to party with him often that year. In all probability, Josh would not have made it into engineering school if CJ had remained his roommate. But there was no chance of CJ rooming with him after their final bash.

Had CJ ever forgiven him?

Josh Googled the Kansas City architectural firm listed and read the brief bio on Curtis. Looked like he'd done okay for himself, despite the setback. Josh sent off a brief email to CJ, acknowledging they were both working on the same project, and asked if he'd like to get together when he was in Maple Valley. He pressed send and returned to the Memorial Hospital file. As he flipped through the documents, he tried to get centered on his job.

A few hours later he realized it was time for lunch when there was a light knock on the door. "Come in," Josh called.

Jaleen hesitated in the doorway. "There's a Mr. Petrowski here. I'm not sure what he wants. Something about an investigation on the Memorial Hospital project …"

Irritation pricked at Josh. However, investigations weren't something that could be ignored. "Send him in," he barked.

A thin, balding man in a cheap pin-striped suit entered as Jaleen held the door for him. "Joshua Nelson? I'm Richard Petrowski." He extended his hand.

Josh stood and shook hands with the man. "Most people call me Josh. What can I do for you?"

Narrow lips curled into a smile that must have been intended to put him at ease. "I've been hired to look into some possible fraud concerning the new wing being added onto Memorial Hospital here in town. I need a few facts verified."

"What firm did you say you were with?"

"Just me. Richard Petrowski. I'm a private investigator." He looked at his watch and smiled again. "It's lunchtime. Can I buy you lunch?"

Josh pursed his lips. Something about this guy didn't ring true. "I don't have much time. I've been out of the office and I'm a bit behind."

"You have my word, it won't take long. And you do eat lunch, don't you?"

"Sometimes." Josh glanced at the plans on his desk. He needed a break. "There's a deli right down the street. Couple of booths that would be semi-private. That do?"

"Great." Richard followed him out.

Josh ordered a turkey and Swiss cheese on ciabatta bread. He tried not to think about the times he had eaten here with Isaiah. His son loved going to work with him when he had a day off from school.

Richard and Josh placed their sandwiches and drinks on the table, slid across the plastic seats, and settled in. Richard asked a few broad questions about Memorial Hospital. Josh tossed answers at him easily. This was general data, nothing that wasn't public information.

Then, leaning forward slightly, Richard asked, "Are you the same Josh Nelson whose son was hit by a car February fourth?"

Josh's breath left him as suddenly as a child who has fallen from a swing onto his back. Fighting for composure, he swallowed with difficulty, laid his sandwich down, and nodded.

"I'm so sorry. I can't imagine what you're going through."

Josh choked out, "Thanks."

Richard shook his head. "And do I understand the woman who hit him got off scot-free? There were no charges filed?"

"None that I'm aware of. There was nothing to substantiate pressing charges. Isaiah went right out in front of her on his skateboard. She couldn't stop."

"You know, there must be more to the story. I bet she was talking on her cell phone or texting, or … something. Not paying attention, you know?"

Josh nodded but still felt uneasy. "Maybe."

Richard leaned in further, his voice low and quiet. "I don't think justice was served, Mr. Nelson. And if you don't mind, I'd like to introduce you to a friend of mine, a lawyer."

"I'm not sure I understand, Mr. Petrowski."

"Please, it's Richard." His hand slid into his pocket and removed a business card. "You have the right to justice. For your son. This man will see that you get it."

"You mean sue?"

"Let's just call it forcing the courts to bring justice for your little Isaiah."

Josh glanced at the name on the card before tucking it into his shirt pocket. "I'm not sure about this. I'll talk to my wife."

"Certainly." Richard picked up his sandwich. "I'm sure she wants what's right too. Talk it over and then call Frank. He'll help you."

Josh bit into his sandwich and chewed, a tiny frown pinched between his eyebrows. They finished their lunch while discussing various aspects of the hospital addition, but nothing more was mentioned about an investigation.

The men shook hands before leaving and, as Josh walked the two blocks back to Delta Engineering, phrases like *right to justice* played in his head.

CHAPTER 15

The email came on Monday.

Thanks for signing up to volunteer at The Lighthouse. We have received several large donations of clothes and need two or three people who can help sort and organize our clothes closet. If you can come Thursday, February 17th anytime in the afternoon, your assistance will be greatly appreciated. Volunteer Coordinator, Stacy Maher.

Emily reread it as she nibbled thoughtfully on her fingernail. This was something she could do. She'd been organizing clothes since she was five years old. Nate didn't need to know she was doing another volunteer project. She would let him think she was working late.

On Thursday, when Emily pulled into The Lighthouse, she found a spot to park toward the back, hidden from the street by some bushes. She felt a little tug of guilt. She and Nate had always vowed to be honest in their marriage. But the good she was doing certainly outweighed a harmless deception, didn't it? Emily hurried inside.

The receptionist was the same one Emily had met a week ago. Her smile made Emily feel like she was a long-lost friend.

"Here you are again. How can I help you today?"

"I got an email from a Stacy Maher. I think I'm going to help her with some clothes."

"Oh, of course." The young girl nodded knowingly. "You get to work in the clothes closet. I'll tell Stacy you're here." She bounced up and hurried down the hall.

Minutes later, a tiny woman with a frizz of bright red hair bustled up to her.

"I'm Stacy Maher." Her smile beamed from a softly wrinkled face.

Emily held out a hand. "I'm Emily Adams. I got the email about your needing help organizing clothes."

"Wonderful!" Stacy pumped Emily's arm up and down. "Follow me."

The clothes closet was a dingy basement room that smelled slightly stale. Racks of clothes lined one wall, tables held haphazard piles of clothes, and jeans tangled around delicate lingerie and winter coats.

Stacy swept her hand out like it was a showroom. "This is our clothes closet. I'm so glad you came to help. I was beginning to think my email had been lost in cyber space. These clothes," she shoved a large cardboard box forward, "need to be hung on the racks. Take empty hangers from wherever you can find them. Some of the girls will be down to help later. They're in meetings right now."

"Okay, I think I can handle this." Emily picked up a bright red cocktail dress and slid the clothes on the rack apart to reach an empty hanger.

An hour later the box was empty and her back ached from all the bending. While she worked, a few young women filtered in. Some stood at the back of the room talking, while one tall African-American woman appeared to be shopping. A very thin blonde woman with a prominent baby bump folded clothes at one of the tables. As Emily watched her, the surge of pain that followed took her by surprise. Pregnancy was not an option for her. Not now. She pushed the empty box under the table and shoved her longings away as well. She glanced at the clock on the wall. If she left right now, she could probably beat Nate home and he would never know she stopped here.

Stacy Maher's red head suddenly bobbed into view. "Oh, you are a dear. Is that whole box empty? Do you have to leave yet? If you have time, you could help Sherry fold the clothes on that table." Stacy waved toward the table with the pregnant woman.

"Ummm, sure." There was still good to be done. She could push her feelings aside and do it. Emily worked her way around to the table.

"Hi, Sherry. I'm Emily." She offered a smile to her folding partner, but the woman kept her eyes on the table, wadding the clothes in a rather rough way. Maybe she didn't hear the greeting.

Emily began to sort, fold, and stack the clothes in an orderly fashion.

"Let's put the shirts on this side and the jeans over here," she suggested.

Sherry lifted her eyes, but seemed to focus on something behind Emily's head. One corner of her mouth twitched up. "Let's not."

Emily lifted a pair of jeans from the pile, shook them and laid them on the table. She smoothed out the wrinkles before folding them in half, then in equal sections. "See, they'll stack much better if we do."

This time Sherry's grey eyes narrowed slightly before they gazed directly at Emily. "Listen, Emily." Her voice pronounced the name like a dreaded disease. "I don't need you to tell me how to do nothin'. You're just some rich do-gooder, come down to The Lighthouse to make you feel good about helping all us poor, miserable addicts."

Emily gulped and worked to keep her surprise hidden. "I'm just a volunteer. Stacy suggested I come over here to help you."

Sherry slapped another wadded up shirt on the table. "I can fold these clothes fine without you."

"Sure. Sorry." Emily gave a weak smile and placed the folded pair of jeans on the stack before she turned and walked to the door.

Stacy apparently saw her leaving and weaved her way through the tables to reach the door first. "Emily, thanks so much; you were a great help today. I know all the girls here appreciate your volunteering."

"I loved every minute of it." Emily covered her lie with a smile.

Before she left the building, she checked her phone. There were three texts from Nate asking when she would be home.

On my way, meeting @ work. She sent the reply and hurried out to her car.

CHAPTER 16

J osh leaned back in his chair and waited for Stephani to pick up the phone. He dreaded this time of day. While he was at work, there were distractions, things to accomplish. But at home, there was only the emptiness, the vacuum where Isaiah had been, sucking every bit of life from him.

"Hi, honey." He forced a bit of cheerfulness into his voice, for her sake. "How about if I pick up sandwiches on the way home? I don't think I can take another of Lucille's casseroles."

"Sandwiches will be fine, but don't you dare tell her."

Although most of the church members had moved on with their own lives, Lucille still arrived on their doorstep with a casserole every few days. Tater Tot Casserole was good, but after the third one, Josh wanted to say, "No, thanks." Stephani wouldn't let him do it because she knew it would hurt Lucille's feelings.

"My lips are sealed. I will accept the Monday casserole with a smile of thanks for the rest of my life, if needed. When are you coming?"

"I need to re-shelve a stack of books and then I'll be home."

Stephani's job as a part-time children's librarian had been perfect, allowing her time as needed to be home with Isaiah. After the funeral, Josh wasn't sure she would want to return to work where she would be around other people's children, but she seemed as eager as he was to leave the emptiness of the house that used to be a home.

Josh stopped at Jen's and ordered two Mediterranean turkey wraps to go. He drove home, taking the longer route to bypass Memorial Hospital and the memories he wanted to avoid.

At home, he laid the sandwiches on the table and pulled iced tea for himself and water for Stephani out of the fridge. As he headed upstairs to change, he paused before the door to Isaiah's room. He didn't know when, but Stephani had closed it, probably to spare them the pain of seeing the place their child should be.

When he opened the door and stepped in, a wave of pain washed over him. His knees buckled and he sat down on the rumpled, blue-plaid bedspread. A pair of Isaiah's pajamas lay on the floor. Josh picked them up and held them to his cheek. They still held the fragrance of his son, and he breathed it in as tears ran down his face.

Josh folded the pajamas as gently as if somehow Isaiah were still in them. He tucked them under the pillow, wiped his eyes, and stood. Stephani would be home soon. He needed to be strong for her. He bent down to pick up a stack of books and school papers piled by the bed.

Isaiah had been working on a report for Black History month. He'd chosen to report on Martin Luther King. Isaiah had picked him because he admired his faith as well as his accomplishments. He unrolled the poster his son had made using pictures they'd printed out together on the computer. Isaiah had labeled each picture and drawn a detailed timeline of King's life. In each corner, dialogue bubbles held quotes from King's speeches. In bright red marker Isaiah had printed the words: *We will not be satisfied until justice rolls down like waters and righteousness like a mighty stream. Martin Luther King*

Isaiah had never given his report. He'd never gotten to share the carefully crafted poster. What kind of justice was that? Josh smoothed out the poster and used a spare push pin to fasten it on Isaiah's bulletin board. He closed the door behind him with a soft thud.

In the bedroom, Josh changed into jeans and a blue pullover shirt, and stuffed his dirty clothes in the hamper. When he got back downstairs, Stephani was coming in the door. She dropped her oversized bag, filled to overflowing with children's books, on the counter. She used to read them with Isaiah, letting him help her choose what new books to order.

"How was your day?" she asked, reaching for the water.

"Not too bad. I didn't get much accomplished, though."

"I feel like I have to drag myself through the day. I'm exhausted, but yet when I lay down to sleep, I can't." Stephani slid down in her chair.

Josh sat opposite her. "I know. Would it help if I slept in the guest room? I don't want to keep you awake when I get up and wander."

Stephani reached across the table and laid her hand on his arm. "No, I want you near." She opened her water and took a sip. "Thanks for getting the sandwiches. Do you want to ask the blessing?"

"You go ahead."

Stephani prayed the short prayer they'd used since Isaiah first learned to talk. When Josh opened his eyes, she was crying.

He bit into his wrap, then caught a stray black olive that slipped onto his shirt. "I had lunch with a guy named Richard Petrowski last Monday. He gave me the card of a lawyer."

Stephani sniffed and unwrapped her sandwich. "A lawyer? Whatever for?"

"In case we want to file a lawsuit."

"I'm lost. Why would we file a lawsuit? Who would we sue?"

"The driver of the car."

"The young woman? But the police didn't file any charges against her."

"This would be a civil suit. It has nothing to do with whether she's charged or not." Josh went to the pantry and came back with an open bag of Doritos. He spilled some out on his plate and handed the bag to Stephani. "I'd like to talk to the lawyer. Pastor Allen said we should talk to someone about the accident."

"I don't know, Josh. I don't think he meant a lawyer." Stephani's eyebrows drew together in a little frown.

"Richard said it would bring justice. That we had a right to justice."

Stephani sighed. "If it makes you feel better, we could talk to this lawyer. But I don't want to sue anyone."

"Okay, fair enough. We'll just talk to him and see what he has to say. I'll call him tomorrow and set up an appointment. I think he's somewhere in Kansas City."

They finished their sandwiches in silence, each lost in their own world of grief.

CHAPTER 17

Emily sank into the cushions of the Taurus and leaned back. The harder she tried to catch up at work, the more she fell behind. People were still cautious around her, some asking if she needed anything, or if she was okay. Some blatantly avoided her, but that didn't stop them from requesting a report, an insurance form, or information on a 401K.

She started the drive home. When she passed The Lighthouse, she felt a tug of guilt. She'd gotten another email asking for volunteers at the clothes closet. Maybe sometime next week things would let up at work. Maybe the disagreeable pregnant woman was no longer there. Maybe …

Nate met her at the door. His kiss asked for a little more than she felt she could give. She turned in his arms and stepped away.

Disappointment clouded his eyes for a moment, but he recovered quickly. "How about we go out tonight? It's Friday and I have a reason to celebrate."

"You make a sale today?" Emily dropped her things on the kitchen table and opened the refrigerator.

"The commercial building on Valley Drive that I've had listed all winter? I had some lookers today. The people from that place you asked about volunteering. The Lighthouse? They want to expand. I guess the rehab business is good."

Emily's head popped up and she studied Nate's expression. "Ummm. Good. I'm glad you're finally getting some interest. But I can't go out tonight. I'm helping at the elementary book fair. They were short of volunteers, so I said I could work it. Are we out of Diet Pepsi?"

Like a storm cloud darkening the sun, anger rushed across Nate's face.

"You're helping at the elementary school? Emily, you've either worked late or helped somebody every night for two weeks. Did it ever occur to you that your husband would like to spend some time with you?"

Emily shut the refrigerator door. "It's not the way I would choose to spend a Friday night, either. I like to spend time with you too, Nate, but they really need help. So I'm going." She headed down the hall to the bedroom. At least she could change from dress clothes into jeans and be more comfortable.

Nate's voice, harsh and loud, carried down the hall. "I'm going to the store. I'll get Pepsi and something for my supper. I'll see you when you get home." The door slammed behind him.

For a moment, Emily wavered. Didn't Nate realize she'd rather spend the night with him? She remembered past Friday nights with him at their favorite restaurant, a tiny little retro diner with great burgers and thick, creamy shakes. They would eat and play oldies songs on the authentic juke boxes, singing along until they collapsed in laughter. But tonight she was needed at the book fair.

A few minutes later, dressed in her favorite jeans, a pale yellow pullover shirt, and some cute strappy heels, she was in her car headed back to the school. When she got there, she parked and hurried in. Although her office was in an adjacent building, she rarely had a reason to be in the elementary wing, and she was unsure where the book fair was held. A couple with two children, a boy and a girl, entered after her, and the children skipped down the hallway to the right. The parents ambled in the same direction, so Emily followed them.

After several turns in the hall, Emily found a room with posters announcing *Book Fair* on the door. The large room appeared to be the library. In front of the shelves of books to check out, portable shelving stood in every available space, stacked with hundreds of books, each one with a bright cover. Parents and children roamed freely, browsing through the books and other items for sale. Emily located the woman in charge, a teacher she thought was the librarian.

Emily put on what she hoped was a pleasant smile. "I signed up to help tonight."

"Great." The woman consulted a list of names taped on the wall. "Emily Adams, right?" At Emily's nod, she continued. "Grace and Natalie are running the cash register, Suzanne is helping with checkout, and Phil is sacking. Why don't you roam around and see if anyone has questions or needs help picking out books?"

"Okay," Emily agreed, wondering how she was going to answer questions when she didn't know what she was doing.

She wove through the thickening crowd of families—fathers with toddlers in strollers, mothers reading out loud from picture books, and children everywhere. She hadn't considered what this job would do to her emotions. No one seemed to need her assistance. A steady stream of parents lined up to check out, all with children who clutched books they wanted to purchase.

A small girl with a tumble of brown curls down her back was thumbing through a shiny new copy of *The Cat in the Hat*. Emily bent down, "Can I help you?"

She looked at Emily, dropped the book on the floor, and with a wail, fled around the corner and into the arms of a woman with brown curls just like hers. Emily mouthed, *I'm sorry*, and re-shelved the book.

She asked a couple more families if they needed help, but no one did. Then a woman with two girls tugging on her hands asked where the *Boxcar Children* books were. After wandering around the shelves for a while with the mother and girls in tow, Emily finally had to direct her to the librarian.

Her feet hurt and she felt useless. She wandered to the back of the room and leaned against a wall. Emily slipped one foot out of her shoe and bent to rub it.

"She's the one that hit the Nelson boy, I'm sure of it." The whisper came from the other side of the shelf of toddler books Emily stood behind.

"He died, didn't he?"

"Yes, he did."

"Why is she here?"

"She never got charged, but I'll tell you what I think …"

Emily didn't want to hear what the woman thought. She slipped her foot back in the shoe, heat rising in her cheeks, and hurried to the front of the room where the checkout line was.

"Can I help someone up here?"

Phil Jenkins, the sixth-grade teacher, handed her some bags. "The crowd's thinning out. If you take over for me, I can get home in time to do baths and read the bedtime story to Abby and Marie."

"Be glad to." Emily scooted around behind the table that served as a makeshift counter and bagged the piles of purchased books. She scanned the crowd and wondered which faces matched the whispering voices. The feeling of guilt was a weight far heavier than the sacks she handed out.

When the last family left, lugging three sacks of books between the same number of blonde-haired children, Emily sighed with relief.

"Thank you all, so much." The librarian's smile included all of the volunteers as they collected purses and jackets.

★★★★★★★

Nate must have already gone to bed, Emily thought as she took off her shoes and rubbed her feet, wishing she could massage her emotions. She paused to look at a stack of mail on the table before heading to the bedroom. A card addressed to her in her sister's handwriting peeked out from under a flyer from the local grocery. She pulled it out. Andrea lived with her husband and two teenage boys in a small suburb of Kansas City, three hours away. She remembered Nate called her after the accident, when he was attempting to get her out of bed. Although she and her sister were the best of friends, she couldn't talk to her then.

She slipped her fingernail under the flap and tore it open.

On the front, a kitten dangled from a tree branch by its front paws. *Hang in there,* read the caption. Inside, *I'm praying for you!*

Emily tossed the card to one side. *Praying* for me? What good will *that* do?

CHAPTER 18

Emily reached over Nate to silence the alarm. As she slid out of bed, he sprawled into the warm spot she left. At least his anger seemed to have abated by the time she got home from the book fair. Even when she reminded him about the Habitat for Humanity house, he didn't explode as she half expected.

He even asked her, "You want me to come and help too?"

"No, it's just a group from the school. You'd feel out of place." Emily felt guilty, especially since Jim had issued the invitation to both of them, but somehow if Nate came, it would no longer be *her* good thing to do.

She stood at the open closet door, puzzled over what was appropriate to wear when building a house. A quick peek out the window told her the sun was up, and she knew the forecast was for a warm, almost spring-like day. Finally, she chose some faded jeans, a soft tee shirt, and a pair of blue crocs. She filled a travel mug with coffee, pulled on a fleece jacket, and hurried out the door.

When she got to the construction site, people were everywhere. Several men and women wore bright, lime green tee shirts that signified they were in charge. The house sat in the center of the activity like an oddly shaped box, wrapped in a puffy, silver quilt. A truck carrying bundles of shingles stacked on pallets pulled to the front curb. With a series of warning beeps, it backed into the driveway.

Emily approached a large man in overalls and the official lime green tee. "Hi, I'm one of the volunteers from the school. Emily Adams."

"Great." The man reached out a beefy hand that swallowed hers as he pumped her arm up and down. "I'm John. Welcome to Maple Valley's first Habitat for Humanity home. Our goal today is to get this baby shingled, insulated, and sided. Next week we'll get the drywall up and have the family moved in by summer. Ever laid shingles, missy?"

"No, I haven't," Emily said, eyeing the height of the roof.

The man laughed as he followed her gaze. "Well, if you're not inclined to climb up on top of a house, we have things to do inside. Let me introduce you to Jordan. He's the foreman."

Emily followed John inside the house, stepping over piles of sawdust and construction materials. Jordan was a short man, wiry and very efficient. He handed her some gloves and showed her how to pack insulation between the studs, with a strict warning not to touch the exposed fiberglass that looked like pink cotton candy. While Jack Benson, a middle school teacher, rapidly cut pieces of insulation from a gigantic roll, she stuffed them awkwardly in the gaps. As hard as she tried, pieces of the insulation stuck to her clothes and skin. By the time someone called "coffee's ready," her arms and hands itched.

She went to the front room where a pony-tailed woman with a cheerful smile had set up a pot of coffee. She was filling Styrofoam cups with the steaming, dark liquid. Boards across two saw horses provided a makeshift table and were laden with an assortment of donuts, bagels, and muffins. Emily took one of the cups and sipped from it gratefully. She selected a cinnamon-raisin bagel and nibbled it, watching her fellow volunteers. Several teachers greeted her warmly.

All too soon, everyone tossed cups in the trash and hurried back to their assigned jobs.

"Ready to go?" Jack asked her.

"Sure." Emily set down her still half-full cup, wiped her mouth with a napkin, and followed Jack. Shortly after she began stuffing the walls with insulation, Jordan appeared.

"Emily, right?"

"Yes." She wondered if he was going to correct her on her insulation stuffing technique.

"We're a little short of help outside. The siding just arrived and I had to pull some of my roofers to work on it. Can I put you to work shingling?"

"On the roof?" Emily's voice squeaked.

"It's okay. The other two up there know what they're doing. You'd just assist them."

"I guess I could try." Emily wondered if volunteering for something that scared you witless somehow counted more. Jordan led her outside where a ladder leaned against the side of the house. She took a deep breath and started up. One step, two steps, then, a few rungs later, she could see over the top of the house. Two men were on the roof—Keith Taylor, a high school science teacher, and a man she didn't know. Keith was placing shingles in a row while the other man had a device that shot nails to hold the shingles down. Emily waited, clutching the top of the ladder, not sure how to get from the ladder to the roof.

Keith must have noticed her waiting. "Hey, Emily, you our other shingler?"

"Ummm, I guess. Jordan asked if I would come up and help." Emily paused to see if the men would notice her dilemma. They obviously didn't. "I don't know how to get up there."

Keith dropped a handful of shingles and came over to the ladder. "Put one hand here. Hold on to me. Put your foot here. Okay, now step up."

Now on the roof, Emily tried not to look down or think about how high she was. Her feet stepped cautiously over to where the men were working.

Keith showed her how to line up the shingles. He used the nail gun to fasten them down and the other man, who introduced himself as Levi Cummings, carried the shingles and helped Emily keep them straight. The sun shone warm and soon Emily was sweating. That made her itch more, but she couldn't stop to scratch, or even rest. Her back ached from bending over. Just when she thought she was going to have to ask for a break, she heard a bell and a shout.

"Lunchtime!"

Keith guided Emily to the edge of the roof and down the ladder. In the coffee room, someone had laid out sandwiches, chips, fruit, cookies, and sodas. Emily took a sandwich and an apple, but she was too tired to be very hungry. She drank the soda and forced some of the sandwich down before throwing it away. She leaned back against one of the walls and struggled to keep her eyes open.

"Careful. If you get against that insulation, it will make you itch," a woman remarked as she walked by.

Yeah, I know, Emily thought as she scratched one ankle.

Long before she was ready, people moved back to their positions and started to work. As she climbed the ladder, she saw Jim Van Scoy helping with the siding. It seemed odd to see him in jeans and a tee shirt. When she managed to get back on the roof, by herself this time, Keith handed her the nail gun.

"Ever use one of these?" he asked.

"Are you kidding?" She yelped as she took the heavy tool and it pulled her hand down, scraping her knuckles on a pile of shingles. "This is the first time I've done any of this stuff."

"Well, Levi had to leave, so how about if I show you how to do this? I'll line them up and you nail them."

Emily tried, but using the nail gun was awkward and her petite hands had difficulty wrapping around the handle. After nailing one long row of shingles, she stood to stretch. When she knelt down again, her smooth-soled shoes slipped on the gritty surface. She scrambled to maintain her balance and Keith shot out a hand to catch her. She grasped it tightly, but not before her foot kicked out and hit the stack of shingles at the edge of the roof. As if in a slow motion replay, Emily watched them slide. Keith made a heroic grab for them, but because he had stepped over to assist her, he missed. As the shingles tipped over the edge and tumbled down, he had the foresight to holler, "Look out below!"

They both peered over the edge of the roof to survey the damages. The shingles had scattered everywhere, and many of them had cracked or broken. But that wasn't the worst. On their plummet to the ground, the shingles had hit directly in the middle of a box of siding held between two saw horses. The entire box was bent and no longer looked usable.

Keith looked first at Emily, then the damage below.

Someone shouted, "What's going on?"

Emily covered her face with her hands and wished desperately to disappear. Within a minute, Jordan was on the roof. "Want to try insulation again?"

"I'm so sorry, Jordan. Unless you want to fire me, I think I can finish this."

"No, we never fire our volunteers. Of course, we've never had a volunteer break a stack of shingles and an entire box of siding in one fell swoop."

"I promise I'll be careful."

Jordan looked at Keith. "Keep her out of trouble, okay?"

****

Two hours later, Emily not only itched, her knuckles were bleeding, her hands throbbed, and her back ached. She climbed down the ladder, carefully placing each hand and foot. On the second to last step, she misjudged and tumbled down, falling hard on her backside.

Keith jumped off the final steps of the ladder and hurried to her. "Are you okay, Emily?"

She tried to laugh it off, but in the middle of the laugh, a sob caught in her throat. "Yeah, I'm okay. Only my pride is injured. And I'm more tired than I've ever been in my whole life."

"You did a good job up there." Keith held out his hand, pulled her to her feet, and gave her a pat on the back. "Only one bundle of shingles lost."

Emily tried to smile at his teasing, but somehow felt everyone was relieved to see her go. She limped to her car and drove home, hoping Nate would agree to get a pizza or Chinese take-out. She had muscles hurting in places she didn't even know she had muscles. All she wanted was a hot bath and her bed.

"Nate? I'm home." She found him in his recliner, watching a hockey game.

"You finally decide to come home?" he asked with a frown.

Emily frowned back. "You knew where I was—the Habitat house."

"I didn't realize you'd be gone the entire day. Aunt Grace came this afternoon."

Emily's heart sank. Nate's Aunt Grace spent the winters in Texas and always stopped to see them on her way home to Minnesota. She'd sent a letter saying what day she planned to be there. Nate had read the letter to her a couple of weeks ago. And now she'd missed the visit.

"Nate, I'm so sorry. I forgot." She wished he would hold out his hand to her and tell her it was okay, but he didn't. She shuffled down the hall to the bathroom, ran the tub full of hot water, and sank down in it.

How could doing something so good go so terribly wrong?

CHAPTER 19

Josh kept his arm around Stephani as they approached the offices of Stevens and Bloyer, Attorneys at Law. They had driven three hours to the outskirts of Kansas City, then down several streets lined with used car lots and neglected apartment complexes. After locating the address, they pulled into a weedy parking lot in front of a small stucco building. Drips of paint on the sidewalk indicated that it had been recently painted a rather garish turquoise.

"I don't feel right about this," Stephani hissed.

"Let's just hear what he has to say." Josh squeezed her shoulder, hoping to give some reassurance. "Frank said they only want to help."

"What can they do? Nothing will bring Isaiah back." Her words ended in a little sob.

Josh held the door for Stephani. When they entered a small waiting area, dim lighting and the smell of fingernail polish filled the room. A young platinum blonde in a low-cut blouse smiled brightly at them.

"May I help you?"

Josh took a step forward. "We're Josh and Stephani Nelson. We have an appointment with Frank Stevens."

"Oh, yes, Mr. Stevens is expecting you." She wiggled her way out from behind the desk and stood, revealing a skirt so short Josh averted his eyes.

"Right this way, please." The room she led them to was furnished with cheap furniture and smelled of smoke. "Have a seat. Can I get you anything? Coffee? Tea? Water?"

"No, we're fine," Josh answered for both of them as they settled onto a leather sofa.

Frank Stevens entered immediately. Not a large man, he still filled the room with his presence. His gray, well-tailored suit fit perfectly, and his dark hair with a bit of silver at the temples, was trimmed to perfection. A broad smile showed white, even teeth. Both Josh and Stephani rose to their feet as he strode across the room.

"Mr. and Mrs. Nelson, I'm Frank Stevens." He shook hands with both of them, holding Stephani's hand in both of his as he said, "I am so sorry. I would never presume to say I understand your grief. Your loss must be unbearable. Let me assure you, my partner and I will do everything we can to spare you further pain. Our mission is to help those who are hurting and to ensure that justice is served. Please, sit down."

Frank took a seat in an armchair, facing them across a glass coffee table. Stephani sat close to Josh, sniffling a little and rummaging through the purse on her lap. Frank slid a box of tissues across the table. She took one and nodded.

"Do you have a picture of Isaiah?" Frank's voice was gentle.

Stephani flipped through the items in her purse and pulled out a billfold-sized school picture, Isaiah in a blue striped shirt, one tooth missing. Forever smiling. Forever ten.

"What a handsome boy. Looks like his dad." Frank glanced up at Josh as he handed the picture back to Stephani. She took one last look before tucking it away in her purse.

"Yeah, we got that a lot." Josh put his arm around Stephani and squeezed her shoulder.

Frank started a recorder. "Mrs. Nelson, I'd like you to tell me about the accident in your own words."

Stephani took a breath and sat up straighter. For a second, Josh thought she might bolt from the room, but her shoulders relaxed and she relayed the details, punctuating her story with quiet sniffs and discreet swipes with the tissue. Josh took over the story when she reached the point where he arrived home and found the ambulance loading his son. As he talked, Josh found it difficult to share the story of his son's death with Frank, although he appeared sympathetic.

When they finished, Frank allowed them a moment as he bowed, almost prayerfully, over his hands. He raised his eyes to theirs and spoke in a quiet but firm tone. "Your son's death should not have occurred. I read the police report and I believe failure to press charges was a travesty of justice. In my opinion, if we take this to trial, show the jury your son's picture, they'll award you millions."

Josh felt Stephani's body stiffen. "Money? You think we want money for our son?"

Frank's voice was like thick cream. "Mrs. Nelson, may I call you Stephani?" She nodded. "Stephani, I know there is no amount of money that could bring Isaiah back. We only want some consequences for the woman who took your son's life."

"But … but … she did nothing wrong."

Josh leaned forward, flexing his fists. "She killed our son."

Stephani's ponytail shook as she turned to him. "Josh, you can't feel that way. It was an accident. We should have forbidden Isaiah to ride his skateboard at the end of the driveway. We were at fault."

Frank laid his hands palm down on the table and leaned toward them. "Sometimes we blame ourselves for events we can't control, Stephani. But, trust me; this had nothing to do with you or Josh." He paused and cleared his throat. "Our firm can help you. Filing a wrongful death suit can bring closure for you, begin the healing process. We only exist to promote justice."

Josh nodded and asked, "How would it work?"

Frank leaned back and folded his hands in his lap. "We would file the paperwork for a wrongful death suit from our offices. Now, you have up to two years to file, but the longer you wait, the more chance there is that any evidence will disappear. There are two factors to consider in a wrongful death suit—economic and noneconomic. Since you lost a child, the economic factors are less relevant, but you did have the funeral and burial to pay for. And the hospital costs. These are tangible expenses."

Josh nodded again, but remained silent.

Frank continued. "The noneconomic factors are the ones we would focus on, and these are immense. You have loss of love, companionship, affection—and we can ask damages for your mental anguish." He paused and looked at Stephani, who dabbed at her eyes with the tissue.

"We can also ask for punitive damages. If we can prove the driver of the car was at fault, and I think we can, we'll ask for a settlement for that as well."

Josh glanced sideways at Stephani. Her eyebrows were knit together in a frown and her head shook slightly. He reached for her hand.

"If you have already decided this is what you want to do, we can start the proceedings today. If you need time to process all the information, that's fine too, but we don't want to wait too long and risk losing evidence."

"If we decide to file, how long will it take before it goes to court?" Josh asked.

Frank laid out the probable timeline and what would happen at each stage.

"We're not going to make a decision today." Stephani's voice was soft, but Josh knew if she'd made a decision, she would stick to it.

"That's fine. We'll give you folks a little time. This is not easy. You'll make the right decision; you'll choose justice for your little boy."

Josh stood, and the men shook hands. "Thanks for taking time to meet with us, Frank."

Frank smiled and nodded at Stephani. "We'll be in touch."

Stephani led the way out of the building, her jaw set and her shoulders back. In the car, she snapped her seatbelt and swiveled to face Josh. "They don't want to help us. They just want money."

Josh started the car and pulled out into traffic toward Maple Valley. "They're a business. Yes, I know they want to make money. But this is not about money. It's about what's fair and just and right."

Stephani stared out the window. "Fair and just and right is not suing an innocent person."

"Is she innocent?"

Stephani didn't answer.

CHAPTER 20

Emily tightened the laces on her new fluorescent yellow Nikes and ran a few steps to try them out. They felt good. She'd finally gotten caught up at work and had left every day this week by five. It gave her plenty of time for running and when she didn't run, she could volunteer an hour or so at The Lighthouse. She'd also been trying to spend time with Nate. After she missed Aunt Grace's visit, there had been a few frosty days, but he seemed to have forgiven her.

She could easily run four or five miles now, and she felt confident about the Run for SIDs, less than a month away. People at the office, even the janitor, had pledged generously. Emily was excited about doing something that would help so many.

Her usual training route took her through their residential district, onto a bike path that meandered through a wooded park, out beyond the high school to a rural area, and then along a well-lit paved road back to town. It was about five miles, but she could lengthen or shorten it by looping around a few extra blocks or taking a shortcut on the path through the park.

She locked the door, stretched, selected an upbeat song on her iPod, and started out. When she ran, her head cleared, and the nightmare images disappeared. Even the weight of guilt temporarily subsided. Emily switched songs and picked up the pace. She loved the slap of her shoes on the asphalt and the rhythm of her breathing. The chilly night air made her breath appear in foggy little puffs. At the halfway point, she slowed down and took a drink from the hydration bottle hanging at her waist.

The rustle of weeds in the ditch beside her and a slight movement caught her eye. Her heart lurched. She'd never been afraid on her nightly runs, but she'd never come face-to-face with a skunk or other night critter either. Muscles tensed for flight, she waited. The grasses twitched again. With all of her senses on alert, Emily removed her ear buds and stood very still.

A tiny, wet, bedraggled head, mostly ears, emerged from the grass, and yowled loudly. Emily laughed in relief. It was only a kitten. At the sound of her laughter, the kitten disappeared again in the clump of grass. Emily squatted and coaxed. "Here kitty, come here, sweetheart."

The kitten poked out again, and Emily looked around. They were past the high school, at least a half mile from any houses. Who could it belong to? She reached out a tentative hand and as the kitten was set to scuttle back in the grass, scooped it up. Terrified, the kitten used everything it had to squirm out of her grasp. Emily cradled it close and rubbed the wet head until the kitten calmed somewhat. It looked much too young to be on its own. Emily stepped down into the ditch and parted the grass with her foot. There was no mother cat, no other kittens, just an empty cardboard shoebox with a rag stuffed inside.

Back on the sidewalk, Emily peered down at the soggy ball of fur. She tucked the kitten under her sweatshirt and started toward home. She could feel the kitten's heart pounding through her tee shirt, but at least it no longer struggled to escape.

When she turned into the driveway, the bluish light of the TV shone from the family room. Nate was home and probably worried. She'd taken far more time than her usual run, walking so as not to jostle her passenger, who now seemed to be sleeping.

She used her key to enter the front door. "Nate? Can you bring me my car keys?"

Nate came into the hall, combing his fingers through his hair. It looked like he'd dozed off. "Where have you been, Emily? It's late." The sound of a hockey game blared from the family room.

"I, ummm, found something."

"Found something?"

Emily lifted the edge of her sweatshirt. The kitten blinked sleepy eyes, then, seeing Nate, erupted with a fierce hiss. Emily covered the ball of fur again. "It was in the ditch way out by the high school. It's so tiny, I couldn't leave it there."

"A cat, Em?"

"A kitten. A tiny little kitten. It probably got lost. We'll put something in the paper and find its owners. And besides, we talked about getting a pet."

"We were supposed to get kids first and then get the pet for them."

Emily felt a stab of guilt as she thought of the foil packet in her bathroom drawer. "I need to get some cat litter and food—even if it's just here one night."

Nate sighed. "Make me a list; I'll go. The cat looks comfortable and it doesn't make sense to disturb it."

Emily moved to the kitchen and grabbed a pad from the counter. She jotted down the items they would need and handed it to Nate. "Thanks," she called as he headed out the door. Moving carefully, she opened the fridge and took out some leftover Chinese. She heated it in the microwave and ate it standing at the counter. The smell of food must have awakened the kitten. She could feel it moving against her stomach. For the briefest of moments, she wondered what it would feel like to have a baby moving against her. Then an image arose of the boy's startled face, and she knew she would never know.

Nate came through the door with several plastic bags. He unloaded them and stacked the food, bowls, cat litter, and a box on the counter. A lopsided grin lit up his features as he took out a small, pink ball with a bell inside. "I thought the scrawny little thing needed a toy."

"Awww." Emily gave him a peck on the cheek before she hurried to fill the litter box and place it on the floor. She opened a can and scooped a small amount of food into the bowl. Pulling the squirming kitten out from under her shirt, she set it gently on the floor. "Here you go. Litter box and food. What more could any rescued cat want?"

The kitten wobbled toward the food and, after a tentative sniff, began eating. After emptying the bowl, it backed away, sat in the middle of the floor, and gave a few swipes at its wet fur with a miniscule tongue. When Nate and Emily laughed, the kitten flattened its huge ears and scurried under the kitchen table.

"It's pretty scared. I don't think it's been around people a whole lot." Emily took a bite of cashew chicken.

"Which dramatically reduces the possibility of finding an owner."

"Do you mind?"

"Having a cat? I guess not. I'd rather have a kid, but maybe this is a good way to start. No signs yet?" Nate looped his arm around her and patted her belly.

Emily moved away and stirred the dish of Chinese with her fork. "No, not yet."

"Maybe we just need to try harder."

Emily knew Nate was studying her, but she refused to meet his eyes.

CHAPTER 21

"*Si, me gustaria una ensalada para el almuerzo.* Yes, please give me a salad for lunch," Carrie Ann spoke slowly. She smiled and nodded at the students sitting across the table from her as they echoed her words.

"That was perfect. And that's all for today. You're dismissed." Carrie Ann closed the language book. "Miguel, could I talk to you for a minute before you go?"

"*Si.*" Then, enunciating each word with care, he spoke in English. "Miss Carrie, what do you need? I will be happy to help you."

"Nice English, Miguel. I have a question for you." Carrie Ann moved to the door, ruffling hair, or giving a pat to each boy or girl as they slipped out.

When everyone else had gone, she turned to the boy at her elbow and continued in English, speaking so the boy would understand. "Have you seen Juan? This is the second day he has missed English lessons, and that's not like him. His arm is healing okay, isn't it?"

The dark head dipped and his eyes avoided hers. "No, Senorita Nelson, I have not seen Juan." He turned and was almost to the door when she caught him gently by the arm.

"Miguel, I don't believe you are telling me the truth. What do you know about Juan? Is he in some kind of trouble?"

The dark brown eyes rose to meet hers. For a minute, Carrie thought the fear she saw in Miguel's eyes would impel him to run. But then he nodded. "*Si*, there is trouble. Juan works for Eduardo."

Carrie Ann released Miguel's arm. "A job? He never said anything about a job. That's good, right?"

A sad look clouded the boy's eyes. "Eduardo is not a good man. He will keep Juan from coming to the Outreach Center. He has ways."

Carrie Ann's heart beat faster. She knew she should not get involved. Her job was to teach English, serve meals, and try to find limited resources in a country that did not care if children lived on the streets and were trained in a university of crime.

"Miguel, tell me where he is. Let me help him."

"No, Senorita Nelson, it would not be safe for you to go there." Miguel shook his head, dark hair flying.

"You let me worry about that."

"No, I cannot." Miguel turned to leave, but Carrie Ann reached for his arm again.

"I will be fine. Just tell me where Juan is."

"*Olmo Calle.* There is a tall apartment building, lots of windows. The alley that goes behind it has lots of dumpsters. Lots of places to hide. Several kids live there." Miguel mumbled the address before he fled out the door and down the street.

Carrie had a vague idea where Olmo Street was. And she thought she could make it there and back to her apartment before dark. She pulled out the map of Bogotá she kept in her purse and studied it. Jeremiah and Rose had left early that afternoon to attend a meeting with some of the city officials, so Carrie locked up, but not before slipping some bread and clean bandages in her bag.

She walked briskly and was soon in an unfamiliar area of town. Stale cooking odors drifted down from the apartments. Garbage littered the sidewalk. Bars covered the windows of retail establishments.

"*Que' Cabron!*" The Spanish curse echoed shrilly over the street. A door slammed and all was quiet.

The afternoon shadows deepened. Carrie Ann shrugged off a feeling of uneasiness and clutched the bag draped across her shoulder. At the corner, she paused. A sign identified Olmo Street. This must be the apartment building Miguel mentioned. The dirty stucco structure had ramshackle balconies hanging from each apartment. The entryway contained boards fastened where there had once been glass. Most of the windows were shrouded and dark.

Behind the apartment ran the alley, lined with battered dumpsters. On the other side of the alley loomed several abandoned warehouses. Broken glass littered the sidewalk and the reek of garbage in the dumpsters gagged her.

She peered into the alley. Was this where children actually lived? She could see some cardboard boxes stacked beside one of the dumpsters and some piles of filthy clothes.

The traffic on this street was minimal, and there were no other pedestrians. When a dog barked, Carrie Ann jumped. She shook it off and laughed at herself for being so nervous. She forced her feet to move into the shadows of the alley.

At first she thought her bag had caught on something. When she turned to give it a tug, she saw him. White teeth flashed in the dark as he leered at her. Her bag was held tightly in his fist. Carrie Ann started to scream, but his hand, smelling of cigarette smoke and grease, closed over her mouth. Her stomach lurched and threatened to spill its contents. Large arms wrapped around, pinning her hands tightly to her sides. He began to move further into the alley, half carrying, half dragging her.

She wasn't going without a fight. She tried to bite his hand, but it held her jaw. Carrie Ann kicked and thrashed as she attempted to loosen his hold. When the shadows of the buildings swallowed them, her feet were jerked out from under her and she fell. When her head hit the rough brick surface of the alley, darkness swirled into her brain and she lost consciousness.

****

Carrie Ann roused with a whimper. How long had she lain in the alley? Was her attacker still near? She stifled the scream lodged in her throat. As she came to full consciousness, the pain surfaced. Her legs were cool and she felt about the dark alley for her clothes. The flowered skirt was wadded in a pile nearby. She grabbed it and eased it over her hips, wincing at the pain that shot through her body. She raised one hand to feel the throbbing lump on the back of her head and struggled to her feet. Her underwear was nowhere to be found. Awareness of what had happened exploded and she screamed out, "Help!"

No one appeared, and with a rising fear of alerting more degenerates to her situation, she calmed herself with several deep breaths. Clutching the torn remnants of her blouse around her, she peered up and down the dark alley for any sign of her attacker. She was alone.

Oh, God, help me.

Her entire body felt battered, but nothing seemed to be broken or bleeding. Oddly, her bag was lying against the dumpster, the contents spilled on the brick. She rifled through the pile. The small amount of pesos she carried had been taken, along with the package of bread. She stuffed everything else back inside.

Carrie Ann limped toward her apartment, the agony of every step reminding her of the assault.

★★★★★★★

Carrie Ann sat on her bed wrapped in a thin blanket, a cup of tea warm and soothing in her hands. Rose sat close with a comforting arm around her, while Jeremiah paced between the door and the kitchen in the small apartment.

"They said they will look into it. But that's a lie. The police don't care. Rapes, assaults, children getting murdered … they're too busy getting their own deals from the drug lords."

Rose spoke up, her voice soft and gentle. "Jeremiah, we can't solve all the problems in Columbia. Let's just take care of the flock God has given us."

Jeremiah looked at the two women, his eyes blazing with anguish. "But we didn't. Carrie Ann …" His voice trailed off and he turned away. "We go to the police and they tell us what they think we want to hear, but they have no intentions of doing anything about it."

Carrie Ann set her teacup on the nightstand. "You're not responsible, Jeremiah. I knew it was foolish to be on Olmo Street, but I was so worried about Juan that I went anyway. Not only did I not find him, I caused you trouble."

"No, Carrie." Rose hugged her tighter. "Don't talk like that. You didn't cause anything. Wanting to find Juan was a caring thing to do. You tried to help one of our boys. We're angry because you got hurt and we need to do what we can to help you heal."

"I'll be okay. I'm tougher than I look. Maybe if I just had a day to sleep. My head still hurts." She rubbed the place her head had hit the pavement.

"What do you mean a day?" Rose interrupted. "You're taking the rest of the week off, for sure."

Carrie Ann shivered and pulled the blanket tighter. She'd never been afraid to be by herself, but the little apartment now seemed filled with dark shadows and possible intruders.

As if she could read her thoughts, Rose asked, "Why don't you gather the things you need for a few days and come to our apartment? You'll be with us during the night and closer to the Mission so I can check on you during the day."

"Oh, I couldn't put you out that way," Carrie Ann protested.

"It won't be any trouble at all. We have a pullout couch in the living room. Jeremiah and I can sleep on that and you can have our bedroom."

"I won't take your bed, but maybe it would be a comfort not to be alone tonight." Carrie Ann looked at the darkness outside her window.

Rose patted her hand. "Are you sure you don't want to talk to the counselor the doctor suggested?"

"No." Carrie Ann took another sip of tea. "I don't want to discuss it with strangers."

Jeremiah turned abruptly and faced Carrie Ann. "That's it!"

"What?" both women asked in unison.

"We'll send you stateside. We'll bump up your furlough a few months. You go home, spend time with your family, see a counselor, and rest up."

"I can't leave now. We just got rolling on the morning English lessons. And I have fifteen children who come regularly for the math classes in the afternoon. And Juan is …"

Jeremiah interrupted in a firm, fatherly tone. "Yes, you are going home.

I will not change my mind on this one. Rose can take over the English lessons. I can cover some of the afternoon classes, and we'll find Juan."

Rose nodded and patted Carrie's shoulder. "It will be good to have your family around to help you, Carrie Ann. What happened is not trivial. You do need time to heal. I'm not the teacher you are, but I'm sure the kids and I will do fine. And in a few months, if you're up to it, you can return and jump right back in."

"But," Carrie Ann sputtered, "my family's not expecting me until summer."

Rose chuckled softly. "And do you think if you made a telephone call to your mom and told her we'd moved your furlough up, she would say, 'Oh, no, you can't come yet'?"

"No, she'd be thrilled." Carrie Ann leaned her head on Rose's shoulder. "Okay. I know better than to argue with the two of you." She managed a weak smile. "It will be good to be with my family. I'd like to see Josh; maybe I can minister to him and Stephani. And this is a good time of year to visit the churches that support me. Attendance drops in the summertime."

She reached for her stack of books. "For the English classes, we're ready for lesson thirty-six. The kids will enjoy this one; it tells about soccer games." Carrie Ann showed the lesson to Rose and laid out her plans, including ways to reinforce the teaching.

Jeremiah sank into the basket chair, facing Rose and Carrie Ann. When they were finished he said, "It's settled, then. We'll get you a ticket on the first available flight. How about we spend some time in prayer with you before we get your things and go?"

The blanket fell onto the bed as Carrie Ann stood. "Good idea. Pray that I will be able to forgive him." She reached for Rose and Jeremiah's hands and they moved into a circle of prayer.

CHAPTER 22

Donna smoothed the fur of the sedated black female dog as Dr. Ewing stitched up the incision. She was one of the lucky ones. A young man had spotted her picture on the Internet and drove an hour to the shelter in Maple Valley to adopt Samantha. As one of the requirements for adoption, he was having her spayed. As soon as she recovered, she would go to her new home.

Donna's two-day-a-week retirement job at All Paws Animal Clinic was perfect. There was plenty of variety and she loved it all, but it was a special pleasure to see a rescued animal with his or her new family.

"There you go, girl, no unwanted pups ending up in a shelter." Donna took the needle from Dr. Ewing and placed it with the other instruments she would clean and sterilize later. She helped the doctor move Samantha to a clean cage. One eye was already twitching open as the anesthesia wore off. She gave the dog one more pat before closing the cage door.

"Let's get Rascal vaccinated next," the doctor suggested.

Donna opened the cage and lifted out a shaggy two-month-old Yorkshire puppy. She held him as the vaccinations were administered.

"His owners pick him up tomorrow. I think he'll be glad to go home." Dr. Ewing disposed of the needle and washed his hands as Donna returned the puppy to his cage and gave him a little back scratch.

"Pickles the pug is waiting in exam room one." She picked up the dirty instruments and wiped down the exam table.

When the bell on the front door tinkled, she hurried to greet the next customer. They liked to get patients in as quickly as possible to avoid crowding and possible altercations between pets in the waiting room. A tall woman with strawberry-blonde hair walked in with the tiniest bundle of fur imaginable. The kitten's voice, however, was not small. The yowling filled the clinic. Yvonne, the receptionist, finished getting the intake information and handed the clipboard to Donna.

"Come this way and we'll get you set up in exam room two." Donna set out briskly down the hall and the woman followed, her kitten yowling all the way. When they were inside the room with the door shut, Donna reached out her hand to the kitten. "And who is this tiny baby with the big voice?" She smiled up at the kitten's owner.

"Well, it doesn't exactly have a name."

Apparently deciding it wasn't in danger, the kitten stopped crying and snuggled down in its owner's arms. "We don't even know if it's a boy or a girl. I found it when I was jogging out by the high school. We put an ad in the paper, but so far no one's responded."

The kitten peered out over the woman's arm, gazing at Donna with wide amber eyes. Her owner stroked the gray fur with obvious affection. "I really don't know if we'll keep it, but I thought maybe it needed to be checked over and, I don't know, does it need shots?"

"Let me see." Donna reached for the kitten and, with a practiced turn of her hand, lifted the tail. "Congratulations. You have a girl." She looked the kitten over and smoothed the ruffled fur. "Let's see what Dr. Ewing says, but I'd guess she's about seven or eight weeks old. She's due for her first inoculations and probably needs worming. Did you bring in a fecal sample?"

"Her poop?" The woman's nose wrinkled. "No, I didn't know I was supposed to."

"That's okay. The doctor may ask you to bring in a sample later, or he may just do a general worming." Donna handed the kitten back to her owner. "He'll be here in a few minutes."

Donna glanced down at the clipboard to call the customer by name. *Emily Adams.* "Please wait here, Emily."

The name sounded so familiar. Then a shock of recognition ran through her like a bolt of electricity. Surely it was not the same Emily. Donna stumbled out the door and down the hall. Using the computer, she pulled up the file and double-checked the address. Roosevelt

Avenue. The same address in the newspaper article—only a few blocks from where she lived.

There was an exit door to a small yard where they exercised dogs boarded for short or long-term care. Donna lurched through the door and leaned against the brick wall of the clinic.

God, it was easier to pray for her before I met her. She took deep breaths of the spring air and with each breath came a measure of strength and peace.

Please don't ask me to talk to her. Let her leave the clinic and let me never see her again.

A yellow Lab loped across the pen and dropped a green tennis ball at Donna's feet. He stood watching her expectantly. When she didn't respond, he nudged the hand hanging by her side. She picked up the ball, threw it across the yard, and watched him gallop off.

Lord, let me be as eager to do your will as this Lab is to chase a ball. Give me your eyes to see Emily as you see her. And help me to forgive her.

After a few moments, Donna reentered the clinic. She went to the reception area and, since there were no patients waiting, busied herself filing charts and organizing shelves of veterinary supplies. It was simple to stay bent over the file cabinet when Emily came to check out. Yvonne took her payment and thanked her. When the bell on the door tinkled again, Donna stood up. Emily was leaving, shielding her kitten, as a huge Doberman dragged its owner inside.

"Hello, Bubba." Yvonne greeted the Doberman and his owner. "Donna, will you check for Bubba Dowling's file?"

Donna had the file in hand when Dr. Ewing hurried in from the back carrying a small bottle. "Has Mrs. Adams already left?"

"Yes," both Donna and Yvonne answered.

"I intended to give her this sample of vitamins for the kitten." He turned to Yvonne. "Can you call her sometime today and let her know they're here?"

Take them to her. The thought came loud and clear. Donna remembered the Lab chasing the ball and her own prayer. She took a deep breath. "I could drive them by her house."

"Thank you, but that's not necessary."

"It's no problem. I'd be glad to do it. She only lives a few blocks from me."

"Well, if you want to, go ahead." The doctor handed her a bottle of vitamins.

Donna wished she hadn't volunteered. She didn't want to see Emily Adams, and she certainly didn't want to talk to her. "I'll take them on my way home tonight."

"Thanks, Donna. Go ahead and take Bubba and Tom to room one."

Donna led the way down the hall to the open exam room. She took preliminary information from the Doberman's owner and refused to think about coming face-to-face again with the woman who killed her grandson.

CHAPTER 23

Emily stirred the marinara sauce as it simmered, inhaling the fragrance of the herbs. Nate's favorite dish was spaghetti and meatballs, made with Emily's homemade sauce and topped with freshly grated Parmesan. She'd stopped at the bakery for garlic focaccia bread, and there was fresh lettuce in the fridge for salads. They'd hardly eaten together since she'd started running and volunteering. This afternoon, Nate was out showing houses, but he'd sent a text saying he would be home early. She hoped a special meal would make up for her being gone so much.

When the doorbell rang, Emily laid down the spoon and wiped her hands on a towel. She moved down the hall and was surprised when she peeked out the window. The short, gray-haired lady from the vet's office stood on the stoop. Emily wondered if they'd found something wrong with her kitten, maybe an illness or defect. She threw the door open.

"What's wrong?" she blurted.

The lady looked startled and took a step backwards. Then, obviously realizing what Emily meant, she said, "Oh, nothing's wrong with your kitten." One blue-veined hand waved the thought away. "The doctor intended to give you these vitamins today when you were in the clinic." She held out a small white bottle.

"And you brought them to me?" Emily couldn't believe it. "I don't get that kind of service from my own doctor."

"Well …" The woman twisted the handle of her bag and her lips pursed as if she had more to say. "I wanted to talk to you anyway. May I … may I come in?"

"Ummm. Sure. I'm cooking supper. Come out to the kitchen with me so I won't burn it." Emily led the way and reached to move the newspaper off the kitchen table. "Here, have a seat. Can I get you a glass of water? Diet Pepsi?"

"No, thank you. I'm fine. I just wanted to talk for a minute."

Emily gave the sauce a quick stir, turned down the heat, and then sat at the table, expecting advice on raising a kitten.

The woman took a deep breath and let it out slowly. "My name's Donna Nelson. I am, I mean, I was Isaiah Nelson's grandmother."

Time stopped and Emily was sure her heart did as well. Isaiah Nelson? The boy? With a gasp, she covered her mouth with her hand. The startled face with the blue eyes flashed before her and for a moment she couldn't speak. Then her words came in breathy little hiccups. "Oh. Oh, my. I'm sorry. I'm so sorry. You must hate me."

Donna's soft hand reached out and covered hers. "No, I don't hate you. What happened was terrible, an unbelievable tragedy, but it wasn't your fault." She took another deep breath.

"I ... I forgive you."

For a moment, Emily thought she misunderstood. She raised her eyes to Donna's. "But how can you? What I did was unforgiveable."

"I forgive because I've been forgiven." Donna's gray eyes were wet, but she looked deeply into Emily's blue ones.

Emily drew her hand back. "You didn't hit someone with your car, did you?"

"No, I've never done that. But I've done a lot of things wrong, more wrong than right, I think. But I'm a Christian. God forgave me and He gives me the power to forgive. I've been praying for you."

Tears spilled over and ran down Emily's cheeks. She swiped at them with the back of her hand. "What about Isaiah's mom and dad? How do they feel?"

A tiny frown appeared on Donna's face before she looked down. "Truthfully, I don't know. They may not be ready to forgive."

A yowl preceded the kitten's entrance into the kitchen. Emily reached down and scooped her up. A rumble came from the kitten's throat as she circled once, then curled up in her lap. Emily grabbed a napkin from the holder on the table and blew her nose.

"I'm glad she found you." Donna leaned forward and used one finger to scratch behind the over-sized ears. "Nothing happier than a rescued animal in their forever home."

"She makes me laugh." Emily didn't add that she was nearly the only thing that made her laugh anymore.

Donna stood and gave the kitten one last pat. "I'll get out of here and let you finish your supper." Turning back she asked, "Do you go to church, Emily?"

"No. Nate and I never got into that. Not that it's not a good thing to do. Maybe we'd go if we had a kid."

"You and Nate would be welcome at my church, Maple Valley Fellowship. We'd love to have you." Donna dug in her purse and pulled out a scrap of paper and a pen. She wrote some numbers on the paper and pushed it over to Emily. "Here. This is my telephone number if you want to come. Just call and I'll meet you there."

Emily took the paper. "Thanks for inviting me. Maybe we'll come sometime. I'll talk to Nate about it."

Emily stood, still holding the kitten, and Donna gave her a quick hug before she strode to the door. Emily watched as she got into her car and drove away. For a few minutes she was very still, lost in thought as she stared out the window.

★★★★★★★

Nate couldn't keep from grinning as he got out of the Explorer. He'd been in this business long enough to know when he'd made a sale, and he'd made a sale today. Oh, they hadn't signed an offer yet, but they would. And it was his listing, so that upped his earnings. Maybe he'd take Emily out tonight. She seemed to be better lately—working through the accident. Things were getting back to normal.

"Honey," he called, dropping his jacket over the back of his recliner as he moved toward the kitchen. "Mmmm. Spaghetti?" He wrapped his arms around Emily as she stood at the stove.

She turned in the circle of his arms and kissed him.

"I was going to offer to take you out tonight, but this is even better." He continued to hold her as she tilted back to look at him.

"I know I've neglected you lately, things on my mind, you know, and work. I decided to treat you. You sure spaghetti's okay?"

"More than okay. What's for dessert?" He pulled her close and nibbled on her ear.

Emily gave him a playful shove. "Go change. The spaghetti is ready. I just have to heat the bread."

Nate whistled down the hall as he yanked off his tie and unbuttoned his shirt. He pulled on a pair of jeans and decided it was warm enough for a short-sleeved tee. He stepped into Emily's bathroom for a quick wash of his hands. He was reaching for the soap when he saw them. Lying on the counter by the sink was a small foil package. Birth control pills. Why did she have those out? He turned over the package and realized it was a new prescription, filled that week. And some of them had been punched out. He soaped up his hands, rinsed, and dried them on a pink striped towel.

When he walked back in the kitchen, Emily had heaped two plates with spaghetti and placed a basket of warmed bread on the table. Two crisp salads sat by their plates.

Nate stood with his hands on the back of a chair. "Emily, why are you taking birth control pills again?"

Emily drew in a sharp breath. "What?"

"I went in your bathroom to wash my hands. I saw the birth control pills. It's a new prescription and some of them have been taken. What's going on? Am I mistaken? I thought we were trying to make a baby." Nate's voice had a cold edge.

A small whimper escaped. "After the accident … I just can't … I can't be a mom."

"Don't you think that's something we should talk about? I'm thinking it's my fault we're not getting pregnant and you're back on the pill."

"I didn't know how to tell you," Emily almost whispered.

"What else are you hiding from me, Emily? What other things are you doing behind my back?" He shoved the chair against the table. "I don't feel like spaghetti." Grabbing his car keys, Nate strode to the door and slammed it behind him.

CHAPTER 24

A soft paw batted at Emily's cheek. The kitten sat on Nate's pillow, regarding her new master intently with wide amber eyes. Apparently satisfied that Emily was awake, she yawned and stretched, then hopped off the bed and trotted down the hall, probably heading for the litter box. Emily switched off her alarm. She'd already hit the snooze button twice. Now she needed to hurry to make it to work on time.

In spite of the kitten's yowling, the house seemed strangely quiet. Emily padded in bare feet to the kitchen, but there was no coffee, no newspaper, and no Nate.

In the refrigerator, a container of spaghetti sat cold and congealed. After Nate stormed out Friday night, Emily plopped their dinner into a plastic bowl, ate her salad, and went for a run. When she'd returned, Nate wasn't there, so she'd gone to bed alone. Hours later, the front door opened and closed. She rolled to her side of the bed and heard the spare room door click shut.

Over the weekend, Nate had hosted two open houses. When he'd been at home, he talked only if necessary. Although she'd been extra polite in the hope his anger would subside, he still slept in the spare bedroom. And he'd left the house early this morning. Without making coffee.

If she got out the door in the next few minutes, she might have time to drive through Starbucks and still make it on time. She pulled a container of yogurt out of the fridge and stirred in a little granola. After a couple of bites, she looked down at the kitten yowling at her feet.

"Are you sad too?" She sat at the kitchen table, put the kitten on her lap, and was rewarded with the throaty rumble of her purr. "Now that I know you're a girl, I guess I should name you." She looked at the kitten with her ridiculously large ears. "I think I'll call you Minnie. You look like Minnie Mouse."

Minnie answered with her loud meow.

"Maybe you're more hungry than sad." She filled the little bowl with cat food and set it on the floor, adding the vitamins Donna had brought. Minnie waved her fluffy tail as she crunched the bite-size pieces of cat food.

Emily needed to hurry and get dressed. She pulled on dark blue dress pants and a pale blue shirt, but when she started to fasten the shirt, a tiny white button fell on the floor. She pulled off the shirt, wadded it up, and threw it to one side. She looked for something to match the pants. Frustrated, she stripped again to underwear and chose black pants with a black-and-white shirt. As she buttoned her pants, Emily glanced wistfully at the Nikes tossed in the corner. Running seemed to be the only way she could escape. When she ran, thoughts of work, home, and especially the event that had changed her life, evaporated. But there was no time for a run in the morning. Maybe she could leave work early and take an extra long one tonight. The SIDs event was only a week away. No matter what happened between her and Nate, she had to keep training. She pulled her black heels out of the closet.

With shoes in hand, Emily hurried down the hall. She could put on her makeup in the car while she waited for her coffee at Starbucks. She grabbed for her purse sitting on the hall table and an envelope fell to the floor—a notice that the car payment was due. Nate was supposed to take care of it, but here it was. If the payment wasn't put in the mail today, there would be a penalty, and they couldn't afford that. She stopped to write a check and shoved it in the envelope. Now a trip to the post office was necessary, and it was in the opposite direction of the school. She rubbed a hand across her forehead in a futile attempt to ease the tension.

In the entryway, Emily pulled on her shoes. Just before she stepped out, she glanced up at the tiny message board that hung beside the door. *Bring up books from the basement for pickup on Monday.* Another job Nate hadn't done. She'd sorted the books on Saturday, thinking it was a good thing to do, donating their old college books to a charity. Goodwill seemed grateful and promised a Monday pickup. Nate was to carry the heavy boxes up from the basement. He'd either forgotten or been so angry he chose not to do it.

Emily slammed the door, took off the heels, and went downstairs. The basement was used primarily for storage, but they had talked about finishing a couple of rooms. There was a large open area that would be a great game room. Sitting right where she'd loaded them were three, very heavy boxes. She wanted to leave them, but they were to be picked up today.

After one box was wriggled into her arms, Emily started up the stairs. She shoved the box beside the garage and went back for the next one, stacking it on top. The third box was lighter. With the door open and a box balanced on her hip, she slipped back into her heels. Her free hand grabbed for her purse, but as she hooked the strap over her arm, a streak of gray shot out the open door.

"Minnie! No!" Dropping the box, she went after the kitten. Minnie darted behind a bush.

"Here, sweetie, come here," Emily called, her voice like syrup. Minnie waited until Emily was right beside the bush before she sailed off around the house. Ten minutes later, she finally cornered the kitten under the back deck.

"Minnie, don't ever do that again," Emily scolded, but the kitten just snuggled in and purred. She took her to the kitchen, poured a tiny bit of milk into her dish to keep her busy, and maneuvered the last box outside.

Emily thought about skipping the coffee, but she already had a headache and needed a latte. At Starbucks, she was the fourth car in line. A glance at the clock said she would be late—very late—but there was nothing she could do. Maybe she could slip in unnoticed.

She used the rearview mirror to touch on some eye makeup and lipstick. When the driver behind her tooted his horn, she moved up to the window.

Fifteen minutes later, she burst through the office door. Of all days, Jim Van Scoy stood by Shirley's desk. One eyebrow rose slightly as Emily flew past, but he didn't speak, not even a response to her hurried, "Good morning."

As she powered up the computer, Jim's large frame filled the doorway to her office. "We missed you at the meeting this morning."

Emily stared at him as her mind worked frantically.

"The staff meeting? Scheduled at eight thirty?" The tone of Jim's voice held no warmth.

With a sickening flip of her stomach, Emily remembered. There had been a memo last week. A meeting was scheduled before the office opened, but they would be compensated by being allowed to leave an hour early on Monday afternoon. If she'd remembered the meeting, it would have allowed ample time for a long run. Now, she not only wouldn't be allowed to leave early, she may have jeopardized her job.

"Oh, Jim, I'm so sorry. There's been so much going on, I guess I forgot. My cat got out this morning and I had to chase her ..." Emily stopped as she realized Jim probably didn't care what had made her late. "I'm really sorry. Can you recap for me?"

Jim's stern expression didn't lessen. "Let's meet at eleven."

Emily glanced at her calendar. She could reschedule her appointment with a teacher who needed to make changes to his insurance policy. "I'll be there."

Jim's glare held her fast. "I realize your accident was traumatic, but you cannot let it affect your work. I won't hold you to a different standard because you have things going on in your personal life. I still require you to be a professional."

Emily nodded, unable to look at him. "I know, and I don't expect you to treat me differently. I really am sorry about missing the meeting. It won't happen again. I promise."

"We need the figures for the elementary budget this morning. We can go over it at eleven when we meet." Jim turned and pulled the door shut behind him.

Emily felt a chill of fear as she opened her email and leafed through the inbox. Why was her entire life falling apart? She pulled up the budget and worked all morning without stopping, except when she sent a text to Nate. *Will I c u tonight?* So far, there had been no answer.

At eleven, she hurried down the hall to the superintendant's large office. He was brisk and businesslike as they went over the budget and talked about upcoming projects. Emily was relieved he didn't mention probation or an incident report for her file. After the meeting, Emily returned to her desk. On her phone was a text from Nate: *Showing house b home late.* Emily shoved the phone back into her pocket and stared at the computer.

Numbers floated around in her head like cottonwood seeds in the wind. The afternoon dragged on until she heard chatter in the hallway—the rest of the staff leaving early. Then all was quiet except for laughter on the playground. She raised her shade a tiny bit and looked out. A pudgy little girl tugged her daddy toward the swings. He lifted her into one of the vinyl seats and pushed her. Emily watched as the girl pumped her short legs in the air, squealing with delight. The mother crouched beside a sturdy, dark-haired boy, examining something in his hand, perhaps a caterpillar. They tipped their heads back and laughed at a shared joy.

Emily's chest tightened with sorrow and she turned back to the computer.

Clouds had moved in and a slight drizzle was falling by the time she left the office and headed home. It was dark and damp, so she cut her run short and only went a few blocks before she looped around and returned to the house.

When she got back, Nate stood in the kitchen fixing a sandwich. He glanced up as she came in, but didn't speak to her. He just kept spreading mayonnaise on the bread.

"Did you make me one?" Emily asked.

Nate shrugged. "You weren't here." He layered on some deli turkey and closed the sandwich. "The bread's there."

Emily moved to the counter to work on a sandwich. "I was late to work this morning."

Nate had his sandwich on a plate and was moving to the family room. "Couldn't you get up? I didn't turn off the alarm."

Emily slapped her sandwich together. "I had to write a check for the car payment you forgot and then I carried those boxes of books up from the basement. As I was trying to get the last one out the door, the kitten got out and I had to chase her around the house." Her voice rose as she spoke and the last phrase came out in a shriek.

Nate acted like he didn't notice. "So, did Jim call you on the carpet?"

"I missed a meeting."

"Not sure how you missing a meeting at work is my fault. If you'd reminded me, I'd have paid that bill and carried those books up." Nate flipped on the TV and flopped onto the recliner.

Emily carried her sandwich into the office without another word.

CHAPTER 25

Josh glanced over his emails. He ran on automatic these days, doing only what was necessary at work and home. No thought or feeling— just numb.

There was a memo regarding a meeting at ten with some of the architects from Wallace and Jones Architectural Firm. He remembered the email he had sent to CJ and scanned his inbox. There was no reply.

Josh drifted back to his sophomore year. How many parties had he gone to with CJ while they were roommates? Must have been close to a hundred. They'd partied every weekend he hadn't gone home, that was certain. And most of the parties involved marijuana and some kind of alcohol. Carrie Ann knew what he was doing and tried to talk to him. She even suggested he find a different roommate. But CJ was fun, and Josh had been young and more than a little reckless.

It had ended badly. On a Friday night in early May, CJ decided to throw a party in their dorm room. He always had connections with older classmates who were willing to sell him alcohol and drugs. When Josh returned from class that afternoon, their closet had been turned into a makeshift bar and a large stash of marijuana was hidden in the kitchenette cupboards.

People began arriving early. Some were friends or acquaintances, others Josh didn't know at all. Their stereo was blasting out music by Tupak and Snoop Dog. CJ had schmoozed the resident assistant, so he was confident they wouldn't get a visit or a call to turn down the sound. Soon the air was thick with sweet-smelling marijuana smoke and stale beer. One couple was making out on Josh's bed while others spilled out into the hall.

Sometime around midnight, the phone rang. Josh picked up and the voice on the other end said, "Campus security just pulled up." When Josh repeated the announcement, students fled in all directions, stubs of joints still lit and beer cans half empty. CJ pushed out the screen of their first-floor window and left.

Josh answered the knock and let security in. He'd been the one who stayed—the one who told the truth and faced the music. The college let both of them off with probation and a fine, but CJ never forgave Josh for turning him in. The next year, they both chose other roommates.

David, Josh's new roommate, was a solemn young man who intended to go into the ministry after his undergraduate studies. That year, Josh studied, pulled up his grade point average, and even made the dean's list. Both Carrie Ann and his parents were relieved Josh was finally taking his education seriously.

A year later, he received a scathing letter from CJ. When CJ had attempted to get into the graduate program at a prestigious university, he was turned down and he blamed Josh. In a heartfelt response, Josh asked for forgiveness, saying he only did what he felt was right. The years passed and Josh never heard back from CJ, who apparently refused to forgive him.

In all probability, he would see CJ at this meeting. Josh could be an adult and not let any folly he had participated in so many years ago influence the decisions and work he had to do now. He hoped CJ could too.

A few minutes before ten, Josh scooped up all the papers spread across his desk and stuffed them inside a file folder. He'd prepared a lengthy presentation to state his case to the architects. He had some serious concerns about an entryway in the Memorial Hospital wing. Changes needed to be made and he hoped the alterations would be acceptable without too much argument. With the folder in one hand and his laptop in another, he strode out of his office and down the hall to the conference room.

"Good morning." Josh nodded to Adam, who was setting up an easel with the architectural drawings. More plans, charts, and drawings were spread over the table. Three men from Wallace and Jones sat across from Josh, talking and laughing among themselves. None of them looked up. CJ had packed on quite a few pounds since their college days and the red hair had faded, or perhaps been colored. But Josh would have recognized his laugh anywhere.

Three more engineers filed in, one of them Paul Sturtz, who would lead the meeting. Everyone but Paul took a seat. For a few minutes, the air was filled with the patter of small talk. Josh kept busy looking through his file and didn't participate. He couldn't bring himself to join in, joking around like he used to.

Paul glanced at the clock, cleared his throat, and the room grew quiet. "I think we'll get started. We have a lot to do. Can I get anyone another coffee? Soft drink? Water?"

"I'll take a Mountain Dew if you have one." Josh knew that was the soda CJ would pick. CJ looked up then, and Josh saw a flicker of recognition in his eyes, but no smile or nod of hello.

Paul returned with the can of Mountain Dew and slid it across to CJ. A few others refilled coffee cups from the urn in the corner. When everyone was seated again, Paul said, "Let's have some introductions. Some of us are going to be working closely for the next few months. Tell us your name and anything else you'd like us to know."

When it was Josh's turn, he gave his name and added, "I'm looking forward to working with Wallace and Jones. CJ and I go back a long way. We were roommates at Missouri State."

CJ looked uncomfortable, but he nodded. "That was a long time ago. I go by Curtis now. Good to see you, Josh."

Josh nodded at him in return. He doubted the sincerity of CJ's comment.

After the introductions, Paul shifted to the real reason for the meeting. Time to negotiate changes needed for structural safety of the building, while maintaining the architect's vision. Josh opened his folder. The entry was a small area, but critical.

"We have a problem with the east entry." Josh stood and moved to the easel where Paul had displayed the drawings. "The design of this window will not provide the necessary support for the additional weight of the entryway canopy."

"I think it will," one of CJ's colleagues argued. "This is the window the hospital board wants. They specifically requested that we keep the entryways airy and light."

"You're engineers. Figure out a way to support that design," another architect chimed in.

Josh stood his ground. "It can't be done. The window needs to be changed. You could use a smaller window that will still let in the light, but support the canopy. This is a critical area."

"No!" The first architect who spoke jumped in, slapping his palm on the table. "This design complements the entire entryway. The windows here and here," he pointed to the drawing on the easel, "are the same shape. We can't change one window without changing them all."

"Then change them all."

"That's ridiculous." Someone snorted and Josh knew without looking who it was.

Paul cleared his throat. "This is rather controversial for one little window. Let's table this and have both firms look at ways to compromise. We have some other issues I'd like to get to before we break for lunch."

Josh rubbed his temples. He had the beginnings of a headache. This was normal give-and-take between engineering and architectural firms, so why did it cause his head to hurt and his stomach to tie itself in knots? When the meeting adjourned, two of the architects shook Josh's hand as they left. CJ did not.

CHAPTER 26

Emily carried a warm, fragrant rotisserie chicken to the car. Nate had sent a text saying he wouldn't be home for supper, so Emily stopped at Super Valu. She could slice some of the chicken for tonight's meal and have leftovers another night.

But a run was first. The damp weather had moved out, so it would be a good night for a long run. Emily anticipated the workout—the stretch of her muscles, the runner's high as adrenaline flowed.

When she walked in the door, there was a soft thump as Minnie jumped off the couch or wherever she'd curled up for a nap. She trotted out to greet Emily, stretching, yawning, and twining around her legs as Emily moved to the bedroom to change.

Minnie seemed to know she'd found a forever home. If Emily reached down to pet her, she was rewarded with a loud, rumbling purr. When she sat down to read the mail, Minnie leapt into her lap and deposited tiny, rough-tongued kisses on her chin. It seemed to Emily, however, the cat was the only one delighted to see her come home.

After a few minutes of petting, Emily grabbed her Nikes. Minnie immediately pounced on the laces. When Emily pushed her away, Minnie wrapped prickly paws around her hand.

"Hey! Just 'cause I leave you to run every night is no excuse to attack me."

Emily swooped up the kitten, petted her for a minute more, and deposited her on Nate's recliner. With jacket in hand, she slipped out the door. On the porch, she stretched a few times before she started out. As she settled into the rhythm of running, her legs felt strong and her long strides began eating up the pavement.

Just before she turned into the park, less than a mile into her run,

Emily stopped. The heel of her right foot hurt and she took off her shoe to make sure there was nothing in it. There wasn't. She put the shoe back on, flexed her foot a few times, and set out.

Another mile out and she stopped again. Was the problem with her new shoes? But even when she hobbled a few steps in her socks, her foot still hurt. This didn't seem to be one of those times when you run through the pain. She decided to take a shortcut, cutting through the park on the grass. She ran much slower and favored her right foot.

By the time Emily made it home, she was limping and in a lot more pain. She took off both shoes and collapsed on the couch. Minnie showed her delight by jumping on Emily's chest, where she curled up and purred contentedly.

Later, Emily limped to the kitchen to fix supper, but soon returned to the couch. When Nate walked in the door, she lay stretched out, foot propped on a pillow. She was pleased to see the look of real concern on his face.

"What happened?" he asked.

"I don't know. The heel on my right foot started hurting when I ran."

"Did you take some ibuprofen? Did you ice it?"

Emily shook her head. "No. I kept hoping it would just go away."

Nate went to the kitchen and returned with a bottle of ibuprofen, a glass of water, and an ice pack. He shook out some tablets and handed her the water. "Here, take these."

Obediently, she swallowed the pills as he arranged the ice pack under her foot.

"Brrr," she complained as the ice chilled her foot. "Thanks, Nate."

"I see your cat's doing fine."

Minnie lay in the crook of her arm. Emily scratched behind one of the kitten's oversized ears. "Yeah. What do you think of the name, Minnie? You know, because of her ears."

"Um hmm." Nate didn't seem overly interested. "Is there any mail?"

"Just junk. I put it on the table."

Nate rifled through the pile, came back to the family room, and sat in his recliner. Emily propped up on one elbow, causing Minnie to open her eyes. "Here's the remote."

Nate took it, but laid it on the arm of his chair. "You still going to try to do that run?"

"Oh, I'll be fine by then. The run's still a week away. I'll rest my foot for a day or so."

"Did you make it to work on time this morning?"

"Yes, I did." Emily's irritation returned because Nate hadn't apologized for the boxes of books she had moved.

Nate gazed out the window into the darkness. Why didn't he turn on the TV? When he turned to her and cleared his throat, Emily tensed.

"I don't want you to take this wrong, but I'm going to stay with Stan for a while."

For a moment, Emily couldn't speak, couldn't breathe. His words were like a punch in the stomach. She eased her sore foot off the ice and sat up.

"Why, Nate? We can work through this."

Nate shrugged his shoulders and looked away. "Maybe we can, Emily. I don't know, but I feel like I need some space."

"Space for *what?*"

"Space to think."

"Is there someone else?" Emily whispered.

Nate's voice took on an edge. "No, there's no one else. I'm going to live with Stan," he repeated, as if that explained things. Stan was Nate's friend from college. They occasionally met after work at Jen's for wings or went to a football game on a Saturday afternoon. Whenever Emily saw Stan, he had a different girlfriend on his arm, each younger and blonder than the last.

Anger zipped through Emily. "Are you going to hook up with one of Stan's bimbos?"

"I don't plan on it." The frosty tone in Nate's voice didn't reassure her.

"What about the bills?" She knew her check would never cover everything. Anger and hurt melted away to pure panic.

"I'll continue paying my share."

"What if I stop running …?"

"And lying to me? No, that won't do it. I need some time."

Numbness spread through Emily's body as she watched Nate go down the hall to their bedroom. She heard him open and shut the closet and drawers. When he came back with a duffel bag in one hand, he didn't look at her.

Her panic intensified. "Nate, you don't have to do this. Is there anything I can do to make you change your mind?" Emily's voice pleaded.

"No!" His voice held a finality that chilled her. He put the strap of his bag over his shoulder and walked out.

Emily sat on the couch staring at the door, the throbbing in her foot reduced to nothing compared with the ache in her heart.

Who will take care of me? Who will hold me when I cry?

CHAPTER 27

Ten children made their fingers climb as they sang loudly, "The itsy, bitsy spider climbed up the spout again." Carrie Ann clapped her hands along with them as they finished. They loved the old children's songs she had learned from her mom, and they were great for practicing English.

"Now, how about 'Jesus Loves Me'?" The soft voices rose and echoed in the old coffee warehouse. Carrie Ann knew Jeremiah was in his office listening and probably smiling.

After the assault, she'd taken two days off to rest and sleep, but now Jeremiah had purchased her ticket and she was determined to accomplish as much as possible before she left for home. She and Jeremiah had decided to wait until the end of the month for her to fly, to get the best rates and give her time to get things in order. Her only worry was that Juan still had not shown up for class or meals, and no one seemed to have seen him.

"Great singing. Now, everybody get a pencil. We're going to do some writing."

A chorus of good-natured complaints was heard around the table. Eager as they were to learn English, most of the children didn't enjoy the writing exercises.

Carrie handed out sheets of paper, wishing again she had the unlimited resources of teachers in the States. "Everyone ready? Write, 'I will not complain about writing.'"

The children laughed and went to work. As their pencils scratched away, Carrie glanced out the window. For a moment she thought she saw someone peeking in, but when she looked again, there was no one there. She dictated two more sentences and the next time she looked, she was sure she saw a small dark head in the window.

"I'll be right back. You keep writing. Put down all the English words you know." Carrie Ann dropped the book she was using and dashed outside, just in time to see Juan slip into the alley. She lifted her skirt slightly and took off. A moment later, she wrapped her arms around Juan and they both tumbled to the ground.

Carrie Ann stood, but kept hold of Juan's arms as she pulled him to his feet. "I'm sorry. I didn't mean to tackle you, I wanted to talk."

To her dismay, the boy's eyes filled with tears. "I came to see if you were okay. Eduardo, he tell me you were hurt and you would go away."

Eduardo? Wasn't that who Miguel said was Juan's employer? How did he know about the assault? Carrie Ann took a deep breath to steady herself. "Juan, who is Eduardo?"

Juan hung his head and she barely heard the whispered words. "I work for him."

Carrie Ann bent down to look in his eyes. "Juan, will you come inside and talk to Jeremiah?"

Juan looked over his shoulder. "*Si*, I come talk. Are you angry with me, Miss Carrie?"

Carrie Ann gave him a hug and her heart filled when his arms wrapped around her to return the hug. "No, Juan. I'm not angry with you. I was disappointed when you stopped coming to English lessons."

"*Hola*, Juan." Pencils were dropped and writing forgotten as the children scrambled to greet him. He seemed somewhat embarrassed by their welcome, but responded with a shy smile.

Carrie Ann glanced at the clock. "Class dismissed for the day. Make sure your dictation paper has your name on it. I'll see you tomorrow." She shooed the children out the door, not even taking time to listen to the pleas to tell her a joke.

She turned to Juan, who looked like a whitetail deer, eyes wide, ready to bolt. "Are you hungry?"

Juan hesitated, watching out the window as the children scattered down the street.

"It's okay, Juan, you're safe here."

With a grin, he nodded. "*Si*, I am hungry."

Carrie Ann heated the *pandebono*, a cheese bread, and added *cherimoya* and *guanabana* fruit. Then she heated some of the *ajiaco* she had started that morning for the evening meal. Juan ate like he was starved, and Carrie Ann watched him, questions hammering inside.

When his spoon scraped the bottom, Carrie Ann refilled the bowl. "Finish eating, Juan. I need to talk to Mr. Noring."

Jeremiah was in his office. Carrie Ann knocked, even though the door was open. He looked up with a welcome smile. "Come on in. Who do you have in the kitchen eating an extra meal?"

"It's Juan. I caught him peeking in the window during class this morning. He said someone named Eduardo told him I was hurt and would be leaving. I haven't told any of the children anything. How does he know that?"

Jeremiah stood, a frown creasing his forehead. "Let's talk to the boy. Do you want to stay or do you need to go home? You look kind of pale."

"I'll be okay. I want to hear what he has to say." Carrie Ann followed Jeremiah to the kitchen. Juan was tipping the last of the contents of the bowl into his mouth. Carrie sat beside the boy, with Jeremiah across from them.

"Juan, you remember Mr. Noring?"

"*Si*." Juan's eyes were large, dark pools. Carrie wondered what secrets, what evil they'd witnessed in his short life.

Jeremiah spoke in Spanish and then switched to English. "Miss Carrie tells me someone told you she'd been hurt."

Juan nodded. "Eduardo."

"Tell me about this Eduardo."

Juan's thin shoulders hunched and he studied the floor. He looked as if he would like to disappear.

"Remember, you're safe here," Carrie Ann prompted.

"Eduardo wants me to do work for him," Juan finally muttered.

"What does Eduardo do?" Jeremiah asked.

There was a long pause before Juan answered. "He steals."

"So, Eduardo wants you to steal for him?" Jeremiah's voice was quiet, but Carrie Ann could see a vein pulsating on his forehead and his hands clenched in his lap.

"*Sí*. He gives us boys a place to live, takes care of us, but we work for him. I told him no, but my dad, he's here and then he's gone. I haven't seen him for five, maybe six months."

"Eduardo has more boys working for him?" Jeremiah asked.

"*Sí*." The dark head nodded. "Maybe nine or ten."

"Why did you stop coming to the outreach center?"

Juan looked down at the dirty hands in his lap. "Eduardo told us we can't come here. I said I wanted to come, to learn English and how to get a job, but he said no. He told me you were hurt, Miss Carrie, and you would leave. He said there was no use coming here ever again." The brown eyes filled with tears and he looked away.

Carrie Ann tried to speak, to reassure Juan, but she couldn't. Memories of that afternoon in the alley whirled about her, sucking her down. "Excuse me," she said and fled to the restroom. Carrie leaned against the wall and sobbed out loud, fighting waves of anger and hatred. When the flood of anguish subsided, she used a wad of toilet paper to blow her nose and prayed, "God keep me from hating."

When she returned to the kitchen, Jeremiah and Juan were still talking. She slid into her chair and answered his curious glance. "Sorry, Juan. Someone did hurt me, but I'm okay now. In a few days, I'm going home to see my mom and my brother and sister. But I'm not leaving the Outreach Center. I will be back."

Jeremiah leaned toward Juan. "Do you want to work for Eduardo?"

"No!" Juan's voice quivered and his thin body shook. "But when I try to get away ..." He looked at the remnants of ragged bandages still covering his arm.

Carrie Ann gasped. "Did Eduardo do that to you?"

"No, it was another boy. But Eduardo can *arrange* things."

Jeremiah turned to Carrie Ann. "I don't think we would get any help from the police."

"What he's doing is a crime in any country!" Carrie Ann couldn't control her outrage.

"Please," Juan pleaded. "Don't go to the police. I'll go back. I just wanted to see that you were okay, Miss Carrie."

Jeremiah's fist hit the table and startled all of them. "You won't go back. I'm not sure what, but we'll figure something out today."

"You mean it?" Juan's face lifted as a tiny flame of hope sparked his eyes. "You can really help me?"

"Yes, we will help you. Once we have you in a safe place we will report all of this to the police." Jeremiah's eyes took in Carrie Ann too, and she knew he was hoping somehow, through this, her rapist would be brought to justice.

CHAPTER 28

Josh leaned into the pillowed back of the desk chair and massaged his temples. Another headache was brewing. Although he was grateful for the distractions of his job and had thrown himself into his responsibilities at the office, the suffocating fog of grief was inescapable.

And the continuing conflict between Delta Engineering and Wallace and Jones Architects added additional pressure and stress. The sanctuary of work had become a battleground of conflict. Josh was almost certain Wallace and Jones would have agreed to the changes in the entryway if not for the animosity CJ held against him. How long could someone hold a grudge?

His phone buzzed. "Josh Nelson here."

"Josh, how are you?" The warm tone of the unfamiliar voice on the phone unnerved him.

"Uh, fine."

"This is Frank Stevens. I was calling to see if you and your wife had a chance to talk and if you made any decisions."

Josh stiffened and his hand gripped the phone. "No, Frank. We've talked, yes, but we're not certain what we want to do." That wasn't entirely true. Josh knew exactly what he wanted to do, but he hadn't made much headway in convincing Stephani. "I know every day we delay a decision is a day we waste time—time that could be used to investigate the accident."

"True, but on the other hand, it's a big decision. I don't want to rush you or make you feel pushed. I'm here to help, Josh; I know you want closure."

"Yes, we do. How about if I talk to Stephani tonight? We'll make a decision and I'll get back to you tomorrow."

"Tomorrow will be fine. I'll wait to hear from you. Have a good day."

Josh closed his phone. He didn't think he would ever have a good day again.

He obviously wasn't going to accomplish any more at the office, so he tucked a few things into his bag and closed his laptop. On his way out he stopped at Jaleen's desk.

"I'm leaving for the day. If Charles Benson calls on the new bridge proposal, give him my cell number."

Jaleen flashed him a smile. "Sure. Leaving early to take your wife out for dinner?"

Josh paused in mid-stride. "I hadn't thought of that. Good idea, thanks."

Josh blinked as he pushed through the glass doors and walked into the spring sunshine. When had the leaves unfurled on the trees? He pulled out his phone and punched in the number for the library.

When a female voice answered, he asked for Stephani. She never carried her cell phone with her at work because she felt it would interrupt her time with the kids.

"This is Stephani."

"Hi, honey. How's your day going?"

"Oh, hi, Josh. It's been okay. Story hour went well. At least nobody crawled under the table. What's up?"

"Have you planned anything for supper? I thought we might go out."

"Out? Why?"

"Do I need a reason to treat my lovely wife?"

"I guess not. Can we go to Luigi's?"

Luigi's was Stephani's favorite. She loved the cozy atmosphere in the little Italian restaurant. Their specialty was cavatelli with homemade sausage and marinara sauce. Every meal was served with tender, crusty breadsticks, still warm from the oven.

"Luigi's it is. I'm on my way home now." He used the remote to unlock his car and slid inside. "You about ready to go?"

"I'll finish re-shelving and meet you at home in thirty minutes." Like Josh, Stephani spent more hours at work than she ever had before.

After they said their good-byes, Josh drove home. Facing the empty house was the hardest. It began as soon as he turned the corner onto Eighth Street and built up inside until, when he walked in the door, he had to fight the impulse to scream, smash windows, and throw things. He turned on the TV with the volume on high and headed to the bedroom to change from his dress shirt to a light blue pullover. He retrieved his Keen sandals from the back of the closet. Downstairs, he sat on the couch staring at the TV screen without comprehension as he waited.

When Stephani walked in the door, he realized with a start that she'd lost weight. His wife had always been petite, but tonight her shirt hung on drooping shoulders and her face looked drawn and angular.

She dropped her bag on the counter. "Do I need to change?"

"You look great to me." Josh forced a smile for her.

"Let me at least touch-up my makeup." Stephani grabbed a small pouch from her bag and went into the guest bathroom on the main floor. Other than to sleep, it seemed both of them avoided going upstairs and passing the room with the closed door.

At Luigi's, the hostess seated them in a booth in the far corner. A candle in a wine bottle cast flickering shadows on Stephani's face. Josh inhaled the warm fragrance of marinara sauce and fresh bread and relaxed a little. Both he and Stephani ordered the cavatelli. When the salads and breadsticks came, they ate with little conversation. The silence wasn't uncomfortable, but an aura of sadness hung over the table like a cloud. Josh reached across and laid his hand on Stephani's arm. "Will we ever get through this?"

When Stephani lifted her eyes to meet his, they were filled with unspeakable sorrow. "I don't know, Josh. I don't know how to go on without Isaiah."

"I miss the stupidest things." Josh paused as the waitress brought their meals. "I miss the tennis balls hitting the side of the garage when he practiced his pitching. I miss the TV being used for video games when I wanted to watch football. I miss the whining at bedtime. I miss wrestling with him in the family room, and you worrying we would break something ..." Suddenly Josh's throat was so thick he couldn't talk.

Stephani sniffed and reached for her napkin. "I'm dripping tears in my plate."

Josh's attempt at a laugh sounded more like a snort. He tried a bite of pasta, swallowed hard around the lump in his throat, and swiped at his mouth with the back of his hand.

"Stephani, I want to file the suit. I want that woman to pay."

"Why, Josh?"

"What she did was unforgiveable."

"I don't know. I'm not sure we should feel that way."

"Stephani, look what she took from us."

"Isaiah went in front of her. She couldn't stop. There was nothing she could do."

"Maybe she could have. We don't know for sure. Don't you want justice?"

Stephani moved the food around her plate with her fork, but she didn't take another bite.

Josh pushed his plate away. "I'm not hungry. Let's take the rest of this home."

Stephani laid her fork down and dabbed her face with the napkin before speaking. "If you really think we should sue, I'll go along with it. Have you talked with your mom?"

"Mom? About what?"

"About suing."

Josh frowned and reached for his wallet. "I don't really think it's any of her business."

"Maybe not, but we can at least discuss it with her. She's a smart woman. Why don't you talk to her? We're supposed to have dinner there Sunday when Sara and the girls are here."

"I'll think about it." Josh signaled for the waitress, asked for a take-home box, and handed her his credit card. "But my mind's already made up."

CHAPTER 29

Emily's dreams faded and the realization that Nate was not beside her, not even in the house, shocked her awake. She swung her legs over the side of the bed, careful not to hit Minnie, who waited on the floor. Gingerly, she stood on her sore foot to test it out. It was a little better. After limping to the kitchen, she fixed Minnie's breakfast and then grabbed a granola bar. She would get coffee on the way. Despite an injured foot, she could not be late to work again.

She walked in the door fifteen minutes early with her Starbuck's cup, pausing at Jim's office door to say, "Good morning." It never hurt to let the boss see her at work ahead of time.

She was working on the payroll when Amy stuck her head in the door. "You're hard at it already?"

"Yep. Now that the weather is warmer and it's staying light longer, I like to get out of here in time for a run."

"Want to go to Jen's for lunch?"

"Sure." She needed time to get away and be with a friend.

Four hours later, Emily didn't need to look at the menu to order her favorite: sliced turkey on flatbread with lettuce, tomato, and pickles. She got a drink from the fountain and slid into the booth opposite Amy.

"It seems like ages since we've gotten away for lunch. You've been holed up in your office and working, like, crazy hours." Amy chattered away, not even slowing down for a response from Emily. "I have to leave early to pick up Rachel. If I'm not there shortly after four when she gets up from her nap, she gets real mopey. She's getting so cute. Oh, wait, have I shown you the latest pictures?"

Emily took the cell phone and scrolled through ten or twelve baby photos before the server brought their sandwiches.

"Is she walking yet?" Emily pulled a pickle from the edge of the sandwich and ate it.

"Not yet, but she's so close. The other night we were in the family room downstairs …"

Amy went on and on and Emily stopped listening, remembering how Nate wanted to buy a new camera last Christmas because, "…next Christmas we might be taking baby pictures."

"Are you okay?" Amy was eyeing Emily and her uneaten sandwich with concern.

Emily took a bite and swallowed hard. "Yeah. Sure. I have a lot on my mind, that's all."

****

By four o'clock, Emily could walk without pain, but running probably wasn't a good idea. Perhaps if she gave it a day's rest, she would still be able to do well in Saturday's race.

For a second, she planned a great dinner in her head. And then with a jolt, she remembered Nate would not be home to eat with her. The idea of spending the entire evening alone with only Minnie to keep her company was not very appealing.

Emily scrolled through her contact list and sent a quick email to Stacy Maher. *I have a little extra time this week. Can you use some help?*

In less than ten minutes, she had a reply: *Thanks for the offer. I do need help. Our cook's assistant cancelled at the last minute. Could you work in the kitchen tonight?*

Guess I'll be cooking after all, just not at home, Emily thought. *I hope I can avoid seeing that Sherry.*

When she pulled up to the Lighthouse, she parked out front. No need to hide the car this time. Inside, she gave her name to the receptionist, a woman she hadn't seen before, and waited while she called the kitchen. A few minutes later, a large Hispanic lady appeared. Her dark hair was held back in a fat ponytail and her bulky arms were wrapped with tattoos.

She looked Emily up and down. "Stacy said she found a volunteer for me. My regular gal called in with sick kids. I sure hope you know your way around a kitchen."

"I, ummm, I know how to use a microwave," Emily offered.

"Come on. I guess you can learn." She led the way through a series of doors and hallways, with Emily close behind.

The huge room was filled with the odors of cooking. Pots and pans bubbled on the stove. Emily looked for a place to put her purse and sweater. Finally, she shoved them into a corner on the counter.

"My name's Emily." She felt a little bit in the way as she awaited instructions.

"I'm Rosa." The voice was gruff, but her smile warm and quick as she handed Emily some plastic gloves. "Think you can get the salads in them bowls?"

Emily nodded and set to work chopping lettuce into bite-sized pieces and filling the pale green bowls. Rosa moved about the kitchen like a general marshalling her troops. She stirred, scooped, lifted, poured, and banged pots. When three young women arrived to set tables, she barked orders at them, but Emily also saw her give one of them an affectionate hug.

Soon, a long line of women of all ages and sizes, threaded noisily down the stairs. Most of them chatted with each other as they grabbed trays from a stack. Rosa showed Emily how to stand at the counter and place a piece of crispy, fried chicken and a scoop of potatoes on the plates. Rosa gave out green beans, bowls of salad, a piece of chocolate cake, and a greeting for each woman. Sherry passed by and Emily pasted on a smile, but Sherry didn't look up from her tray. By the time the last resident had filed past, Emily's arm ached from the heavy spoons and her mouth felt tired from so much smiling.

"Ready to eat?" Rosa gave her arm a nudge with her elbow. "The fruits of our labors, *si*?"

After smelling and scooping all the chicken and potatoes, Emily wasn't sure she wanted to eat any of it. But she didn't want to refuse Rosa's cooking, either. She reached out and took a pink tray from the stack. "Sure."

After the residents ate, they sat at their tables talking until a buzzer rang. Everyone filed out quickly, except for two women who must have been assigned to help Rosa clean up. One of them was Sherry. They moved to the kitchen and began running water. Perhaps she could finish and slip out without interacting with Sherry.

Emily licked the chocolate cake crumbs from her fork. "That was good, Rosa."

"Thanks. And thanks for your help." Rosa's brown eyes twinkled. "I taught you pretty good, didn't I?"

"You run a very efficient kitchen. I was glad to help."

"Can you take my tray with yours into the kitchen? I've got some paperwork to do."

"Certainly." Emily stacked the trays and dirty dishes so she could carry both at once. Rosa disappeared into a small room off the kitchen, while Emily carried the trays to the kitchen. Sherry and the other woman were nowhere to be seen. She remembered her purse and sweater and went to the corner where she had left them. A huge puddle of dirty, soapy water covered the counter and dripped to the floor. Her sweater and purse were soaked.

Emily retrieved her sweater, wrung it out as best she could and hung the dripping garment over her arm. She picked up her purse and retreated from the kitchen.

In an area outside the facility reserved for women who smoke, Sherry and the other kitchen worker stood with lit cigarettes.

A rush of anger surged through Emily and she held up her dripping sweater. "You slopped water all over the counter. My sweater was on it."

Sherry removed the cigarette from her mouth and sneered at her. "Well, if it isn't the do-gooder, back for another fix. Hey, I'm sorry about that sweater. Hope it wasn't expensive."

Not wanting to cause trouble, Emily struggled to shrug it off. She deliberately closed her mouth and started toward her car. Then, turning, she shot back. "You really shouldn't be smoking when you're pregnant. It can hurt the baby."

Sherry took a step toward her. The hand with the cigarette pointed at her. "You got kids?"

Emily felt herself deflate. "No, I don't."

"Then don't be telling me anything about 'em. You don't know nothing."

Emily turned and walked to her car without another word.

★★★★★★★

Nate opened the door and stepped into the house. He had an appointment at seven, when he hoped to help a potential buyer write up an offer, and he'd forgotten to pack any ties. He usually didn't wear one, but this client was too important to risk offending.

The big-eared kitten padded down the hall, stretching and yawning. Nate tossed the mail on the kitchen table and stooped to give her a pat before heading to the bedroom. The bed was neatly made and the floor tidy. No piles of his dirty socks. *Emily must appreciate that. Wonder where she is? Probably working late or helping out somewhere.* Always time for everyone and everything but him.

Nate chose three ties to take with him and knotted a fourth one around his neck. The cat had followed him, meowing pitifully. He checked her dishes and she still had food. "Sorry, cat, I've got an appointment. You'll have to wait for attention until Emily gets home."

Fifteen minutes later, he pulled into the Lighthouse parking lot. Good, a spot up front. A blue Taurus was parked across the lot. He glanced at it once without recognition, then looked again and checked the license plate to make sure.

Volunteering where he'd told her not to. He wondered how many times she'd come here and not told him. *Sneaking around again, just like she did with the birth control pills.*

He slammed his car door, locked it, and strode into the main office of The Lighthouse.

An hour later, sale secure, he got in his car and turned toward Stan's house. Emily's car was no longer there. He hoped Stan was around to celebrate a sale with him.

CHAPTER 30

Saturday morning, Emily almost pushed the snooze button before she remembered. *The SIDS run.* Unaccustomed to rising so early, Minnie blinked from her spot on Nate's pillow. Emily eased her legs over the edge of the bed and tested her foot. No pain. Minnie leaped down and led the way to the kitchen with her tail waving like a fuzzy flag.

While the coffee brewed, Emily fed Minnie and laid out her own breakfast—yogurt, granola, red grapes, and a cheese stick. She opened the front door, grabbed the newspaper, and flipped through the pages as she ate.

Faint streaks of pink in the east signaled the dawn as she drove downtown. Emily felt strong and confident. *I can do this.* The run began at Center Park, then looped around the town. No further than her daily runs before the problem with her heel.

At the registration table, she picked up her packet. Number seventeen. Feeling a little fluttery, she pinned it on her tank top and took off the sweat pants that covered her shorts. The chilly air raised goose bumps on her arms and legs, but she knew she would warm up quickly when she started running. Everywhere, runners milled around. Some stretched, some downed energy drinks, some just stood and chatted. Emily found an uncrowded spot and lifted first one knee, then the other to her chest. She wiggled her foot. It still felt okay.

Next to her, a young man in running attire jogged slowly in place. A woman with a sleeping baby in a stroller watched him. Placing her hands on his chest, she straightened his number and kissed him. "See you at the finish line."

Emily's heart twisted. She looked away and edged toward the

starting line. The runners crowded together, jockeying for the best position.

When the gun went off, Emily surged forward with the crowd. She was behind a tall, older man in an orange tee shirt. His muscled legs indicated he'd been a runner for a long time. With lengthy strides, he quickly pulled away from her.

As the pack of racers left the park and headed down the wide expanse of Main Street, they eventually thinned out. Emily concentrated on hitting her own pace and maintained a position towards the middle. The sound of hundreds of running shoes drummed in her ears. The noise was pleasant and the sun felt warm on her bare arms. Her muscles felt strong, and she was convinced this was the day—her time to do a good thing.

Emily nodded at the policemen who blocked traffic at the intersections to make sure the runners were safe. She wondered if Chief Geiken was at one of the corners, not sure if she hoped she would see him or not.

When Main Street left the city limits and became Highway Twenty-two, the course turned and followed residential streets for a couple of miles. It circled the high school on the same street where Emily had found Minnie. The last stretch was on a narrower street that ran past a few businesses. From there it turned and ended at the park.

Emily breathed easier as she approached the first water station. Not concerned with coming in first, she slowed enough to grab a bottle and gulp down a few ounces before she tossed it into a recycling can. Posters were planted in the yards to encourage the runners and she picked up her pace. She was a little over halfway to the finish. With the back of her hand, she wiped a sweaty forehead and focused on keeping her breathing even. As Emily made the turn around the high school, she felt the first twinge in her foot.

Just ignore it. Run through the pain. You can do this. Only a little further.

She was almost to the last stretch, the road past the strip mall, when a sharp pain shot through her foot. Emily tripped and slowed, then stepped to the side out of the way of other runners. She untied her shoe and rubbed her foot, hoping the throbbing would stop. When she put her shoe back on, the pain intensified. Maybe I can just finish the race at a walk. After one hobbling step, she gasped. Beside her, other runners streamed by, some of them casting curious glances her way. She hopped to a grassy spot beside the road, sank down, and fought the tears that filled her eyes.

It seemed like hours before the sag wagon, a white Suburban, arrived to pick up stragglers and those who could not finish. The driver saw her and slowed. "Need a lift?"

Emily nodded. "I hurt my foot. I don't think I can walk."

"Stay right there, we'll help." The driver, an older man with a shiny, balding head, swerved to the curb, put the vehicle in park, and hurried out. A young woman hopped out of the passenger side. The man gave her his hand and pulled her to a standing position. With one person on each side of her, she limped to the Suburban. They boosted her up and she sank into the seat.

"I didn't finish." She tried not to whine.

"That's okay." The young woman's voice was soothing. "This is a charity run. You did get some pledges didn't you?"

"Yeah, I guess that's something." Emily sighed as she still worked to hold back the tears.

"Well, that's what counts, raising money to help fund research for SIDS." She looked out the window before turning to look at Emily in the backseat. "I lost a baby to SIDS three years ago. I still grieve for him and want researchers to find ways to prevent others that pain."

"I'm so sorry." Emily felt very small. How would it feel to lose a baby you had carried inside you? Or a ten-year-old child?

They parked by the registration table. Emily accepted the support of the man's arm to get out. "Thanks so much," she said to her rescuers.

The young woman looked concerned. "Is someone here for you? Do you need help getting to your car?"

"No one is meeting me, but I got here early. My car is right there." Emily pointed to the Taurus. "I think I can make it."

"You should get that foot looked at today."

"I will. Thanks again."

Emily hopped to the table and picked up her complimentary tee shirt. She felt guilty taking one when she hadn't finished, but the woman at the table assured her she'd earned it. There was a drawing for some prizes, but Emily didn't stay. Her foot demanded attention.

★★★★★★

Memorial hospital sat back from the street. Red brick buildings with large shade trees surrounded the parking lot and grassy areas. Spring flowers bloomed in containers beside the door. Inside, Emily gave her name and insurance information to the receptionist. She found an empty chair in the waiting area and wondered if she should call Nate. If he were injured, she'd want to know. She didn't know the rules of this new situation. Finally, deciding a text would be okay, she took out her phone and typed: *At hospital hurt foot didn't finish race.* She pushed send and laid the phone in her lap. As she flipped through a home decorating magazine, she listened for the beep that signaled a return text.

"Emily Adams?" The nurse wore scrubs with little bunnies printed on them.

Emily hoisted herself up and tried to put weight on her good foot. "I'm Emily."

"Oh, let me get you a wheelchair." She hurried off as Emily waited, hanging on to an end table to keep her balance.

When the nurse returned, she helped Emily into the chair and wheeled her down the hall into a curtained exam room.

The doctor, a short, stocky man, bustled into the room a few minutes later. His eyes skimmed her chart. "I'm Doctor Robinson." He shook her hand and laid the chart aside. "So, Mrs. Adams, Tell me about this foot injury."

Emily gave all the details she could remember—the pain that started last week, how it got better when she avoided running, and the disaster of today's race.

The doctor nodded as she talked. "Let's get your foot x-rayed and see what we find."

Over an hour later, after waiting first for the x-ray, next for a wheelchair ride back to the exam room, and then for the doctor to return, she heard the door click open.

Dr. Robinson sat on a stool in front of her. "The x-rays showed no fractures, nothing wrong structurally. Let's see where the pain is." He removed her shoe and sock and gently manipulated her foot. "Hurts here? How about here? Not here?" Emily winced and held her breath, her only answer a nod or shake of her head.

When the doctor was finished, Emily picked up her sock, but he stopped her. "Why don't you leave it off? Your foot is swollen. We can get you a padded boot to wear home. What you have is a very common ailment of runners. It's called plantar fasciitis, an inflammation of the plantar tendons. Here's what I want you to do. Use an ice pack on it and take ibuprofen for the pain. I have some exercises for you to do, and if it doesn't get better, I can refer you for a couple of sessions of physical therapy." He handed her a printed sheet. "These are stretches to strengthen the tendons. That should alleviate the pain some. Do them at least three times a day. And I want you to take it easy. No running. You're not a professional runner are you?"

Emily's mouth twisted into a half-smile. "No, I ran in college and just got back into it. I wanted to do something good, so I chose the SIDS run."

"Well, let's choose good things that don't involve running for awhile. Can you do that?"

"Yes, sir."

"Here's the address for physical therapy, in case it's necessary. And, oh, I'll get that boot." He disappeared for a minute and returned with a contraption of canvas, padding, and Velcro. He slipped it on Emily's foot and fastened it. Then he handed her the sock and shoe he'd taken off.

Emily managed a weak smile. "Thanks so much."

The nurse appeared again with the wheelchair. Emily protested, but the nurse assured her it was hospital policy.

Emily drove home, parked in the garage, and hobbled into the house. Minnie was delighted to see her and started yowling. Emily checked her dish, but she still had food. The yowling must have been a greeting, although Minnie always acted hungry. Emily thought about using Nate's recliner, but she couldn't bring herself to do that. She sat on the couch and maneuvered the sore foot up. Finally, she allowed the tears to come. When the streams slowed to a trickle and the sobs became a hiccup, she flipped open her phone.

Still no answer to her text.

CHAPTER 31

Sunday morning, Emily knew she needed someone. Someone to throw their arms around her and tell her she was loved and everything would be okay. She and her sister had always been close, but even more so after their parents died in a car accident when she was still in college. Andrea would comfort her just as she always had.

Emily called Jim and left a message on his voice mail that she had injured her foot and would not be in Monday and possibly Tuesday. Then she called Andrea.

"Hey, Andi." She used her personal nickname for her sister, what she'd called her ever since she could talk. "I was thinking about driving up to see you today. Maybe spend a couple days?"

Andrea must have heard the pain in her voice. "Sure, Sis. What's going on? Are you okay?"

"Too much to tell you over the phone. I injured my foot. It's nothing serious, but I need to stay off of it for a few days. I already called the school and told them I wasn't coming in. If you can put me up, I'll throw my stuff in a bag and leave right away."

"Of course. You're always welcome here. Is Nate coming with you?"

Emily swallowed hard and tried to sound casual. "Nope, just me."

"Okay then." There was a pause and Emily could picture her sister scrunching her face and trying to understand without asking questions. "We're going to church this morning, but we should be home before you get here. So, we'll see you in a few hours. We'll wait dinner for you, so don't stop for fast food on the Interstate."

"Thanks, Andi. See you soon." Emily closed her phone and limped to the closet. Minnie rubbed a soft head against her leg. "Minnie! What am I going to do with you?" She sat on the bed and the kitten jumped to her lap. Minnie settled in with her familiar rumble, kneading Emily's thigh with her front paws. Emily stroked the soft back as she thought about who might be qualified to kitty-sit. Shirley, the receptionist from work, hated cats. And besides, she wasn't sure she wanted people at work to know she'd gone out of town. So that ruled out Amy too. It appeared Nate was out, since he wouldn't even answer her texts. Some people took their pets to the vet to be boarded, but she didn't think the office would be open today.

Minnie looked up at her and yawned, her pink tongue curled in her mouth. Suddenly she knew. Donna Nelson said she should call if she needed anything for Minnie. Maybe Donna could get her into the vet's office or could recommend a cat-sitter. It was still early, but Donna said she went to church, so she was probably up. Now where had she put that paper with her phone number on it?

Emily stood and Minnie slid to the floor with a plop. She looked up at Emily, shook her head indignantly, and sauntered out of the room. After a few minutes of shuffling papers in the office, Emily located the number. She punched it into her phone.

"Donna? This is Emily Adams. I'm sorry to bother you on a Sunday morning, but I've got a small problem with Minnie, the kitten. My husband and I are both going out of town, and I don't know what to do with her. I thought maybe you knew someone who cat-sits."

"Well, they do board animals at All Paws. When do you need someone?"

"I'm leaving today, but I'll be home Tuesday."

"Mmmm. I have keys to the clinic. I could meet you there. No, wait. I know, Emily. If it's just for a few days, why don't you bring her over here? I'd need her food and litter box, of course."

"Oh, I couldn't impose on you," Emily said, thinking it was the perfect solution.

"Not at all. I love cats, I just haven't gotten another one since I lost my old Grayson last winter. What time are you leaving?"

"I could bring her right now."

"That'll be fine. I don't leave for church until nine-thirty. If you come now, I can make sure she's all settled in before I go."

"You sure about this?"

"Yes, I'm positive. Bring her on over."

"I need to get your address."

Emily wrote down the address Donna gave her. As quickly as she could without hurting her foot, she loaded up food, bowls, litter box, and Minnie's favorite toy, the little pink ball.

When Emily put her in the car, Minnie paced back and forth on the seat, protesting loudly. "Do you think I'm taking you back to the ditch, girl? No, you're going to spend some time with that nice woman, Donna. And I'll be home soon. I need to get away for a few days." Minnie's cries continued all the way to Donna's small brick ranch.

As she lifted the kitten from the car, Emily felt a wave of guilt. What was she doing? Abandoning the only one that hadn't deserted her? But she carried Minnie to the house anyway and rang the bell.

Donna opened the door, her broad smile welcoming them as she held out her hands for the squirming kitten. When Emily turned to get the litter box and food, Donna asked, "What did you do to your foot?"

"Oh, it's nothing serious. I hurt it running and I need to stay off of it for a few days. So I'm going to my sister's house in Kansas City. I'll let her take care of me."

Donna put Minnie down to explore while she took her supplies. "Well, you have a good time and don't worry one bit about Minnie. We're going to enjoy each other."

Back at her house, Emily tossed some clothes and toiletries in a bag. In only a few hours, her big sister could tell her what she needed to do to make everything right again.

****

Nate unlocked the front door of the tiny bungalow. He didn't expect a big crowd for this open house, but he always wanted to be prepared. He was pleased to see the owners left it as he suggested. They'd cleaned thoroughly, de-cluttered, and even added vases of fresh flowers. Nate opened a window to bring in a little of the warm spring breeze and laid out brochures listing the house's amenities. He glanced out at the back yard and smiled to see the lilac bushes heavy with blooms.

Out of habit, he reached in his pocket for his cell phone to check the time and almost swore as he remembered. Saturday morning, he'd been talking to a client as he wove his way through Stan's cluttered kitchen. When the conversation ended, he laid the phone down, reached for his cup of coffee, and knocked the phone into the sink full of dirty water. The phone was now totally dead and, because of the open house, he had to wait until Monday to get it replaced. He missed the tidy home Emily insisted on.

The front door opened and Nate greeted a young couple. They began to browse through the little home, the first in a steady stream of lookers.

When a silver-haired couple came late in the day, Nate eyed them curiously. Hadn't they been there earlier? But this time they had a younger man with them.

"Excuse me." He extracted himself from a conversation with a woman he was sure was just a curious neighbor, and approached the couple. "Could I answer any questions about the house?"

"You sure could, young man." The gentleman, who looked like he was well into his seventies, wore overalls and a corn-seed hat. "I'm Daniel Anderson and this is my wife, Marilee. We're looking to move to town. This here's my son, Dirk." He indicated the younger man, who looked slightly embarrassed. "He's buying our farm."

"Great. I bet Dirk will take good care of that farm. And this would be a perfect retirement home—main floor bedroom ... not too much yard to care for ... within walking distance of stores. Did you get a chance to see the storage areas in the basement?" Nate led them around the house again, pointing out positive features and answering Daniel and Marilee's questions.

By the time they left, Nate was fairly sure they would contact him to make an offer. He requested they reach him through email, in case he had trouble getting the phone replaced.

He made one last trip through the house, shut the windows, and gathered up the brochures. For some reason, the potential sale didn't thrill him as much as usual, especially without someone to share the victory.

Why not go by the house and see Emily? He could celebrate with her, ask how her run went, and even see that silly little kitten. Perhaps he had been too harsh about her misleading him. For that matter, he hadn't always been truthful either.

Nate locked up the bungalow, got into the Explorer, and headed to their house. Halfway there, he had an idea. It was still early; he could pick up a pizza to bake and invite himself to supper. He made a U-turn at the intersection and drove to Papa Murphy's Pizza.

"One large Canadian bacon and pineapple," he told the gangly youth who took his order. "And load it up with extra cheese. My wife likes cheese." Nate smiled as he thought about Emily and her habit of twirling the cheese around her finger before she popped it into her mouth.

As he waited for them to make the pizza, he pictured Emily: surprised at first to see him, then happy, and later …

He smiled again.

When they called his number, he paid for the pizza, carried it to the car, and laid it on the front passenger seat. When Nate pulled into the driveway of his house, he could see only one light, the one in the hallway they always left on, even when they were gone. He dug out his key and let himself in through the front door.

"Emily?" Feeling like an intruder, he made his way through the house and looked in all the rooms. No sign of his wife, and stranger still, no sign of the cat. "You didn't take the cat for a walk or a car ride did you?" he muttered. Nate checked the garage and the Taurus was gone too. Where could she be? He tried not to think about the possibility of her with another man.

He fumbled in his pocket for something to write on and found a tiny scrap of florescent yellow paper.

Emily, I came to see you. My cell phone died. Miss you. Nate

Nate laid the note on the table where he knew she would see it and drove back to Stan's. He took the pizza and dropped it into the garbage can in the garage. He wasn't very hungry anymore.

CHAPTER 32

With a sigh of relief, Emily pulled into her sister's driveway and turned off the car. The contemporary two-story tan house squatted on a small green yard. Similar houses crowded close on all sides. Young shade trees were planted everywhere, and bushes or flowers adorned the entryway of each house. Basketball hoops, swing sets, and bicycles decorated the yards. This was a neighborhood of families.

Emily's heel ached, along with her heart. Using the door as a crutch, she eased herself out. Kurt, Andrea's husband, came around the corner of the house.

"Hello, Emily." When he saw the padded boot on her foot, he added, "Are you hurt?"

"Yes, but I'll recover. I thought my big sister would want to take care of me again."

"Of course she will. That's what she does." Kurt lifted her bag from the backseat, hoisted it to his shoulder, and held out a tanned, muscular arm for her to lean on. "This all you have?"

"Yeah." She gave him a wry grin. "I'm traveling light."

"Well, anything you don't have, Andi can loan you. Or you girls can shop for it."

When Emily stepped in the door, Andrea smothered her in a hug. Emily leaned into her sister's embrace and choked back sobs.

"Careful, she has a bum leg," Kurt warned. He held up the bag. "You want me to put this in Trevor's room?"

Andrea stepped back, but still held Emily's hand. "Do you mind sleeping in Trevor's room? The boys can bunk together."

"I don't want to put him out. I could crash on the couch in the family room."

"No. You need a place to get away. What you need is a retreat. Can't offer you that in this crazy house, but at least Trevor's room is downstairs. It is so good to see you." She tugged Emily's hand and pulled her down the hall. "Let's get your leg up. Do you want some ice?"

Emily sank onto a comfortable couch and lifted her sore foot to the cushion. As she watched her sister fill a bag with ice, the tension that had mounted during the long drive melted and slipped away.

Andrea slid the bag of ice under her foot. "So what happened?"

"Would you believe I took up running again?" Emily forced a laugh. "I guess I kind of overdid it. It's nothing serious—plantar fasciitis is the technical term. It's a runner's injury. I'm hoping to give it a rest, heal, and get back to running."

"I want all the details, but if we're going to eat, I need to slap it on the grill. Trevor and Brian have to leave soon. They're playing volleyball with the church youth group this afternoon. Can I get you anything else? Are you comfortable?"

Emily waved her away. "If you leave me alone, I might manage a nap. My cat woke me up early this morning."

"You have a cat? What does Nate think about a cat in the house?"

Emily didn't answer, but her blue eyes filled with tears.

"Oh, honey, we need to talk. You take a nap while I grill the chicken. After dinner we'll send Kurt downstairs to watch baseball, and we'll eat chocolate and talk until our lips fall off."

The couch was soft, the sun coming in the window warm, and before Emily knew it, she drifted off to sleep. She awoke when her two nephews crashed into the room. They skidded to a stop when they saw her.

"Aunt Emily. We didn't know you were here. What's wrong with your foot?"

Emily propped herself up on one elbow. "You two make a lot of noise. What does a girl have to do to take a nap around here?"

Trevor, the younger and taller of her nephews, stepped over the arm of the chair and plopped down into the cushions. "I'm sorry. Were you sleeping?"

"Not really. I just closed my eyes. So what have you two been up to? How's school?"

"Almost over." Brian went to the kitchen and opened the fridge.

Andrea bustled in the door. "Dinner in fifteen minutes. Get out of the refrigerator, Brian."

While her sister set the table, Emily visited with her nephews. She loved these boys. When they were younger, they spent a week with her and Nate every summer. Now they were too busy with sports and high school activities. She missed spending time with them.

"Where's Uncle Nate?" Brian asked. Emily saw Andrea try to shush him from the kitchen.

Emily took a deep breath. She hadn't planned for this. "Uh, he was too busy to come with me this time. He's been showing lots of houses."

Andrea's call saved her from further explanation. "Dinner's ready."

Trevor and Brian each took an arm and almost carried her to the table. The grilled chicken, salad, potatoes, and rolls looked fantastic. Emily hadn't eaten since early morning. Her stomach rumbled in anticipation as she reached for the dish of potatoes, but when she looked up, everyone else had bowed their head.

Kurt smiled at her. "Mind if I say a prayer?"

Flustered, she set the potatoes down and folded her hands. "Oh, no, go ahead."

"Heavenly Father, thank you for this food. Bless it to nourish our bodies. Thank you that Emily can be here with us. We pray you will heal her foot quickly and completely. Amen."

At the "amen," both Trevor and Brian grabbed for the chicken. "Hey!" Andi roared. "Where's your manners?"

Trevor hung his head and asked, "Would you like some chicken, Aunt Emily?"

Emily took a piece and passed the plate back. "So, tell me about this volleyball game."

Brian chimed in. "It's a church league. We play other teams and, wow, are we good." His long arms waved above his head. "I'm the champion spiker. Nobody can return 'em."

Andrea chuckled. "And that's our Brian. Always humble. Pass the rolls, Son."

Brian grinned and handed the basket of rolls to his mom. "If you didn't have the bum foot, Aunt Emily, you could come watch us play."

"Aunt Emily is here to visit with her sister. You guys are not going to monopolize all her time." Andrea stopped buttering her roll and pointed the knife at Brian.

"I wish I could go to the game, but I really am supposed to rest this foot. What other things are you doing this spring to keep out of trouble?"

Trevor pushed a sandy-brown curl off his forehead and leaned toward her. "I'm going to Mexico in June."

"Mexico? What are you going to do there?"

Trevor's voice rose with excitement as he described a youth mission trip. Both boys talked about some end-of-the-school-year events, with Andrea and Kurt chiming in.

Emily ate and listened with longing. *What if I never have a family gathered around a dinner table?*

CHAPTER 33

Donna unlocked her front door and felt, at least for the moment, uplifted and refreshed. Worshiping with her church family temporarily washed away the sorrow and concern for Josh. She looked for Minnie and found her nestled amid the pillows on her bed. The kitten yawned and stretched, then curled up again. She'd made herself at home.

In the kitchen, Donna checked on the pan of lasagna in the oven, breathing in the garlicky fragrance. She pulled vegetables out of the fridge to make a salad. Sara and the girls would be there any minute, and it was always harder to get things done with Jocelyn asking her questions about everything and Tessa requesting a certain toy or book or game.

When the familiar shouts of "Grandma!" rang out, Donna met them at the front door. She knelt down and swooped up the girls, one in each arm, squeezing just a little tighter and a little longer than usual. How precious these two were.

Jocelyn squirmed out of the embrace. "Look, Grandma, I got another super-speller award."

Donna took the rumpled paper Jocelyn handed her and smiled. "Great job, Jocelyn."

Tessa, never one to be outdone, looked for something to share with her. "Grandma, I have an owie. I fell off my scooter." She peeled back a bandage to reveal the tiny scratch.

Donna gave a quick kiss to her knee. "There. Grandma kissed it better."

Sara looked over the girls' heads. "You doing okay, Mom?"

Donna nodded firmly. "I'm doing okay. It's step-by-step, but I know who's holding my hand." She stood up as the girls rushed down the hall to get the toys out of the closet. "I worry about your brother, though. He's so angry."

"Isn't that normal?"

"Yes, anger is normal, but I wish Josh would temper it with what he knows from God's word. He's always been so easygoing. It's hard to be around him now. He's like a stranger in Josh's body."

"Maybe you're expecting too much. Give him a little time. When Greg asked for the divorce, I was furious. I didn't see how God could ever heal that wound. But he has. The girls and I have made a life without him, and I know God has blessings ahead for me."

Donna kissed her daughter's cheek. "You're right. I'll give him some space."

Sara picked up the girls' jackets from the floor where they'd dropped them and carried them down the hall to the bedroom. As Donna returned to the dinner preparations, she heard Sara's delighted squeal. "Mom! You got a kitten."

When Sara entered the kitchen, followed closely by her two girls, she was cuddling Minnie close to her. "She's darling, Mom."

"Yes, she is. Only she isn't mine. I'm keeping her for a customer from the clinic."

"Be gentle with her," Sara cautioned Jocelyn as she handed her the kitten. The two scurried back down the hall.

"Let me hold her," Tessa demanded.

Jocelyn retorted, "I had her first."

Sara helped herself to a cherry tomato in the salad. "You're keeping her for a customer? Why didn't they board her?"

"I think it was a spur-of-the-moment trip. She called this morning wanting to know the name of someone who would take a cat for a few days. So I told her to bring Minnie here. I could always take her over to the clinic, but I kind of like having her around." Donna pulled the pan of lasagna from the oven and set it on the counter before she turned to Sara. "It wasn't just any customer. Minnie's owner is Emily Adams."

"Who?" Sara's eyes widened as the name started to register. "Emily

Adams? The driver of the car? How … Mom, I mean … what are you doing with Emily Adams' cat?"

"It's a complicated story. She came into the clinic a few weeks ago with this kitten she found. I didn't even know it was her, of course, until I read her name on the chart. I still wasn't sure, so I looked up the address and knew it matched. Dr Ewing had a free sample of vitamins for the kitten, but he forgot to give them to her. I offered to take them to her house. I really felt like I was supposed to do it—a Holy Spirit nudge, I think. Anyway, I ended up telling her who I was and we talked. So … when she needed someone to watch Minnie, she called me."

"Wow. I don't know if I could do that."

"Sara, the accident wounded her too. She has to live with the fact she killed a little boy."

"I suppose." Sara dropped her voice to a whisper. "Are you going to tell Josh?"

"It may not come up." Donna hoped desperately that it wouldn't.

The front door opened and Tessa and Jocelyn rushed forward, shoving and jostling to be the first. "Hi, Uncle Josh. Hi, Aunt Stephani. Grandma has a kitten."

"Hello, girls." Josh pulled the door shut behind him.

"I wish Isaiah could see the kitten, don't you, Uncle Josh?" Tessa gazed up at her uncle.

"Tessa, be quiet. You'll make him sad," her sister reprimanded.

Josh knelt down in front of Tessa and gave her a hug. "Yes, I do wish Isaiah could see the kitten. And it's okay, Jocelyn, I like to talk about Isaiah."

Donna reached out to give first Josh, then Stephani a hug. "Jocelyn, why don't you take Aunt Stephani's jacket and lay it on the bed for her? Then you girls come to the table. It's time for dinner. Everything's ready."

The next few minutes were spent getting the food on the table and everyone seated around it. Donna looked at Josh in a silent question. When he shook his head and frowned, Donna stood and said, "I'll say grace. Heavenly Father, thank you for this food. Thank you for my family gathered here. Continue to give us peace and comfort in our loss. Amen." She reached for Josh's plate and scooped a large helping of lasagna.

"I don't like masagna," Tessa said in a loud voice.

Sara took Tessa's plate from her mom and put it in front of her daughter. "It's just noodles and sausage and cheese. See?" She cut off a small bite.

"Try a little bit," Donna encouraged her. "I have ice cream for dessert."

Tessa put a tiny bite on her fork and touched it to her tongue.

"I think it's good, Grandma. I love lasagna." Jocelyn smiled as Donna handed her a plate.

"Eat your dinner, girls." Sara took her own plate and sat down. "So Josh, how's the Memorial Hospital project coming?"

Josh laid down his fork and shook his head. "Not too well, but kind of interesting. Remember CJ Williamson?"

"Your college roommate?" Sara asked. "The one who liked to party?"

"Ummm-hmmm. He apparently managed to finish college. He's an architect now. Works for Wallace and Jones, the firm the hospital hired. We're kind of going head-to-head with them on a couple of issues."

"So, have you talked with him?"

Josh shook his head. "Not outside of a meeting. I offered to get together, go to lunch or something, but I don't think he ever forgave me for not covering for him when he had that party our freshman year."

"Good ole CJ. I'd forgotten all about that. Carrie Ann hated him. She thought he was dragging you into all sorts of trouble."

"I guess I made my own choices," Josh mused. "But it was probably a good thing for both of us when we parted ways."

Donna listened as the conversation ebbed and flowed around her, the girls chattering like squirrels in the trees, and Stephani laughing at something Tessa said. When there was a lull in the conversation, she said, "I have some news from Carrie Ann."

Josh put down his fork and leaned forward. "Are you going to share it or just tease us?"

Donna passed the basket of rolls to Jocelyn. "She called last week and said she's coming home. She didn't say why she wasn't waiting until her scheduled furlough in July. I guess she had an opportunity to get tickets at a good price, so she decided to take it. She felt so bad she wasn't able to come in February."

The table erupted as everyone tried to talk at once. Carrie Ann had always been a favorite. Donna knew a visit from her would be good medicine for their aching souls.

"What are the dates? I'll clear my calendar so I can spend some time here." Sara was already checking the calendar on her phone.

"She flies in Thursday, March thirty-first. Carrie Ann was rather vague on details, so I'm not sure how long she'll be here. It'll be so good to have her home." Donna stood and reached for the dirty dishes. Stephani rose to help. The girls asked to be excused and dashed down the hall to hunt for Minnie.

Josh carried a stack of dishes to the kitchen. "Looks like you have enough help, Mom. Care if I turn the game on?"

"Of course not, dear. Keep the volume down, though, so I don't miss any of the conversation."

Donna put containers of food in the fridge and piled the dishes on the counter. There would be plenty of time to clean up after her family left. "I'll do these later. Let's go sit down."

"Are you sure?" Stephani asked. "We'd be glad to help wash dishes."

Donna wiped her hands on the towel. "Nope. We're sitting. Thanks for offering, though."

Stephani snuggled up beside Josh on the couch; Donna sat in her rocking recliner.

"Things are too quiet. Time to check on the girls." Sara rose from her spot on the floor and left the room.

For a few minutes the frantic activity of the game on the TV claimed their attention. Then, at the same time the station broke for a commercial, Minnie strolled into the room, her gray tail waving in the air as she apparently surveyed the available laps. After a moment, she leaped onto the couch, stepped lightly over Stephani, and curled up on Josh.

"This is the new cat, huh?" Josh tickled under Minnie's chin and she lifted her head in pleasure. "When did you get her?"

Donna took a deep breath and prayed for wisdom. "She's not mine. I'm just cat-sitting. She was a patient at the clinic."

"So, who does she belong to?"

Why did he have to be so direct? She couldn't lie. "It's kind of complicated. Do you want to hear the story?" She wished the basketball game would come back on.

"Sure." Josh wiggled his thumb at Minnie, who rolled onto her back and batted soft paws at his hand.

"A young woman found her in a ditch and brought her into the clinic. I took her information before I realized who it was. The kitten belongs to Emily Adams, Josh."

"What?" Josh's roar brought Sara and the girls to stand and stare in the doorway. He picked up Minnie and deposited her on the floor. "This is that woman's cat? How could you do such a thing?"

Donna kept her voice steady. "She's not a monster, Josh. She needed to leave town and she asked for help from someone she could trust with the cat."

"Does she know who you are?"

"Yes."

"Why would she trust you?"

"Because we talked. I told her I have forgiven her."

Josh spit the words across the room. "I'll never forgive that woman. And as long as you have any association with her, we won't be coming over here. Come on, Stephani. We'll watch the game at home."

"Josh …" Donna's plea hung in the air.

Jocelyn burst into tears. Sara pulled her close with one arm.

Tessa scooped up Minnie. "Why doesn't Uncle Josh like Grandma's kitten?"

Donna followed Josh to the door. Stephani leaned to give her a hug and whispered, "I'm sorry."

"Son, please, let's just …"

Josh's hand gripped the doorknob. When he turned, his eyes were hard and cold. "You may as well know. Stephani and I have talked to a lawyer, and he feels we have a good case. We've decided to proceed with a wrongful death suit. We're seeking justice."

He ushered Stephani through the door, stepped out, and slammed it behind him.

CHAPTER 34

Emily wound her way through the piles of clothes, books, and dirty dishes as she made her way to Trevor's bed. She found her bag and put on the pajamas she had packed. After a trip to the bathroom to brush her teeth, she was ready to sleep. But just as she reached to turn off the bedside lamp, there was a knock on the door and Andrea entered. Without waiting for an invitation, she plunked down on the foot of the bed and tucked her feet under, just like she'd done years ago when she came home from college and the girls caught up on each other's lives.

"So why are you here, Emily?"

Her sister had never been one to beat around the bush.

"I hurt my foot."

Andrea snorted in an unladylike fashion. "That foot is just an excuse. Remember, this is the one person who's known you all your life. What's really going on?"

Emily fiddled with a loose string on the blanket and dug deep for an answer. "I'm not sure. Everything seems to be going wrong in my life."

"Okay, so I'm listening."

"I think it all started with the accident." Emily's hands shook as she told her sister about Isaiah and everything that happened after she got over the initial shock.

"Andi, I still see that little boy's face in my dreams. I don't think I'll ever get over it."

Andrea reached for her hand but didn't comment.

Emily squeezed her eyes shut in an attempt to block out the memories. "The only good thing is my running. It makes me feel better

… helps me forget. I think I can do some good with it, you know, like with the SIDS run."

As Emily talked about her work at the Lighthouse and Sherry's unkind remarks, Andrea occasionally nodded or interjected a question or comment. But, for the most part, she sat quietly and focused all her attention on her sister. Her listening skills were a gift, honed from years as a therapist at a residential school for troubled teens. She did manage a laugh when Emily recounted her day as a volunteer for Habitat for Humanity.

"Now *that*, I would like to have seen."

Emily looked at Andi and her eyes filled. "I keep trying to do what's right, but every time I do something good, I make a bigger mess." She sniffed and tried to halt the tears. She was afraid if she started crying in the presence of her caring sister, she would never stop.

"You've got it all wrong, Sis. All the good works in the world—"

A cautious knock on the door startled both of them. Trevor stood in the doorway. "Aunt Emily, do you mind if I get a book? I have an Econ test tomorrow."

"And you're just now getting around to studying?" Andrea scolded.

Emily wiped her eyes. She knew her sister wasn't too angry. Trevor rarely got less than an A, and was carrying a 4.0 grade average his sophomore year.

"Come on in, we're just talking."

Trevor tossed a few piles of clothes to one side before he found the book. "Thanks," he said. "Sleep tight, Aunt Emily. And don't tell Mom if something crawls out from under the bed."

"Go study!" Andrea rolled her eyes as he left the room. "I wonder what that kid could do if he ever got organized."

Both sisters grew quiet. Emily tried to remember the discussion before Trevor interrupted.

"So what's up with Nate?" Andrea asked.

Emily twisted the blanket with her fingers. Her sister knew she had more burdens to unload, and it all came out in a flood.

"He moved out. We weren't really fighting, you know, just not close anymore. Kind of going our separate ways. He's staying with a friend from college. I don't know how to make it right again, Andi. I try. Now, he won't even answer my texts, so I don't know what's going on." Emily left out the incident with the birth control pills.

"Would he go to counseling with you? Everything you've been through, you need to talk to someone."

Emily let out a soft giggle. "Isn't that what I'm doing?"

Andrea tossed a pillow at her. "Someone other than your sister."

"You don't know how good it feels to talk to you. I haven't had anyone to dump all this on. But you better get upstairs. It's getting late and you have to work tomorrow."

"I do have to go in for a staffing at nine, but I'll probably come home early. Maybe we can have some quality time before the boys get home and take over the house."

"Trevor and Brian are so grown up."

"They are … most of the time." Andrea's pride was obvious in her voice.

Emily held out her arms in a gesture she had used with her sister since they were small. Andrea hugged her for a long time before they said goodnight.

The next day, Emily's foot felt somewhat better. She took it easy and rested all morning, reading and watching TV in the sunny family room.

Andrea arrived home at noon and pulled a battered old wheelchair out of the trunk of her car. "Look what the school let me borrow. Let's go shopping," she suggested.

Not far from Andrea's house was the original downtown area. It had once been a picturesque small town, but that was long before it had become just another suburb the city had swallowed. Now, two brick paved streets were lined with little eclectic shops and restaurants. The sisters had lunch at the Thai restaurant overlooking the river. They spent the afternoon poking in and out of the stores as Andrea pushed Emily in the chair.

Emily found a stuffed gray mouse for Minnie, and Andrea picked up a special folder Brian needed for one of his classes. After spending a long time in a jewelry shop, both of them bought beaded necklaces.

"Oh look," Andrea squealed. She stood in front of The Wooden Cradle, looking in the glass window full of tiny clothes, soft pastel blankets, bright colored toys, and dishes, all piled in and around an antique cradle. "Let's go in."

Emily wanted to get out of the chair and run from the shop, but she only shook her head. "I'm kind of tired."

"Tired? Are you kidding me? I'm the one pushing this monstrosity of a chair. Do you want to go home or stop by and watch Trevor's choir practice?"

"I'd love to see him in action."

"Choir practice it is then." Andrea turned the chair away from the baby shop and headed back to the car.

★★★★★★★

Tuesday morning, Emily's foot felt great. It had been a little tight when she woke, but loosened up after her stretches. She hated to leave Andrea's house. Her visit had been relaxing, which was odd since, most of the time, the house was anything but quiet. With two teenagers, there was always a phone ringing, a knock at the door, or someone coming or going, but Emily had loved every minute of it, even though she and Andi hadn't had time for another heart-to-heart talk.

Now it was time to head home, even though she still had no answers on how to repair her marriage, make things right at work, or make up for the terrible thing she had done.

And she hadn't asked the question she wanted to. Why were Andrea and her family going to church and praying before meals? The two girls hadn't gone to church as children. Their parents had said, "We'll let you make your own decisions about religion." Apparently, her sister's family had made a decision. Church seemed to be a huge part of their lives. Maybe she should try church. It might be another good thing she could do.

When Emily drew close to Maple Valley, she pulled into a rest area and fished her phone from the bottom of her purse. She punched in Donna's number.

"Donna? This is Emily Adams. I'm about twenty miles away from Maple Valley and I thought I would come get Minnie on my way home. Will that work for you?"

"Sure. I'm home. I'll have her things ready when you get here."

"Is she okay?"

"She's fine. I'm really going to miss her."

"I can't thank you enough for keeping her. I'll see you soon." Emily closed the phone and eased back onto the highway. It was silly, but she was excited to see that little bundle of fluff.

When she turned into Donna's driveway, she almost forgot to turn off the ignition in her hurry to see her cat. But when Donna answered the door and she stepped inside, Minnie just waved her tail nonchalantly at her owner and wandered off toward the kitchen.

"Guess she didn't miss me too much." Emily opened her purse. "How much do I owe you?"

"Not a thing. I loved having Minnie."

"Oh, but you must take something. I couldn't … that wouldn't be right. I need to pay you."

Donna shook her head. "Absolutely not. I enjoyed it and I won't take money."

Emily felt overwhelmed. First the kindness of her sister and now Donna. "Thank you. I hope I can repay you in some way. Maybe you'll get a kitten and I can keep it for you."

Donna swooped up Minnie and cuddled her. "That just might happen. This house is going to seem awfully quiet tonight."

Emily picked up the food, bowls, and litter, carried them out to the car, and then returned for Minnie. "Thanks again, Donna." She held out her arms for the kitten.

Donna stood in the doorway. "I'm praying for you, Emily," she called.

Why me? Emily thought as she got into the car and backed down the driveway, ignoring the yowling coming from the back seat. At the house, she parked, carried Minnie inside, and unloaded the car. When she carried in the last bag, Minnie was batting a small piece of florescent yellow paper all around the floor. Suddenly it slid under the stove. Minnie's soft paw reached for it, but the paper was gone.

CHAPTER 35

Josh poured cereal into a bowl and topped it with a splash of milk. He thought about how he and Isaiah used to sit at the kitchen table for breakfast and chart their day as they ate. They always planned one thing to make someone else happy, one thing to make them happy, and one thing to make Mom laugh. Now, Josh stood alone at the counter, wondering how he could make it through another day.

Stephani shuffled in, looking sleepy and tousled in her fluffy blue robe. "Good morning, dear. Are you going with me to the church missions meeting tonight?"

Josh wished he had the desire to sweep his wife into his arms. His own hurt and anger so overwhelmed him, he had nothing left over for Stephani.

"I don't think so. You go without me and take notes, okay? I may be working late."

"Again, Josh?"

Stephani wasn't a nag. She rarely said anything when he worked late, had a meeting, or went out of town. He must really be overdoing it.

"We have lots to do for the hospital project. We're still trying to rework that entryway. But I plan to take off some time when Carrie Ann is in town. I want to see her."

"She'll be staying at your mom's."

He felt an all-too-familiar knot in his gut. "We can invite her over here for dinner."

Stephani just nodded, opened the fridge, and poured a glass of apple juice. She watched him over the glass as she sipped.

"You think I'm wrong, don't you?" Josh pushed his bowl and spoon away, fighting the urge to throw the bowl across the room.

"Wrong about what?"

"About my mom. And that woman."

Stephani came around the counter to where Josh stood. For a moment she leaned against him, her head warm against his shoulder. "You're hurting, Josh. God knows, I am too. We do things when we hurt; we react to the pain."

Josh stiffened and moved away from her ever so slightly. "We meet with Frank Stevens again tomorrow. Are you with me on this?"

"I don't know, Josh. I wish we had more time to think about it. Maybe talk to someone, like Pastor Allen."

Josh's hands fisted. He stared down at them as though they belonged to someone else. "We're doing the right thing. We don't need other people trying to talk us out of it." Glancing at the clock, he hoisted his laptop, leaned down, and gave Stephani a perfunctory kiss. "I better get going. Be sure to let Diane know you won't be in tomorrow morning." He picked up his travel mug of coffee and left.

His job should have been a distraction, a retreat from the grief. But the conflict on the hospital project generated a continual state of frustration. The architects, CJ included, refused to agree to a change and the project was at a standstill.

With a quick nod at Jaleen, Josh ducked into his office. They were meeting again this morning and Josh was no closer to figuring out a compromise. He looked over the file one more time, studying the charts, the figures, the drawings. He flipped it shut and with a sudden burst of resolve, slammed his fist on the closed file. They couldn't give on this one. The entry would have to be changed, and that was that. He strode down the hall and into the conference room.

Paul Sturtz gave him a curt nod as he slid into his chair, but no one else acknowledged his presence. Paul leaned over the table. "Let's get started. I'm ready to wrap up the issues we have on this project, and I'm sure you are too."

Although Paul did his best to keep things mediated, tempers flared. CJ was very vocal, intimating that the engineers' refusal to compromise was a lack of ability on their part to figure out a solution.

Despite Josh's attempts to control himself, when CJ made comments about the engineers' professionalism, he found himself shouting. "It is *not* a lack of ability or professionalism. It comes down to this: we cannot compromise on safety. When we give way on structural components, it damages the integrity of the entire building."

After two hours of heated debate, the Wallace and Jones representatives finally agreed to redesign the entryway using a different style of window. Josh felt no sense of triumph, however. As he was leaving the room, CJ walked out beside him.

"Still looking for ways to hang others out to dry, aren't you Josh?"

★★★★★★★

The next morning, Josh paced from the counter to the patio door. What was taking Stephani so long? They needed to be at the lawyer's office by eleven. He paused to gaze out over the back yard—the wooden fort with its rope ladder up and curvy slide down—the adjustable basketball hoop that Josh had raised last fall—the sand box with a battered yellow dump truck. Isaiah's domain. He turned from the window. He couldn't let his emotions take charge, not today.

"Stephani! We need to go." Even Josh winced at the harsh sound of his voice.

Her voice drifted down the stairs. "Be there in five minutes. We have plenty of time. Get a bottle of water for me, will you?"

Josh pulled the water out of the fridge. His small, burgundy Bible lay on the counter. Funny, he didn't remember putting it there. He wondered if Stephani was trying to drop a subtle hint. It hadn't been opened since February. He pushed the Bible aside while he closed the fridge. Then he jammed it back on the shelf over the kitchen desk.

"I'm ready." Stephani bustled into the kitchen and picked up the water. "Thanks for getting this for me. Are there any muffins left?"

Josh had the car keys in his hand. "We can stop and get something. I need gas anyway."

Conversation in the car was limited. Stephani nibbled on a blueberry muffin and sipped her water. Josh dodged in and out of traffic on the busy highway, the needle on the speedometer going over the marked limit more than once. They pulled into the parking lot of Stevens and Bloyer twenty minutes before their appointment.

Stephani reached for Josh's hand. "Maybe we should pray before we go in."

Josh drew his hand away. "I want to be in there a few minutes early. I need to use the restroom."

When they entered, the receptionist paused and lifted the brush she was using to paint her fingernails. One hand was already painted an odd shade of metallic blue. She waved the hand briefly and Josh wondered if she was drying her nails or greeting them.

"The Nelsons, right? You can go on back to the conference room. Frank, I mean Mr. Stevens," she giggled softly, "will be right there."

"I need to use the restroom." Josh left Stephani standing alone while he went to the small unisex bathroom off the reception area. When he finished, they walked back to the conference room and sat on the couch.

When Frank Stevens entered carrying a thick stack of papers, Josh stood to shake his hand. Stephani kept her hands folded in her lap.

"Josh and Stephani, how are you doing?"

Josh shot a look at his wife huddled on the edge of the couch. "We're just taking one day at a time, Frank."

"Yes, I'm sure. Well, you made the right decision to file suit. This will bring closure for you." He raised both hands, palms outward. "I know it won't bring Isaiah back. You'll still have pain. But there will be the satisfaction of knowing justice was served."

Josh glanced at Stephani again. She sat quietly, staring at her feet. Turning back to Frank, he nodded. "That's what we want."

"Why don't we move to the table? I have the papers for you to sign." Frank led the way to a large, slightly scuffed conference table.

An hour later, Josh and Stephani left the office. As they passed the reception desk, the girl with the frizzy red hair waved one blue-nailed hand at them. This time, certain it was a greeting, Josh waved in response as they went out the door.

As he started the car, Stephani leaned her head back against the head rest and closed her eyes. She was silent all the way back to Maple Valley.

CHAPTER 36

Wednesday morning, Emily slapped the snooze button twice before easing out of bed. She did the stretching exercises recommended by the doctor and realized, after a few sets, she could walk without pain. While dressing, she gazed at the red heels that matched her shirt, but slipped into her padded boot. She told herself this was only temporary, and put her uninjured foot in a black loafer.

She filled Minnie's dish and spent a minute or two stroking the soft gray fur. After rinsing her hands, she grabbed a container of yogurt and a granola bar to eat at her desk.

"Sorry I have to leave again, girl. I'll probably be late tonight too. I can't imagine how much is piled up after being gone. And payroll is coming up next week." She gave one last pat and hurried out the door.

In the office parking lot, she picked a spot close to the front and hobbled in.

"Good morning, Emily," Shirley chirped. "I heard you hurt your foot. Oh, you're still in a boot. Did you finish the race?"

Emily gave her an exaggerated moan. "Can't you let me lick my wounds in private? The race was fun until my foot hurt so badly I couldn't finish." She flashed a quick smile in Shirley's direction. "I do thank you for your contribution to SIDs, though. I'm sorry I let you guys down."

"Hey, I think you're a hero for even trying," Amy said, walking out of the kitchenette area. "I couldn't run across my front yard."

"So how is your foot?" Shirley seemed genuinely interested.

"Better. It's something called plantar fasciitis. The ER doctor gave me ibuprofen and some exercises to do." Emily held the foot out. "At least I can walk now."

"Well, we're glad you're back. It's been crazy here. And I was paranoid that I was going to have to do payroll by myself." Amy plopped down in her office chair and spun toward her computer. "Let's go to Jen's for lunch and catch up."

Emily's mouth watered at the thought of her favorite sandwich and the homemade soups in a bread bowl that everyone loved. "You're tempting me."

"Shirley offered to watch the phones so we could go to lunch early. About eleven-thirty?"

"Sounds great. Let's go." Emily hurried down the hall to her office as fast as her injured foot would allow.

Three hours later, the yogurt and granola bar were still untouched on her desk. She wasn't caught up on the work left undone from her two days off, and she needed to start on the payroll that afternoon. She stood up and stretched.

Amy poked her head in the door. "Ready to go?"

"Yes. I didn't even have time to eat my breakfast." Emily slid the granola bar in her bag and tossed the unopened yogurt into the trash.

"That's what you get for being on vacation for two days," Amy teased. "Want me to drive?"

"Sure. I need to take it easy with my foot."

Amy's red convertible was easy to spot. "I'd put the top down, but …" she looked up at the gray sky, "I don't want rain inside."

Emily slid into the passenger seat with a twinge of jealousy. "The car of my dreams."

"We've had fun with it, but since we're a family of three, we're looking for a minivan."

"A minivan? Next thing I know, you'll enroll Rachel in soccer."

"Don't laugh. They have a league for preschoolers. A couple years from now, I might be a soccer mom."

Emily leaned back and closed her eyes. She didn't want to hear about someone else's idyllic family life.

As Amy pulled into the restaurant parking lot, Emily sat up and opened her eyes. A familiar Explorer was parked out front. A ripple of nervous excitement shot through her ... and then she saw him. Nate strolled out of Jen's in animated conversation with a tall, auburn-haired woman who appeared to be in her twenties. They climbed into the Explorer and drove away, too busy talking to glance toward the convertible. Emily was suddenly aware that she'd slid down in the seat.

"Wasn't that your husband?" Amy was staring at her, her eyes full of questions.

"Yeah. He must be with a client. He's been showing a lot of houses lately." Emily didn't add that he rarely drove clients in his car, preferring them to follow him in theirs. And she had never known him to go to lunch with a client. No longer hungry, she trudged into the restaurant behind Amy.

****

The afternoon dragged by. Emily had difficulty concentrating on work and she never even got started on the payroll. The noise of the children on the playground, something she'd once relished, was loud and annoying. When Jim returned from his meeting in Kansas City, he stepped into her office.

"How's the foot?"

"Much better." Emily pulled her booted foot out from under the desk as if she needed to prove to him her foot was really injured.

"It wasn't a good week to be gone. We'll need the transportation report by the middle of next week. And payroll needs to go out Friday."

"I started work on it this afternoon." Emily nodded toward the computer, wishing she could say, *It's done.*

"Glad your foot's better," Jim commented as he stepped out of her office and down the hall. Somehow, Emily felt he was only glad because it meant she was there to get her work done.

Late in the afternoon, she finally shut down the computer and clicked off the lights. As she walked to her car, she pulled out her phone. She could call Nate, just to ask him who the client was that tossed her auburn curls and smiled at him before getting into his car. Then she thought of her unanswered text messages. She dropped the phone into her bag and drove home to Minnie.

★★★★★★★

Nate took a deep breath and puffed it out in pure relief. Stan's sister, Nikki, had disappeared into the post office while he sat in the car and waited. The silence was lovely. He'd never met anyone who talked as much as Nikki. And he'd listened all afternoon as they looked at house after house. He remembered the quiet give-and-take conversations he used to enjoy with Emily.

After Nikki picked up her mail, he would drop her off at the motel where she was living temporarily. She was looking for the right house to buy before moving to Maple Valley with her six-year-old son. Nate felt his roommate's sister deserved a little extra attention, but it had been a long day. He thought of his comfy recliner and the TV remote. Pulling out his new phone, he checked to see if he had any missed calls. None.

Nikki slid into the passenger seat. "Look at this." She held up a fistful of mail. "All junk. I don't know why I bother going to get it. Hey, thanks Nate, for spending the whole day catering to my whims. We not only got to see houses, but you showed me a lot of the town. That was great. And now I need to choose. I may need to go back a second time. They're kind of all running together. I'm glad I took some pics on my phone, though. I can look those over tonight and write down some pros and cons. And I'll call Kale and talk to him about it. I'm so excited about finally buying my own home. It'll be so much better than an apartment. More room. We were getting really crowded. And better for Kale to grow up here in Maple Valley. He can play baseball and we can have a garden and ..."

As Nikki gabbed away, Nate drove. When he pulled into the motel parking lot, he gave her a forced smile. "Here you go. I'll be in touch. Let me know if you want to go back through any of the houses. It's a big decision."

"Thanks, Nate. You're a nice guy." She paused and looked at him.

"I don't know why you're living with my brother, but I bet your wife misses you." Nikki slipped out of the car, waved at him, and hurried into the lobby of the motel.

Nate sat for a moment before he turned and drove off. Not wanting to face his lonely bedroom, he decided to get some supper before he went to Stan's house. Then maybe he would drive by and see if Emily was home. Maybe she did miss him.

He pulled into a local fast-food restaurant and tried not to remember how long it had been since he had a real meal, one with some vegetables other than fries. He ordered a double cheeseburger combo and sat at a tiny table designed for two. As he unwrapped his food, a man with two small boys tumbled into a nearby booth. Nate tried to concentrate on the cheeseburger, but couldn't help watching as the dad patiently doled out drinks, sandwiches, and ketchup. The boys chattered as they ate. They constantly interrupted each other, demanding their dad's attention. Nate always pictured himself as a father and maybe that was why he felt so betrayed. He'd loved his big family growing up. He was never without a playmate or someone to talk to. He couldn't imagine a life without children.

As Nate took the last bite, one of the little boys leaned close to his dad and whispered something in his ear. The dad leaned his head back and laughed. Then his arm went around the boy in a hug.

Nate wadded up his trash, threw it away, and drove back to Stan's house with a lump in his throat.

CHAPTER 37

Carrie Ann felt a hand shaking her arm.

"I'm sorry to bother you, dear, but you fell asleep and you must have been having a bad dream. You were shouting things in your sleep." A pair of kind brown eyes looked out from behind round, thick glasses. "You just go on back to sleep. Maybe the dream is gone now." The silver-haired woman patted Carrie Ann's hand.

Carrie Ann noticed a few curious eyes flicking in her direction from across the aisle. She sat up and tried to force her eyes to stay open. "No, it's okay. We must be getting close to Kansas City."

The woman squinted at her wristwatch. "I think we land in an hour."

"I'm sorry for bothering everyone. Did I really shout?"

"Not really a shout, just loud talking. You kept telling someone to stop."

Carrie Ann reached into the bag at her feet for a book. She opened it, flipped through the pages, and struggled to focus on the words.

"Would you like a chocolate, dear?"

Carrie Ann looked up from her book to see a bag of Dove chocolates held out to her. "Thanks." She took one, unwrapped it, and bit into the candy, savoring the smooth sweetness. "It's been a long time since I've had one of these."

"Oh, I have to have my chocolate. Keeps me from being a grumpy old lady. My name's Joanne. What's yours, dear?"

"I'm Carrie Ann."

"Are you visiting Kansas City or going home?"

Carrie Ann glanced out the window at the grey clouds floating below the plane. She turned back to Joanne and said, "I'm visiting. I grew up in Maple Valley, southeast of Kansas City, but now I live in

Bogotá, Columbia."

"Columbia. Why, that's in South America."

"Yes, it's been a very long trip."

"What do you do in Columbia?"

The next hour flew by as she told Joanne about her work with the outreach center."What a blessing you are to those children," Joanne exclaimed.

"They bless me too." Carrie Ann thought of her enthusiastic pupils and their smiles in spite of the living conditions. And she thought about Juan, so happy in his new foster home.

When the plane touched down, she felt a moment of sadness as she gathered her carry-on and said goodbye to Joanne, but was soon caught in the stream of people exiting the plane.

She followed the signs toward baggage claim and when she passed the security area, a familiar voice called, "Carrie Ann!"

She turned and suddenly she was running. Like a little girl again, she reached for her mother's arms, hoping for healing in the sanctuary of the warm embrace.

★★★★★★★

Donna knew when her children needed to talk. Ever since they were tiny, she could sense turmoil in their lives. At one time, she even sewed a red plaid Big Feeling Pillow, something they could hold to help them verbalize when their little lives had been turned upside down. As they grew older, Donna learned she sometimes had to wait. Even a Big Feeling Pillow wouldn't help them talk until they were ready.

That was the hard part. Donna knew her youngest daughter carried a terrible burden. At first she thought maybe it was sorrow as she mourned the death of Isaiah. But after a short time of being with her daughter, Donna sensed there was more.

The luggage came and they grabbed the two large bags, loaded them into Donna's Honda, and headed for Maple Valley. Donna kept the conversation light, asking about the Outreach Center, the children, and their classes.

Carrie Ann turned down the volume on the radio. "How are Josh and Stephani doing?"

How like her youngest daughter to always turn the conversation to someone else. Donna eased the car onto the Interstate and sped up before she answered. "They're suffering. Understandably so. And right now your brother is very angry at me. Really, he's angry at everyone and everything. But me more than anyone else."

"Mad at you? Why?"

Donna glanced over at Carrie Ann, then back to the road. It was so hard to talk about. "The woman whose car hit Isaiah came into the clinic with a kitten she found. I met her, we talked, and then, when she asked me to keep the kitten for a weekend, I did."

"Okay, a little awkward, but I still don't know why he's angry with you."

"He thinks we should have nothing to do with the woman. He plans to sue her—a wrongful death suit."

"He's suing? Was she at fault?"

Donna shook her head. "No, I don't think so. The police investigated thoroughly and she wasn't charged with anything, but Josh has to have someone to blame. He's a man and he needs to slay the dragon. Unfortunately, there's no dragon, just an innocent woman who's hurting too."

"Well, that gives us something to pray about. I know Josh as well as anybody, and you can't always reason with him. He has to come to his own conclusions."

A few minutes later Donna could tell that Carrie Ann had nodded off with her head tilted awkwardly against the window. Donna spent the remaining miles to Maple Valley following her daughter's suggestion and praying for Josh.

When they reached home, Donna helped Carrie Ann lug her bags into the bedroom. It hadn't been redone since Carrie Ann was in high school. A banner proudly proclaiming: *Maple Valley Warriors*, still stretched across one wall. Pictures of a young Carrie pirouetting in various sparkly dance costumes decorated the top of the dresser. And several photos showed the twins together—on bikes, with the swim team, and doing sparklers one Fourth of July.

"Nothing's changed in here." Carrie Ann set down her suitcase in the middle of the floor and turned in a circle.

"I can't bring myself to take it all down and redecorate. I know you're not my little girl anymore, but I love to come in here and remember. Besides, Sara's girls stay here and they like to see your stuff."

"When are they coming?"

"This weekend, as soon as Sara gets off work and picks the girls up from daycare. Now, why don't you get your jammies on, and I'll fix us some tea. I even have some mint chocolate chip ice cream if you want a dish."

Carrie Ann laughed—the music Donna had been longing to hear. "Mom, you know my weakness."

Donna hurried off to fix the tea. While it steeped, she dished up two bowls of ice cream. It didn't take her daughter long to reappear, wearing a pair of soft lavender lounging pants and a silky camisole top. She curled onto the kitchen chair and breathed in the fragrance of the orange spice tea as Donna filled two china cups.

Carrie Ann took a tiny sip. "Mmmmm."

Donna placed a dish of ice cream on each side of the table and sat with her fingers wrapped around her cup as if she could draw strength from the warmth.

Carrie Ann picked up her spoon and took a bite of the ice cream. "Thanks, Mom. Nothing like this in Columbia."

"Yes, but it's quiet here. I'm afraid you'll miss your students. How long can you stay?"

"Ummm, not sure." Her eyes met Donna's across the table. "I guess you deserve to know why I'm here."

"Only if you want to tell me."

"I want to, it's just hard to talk about." She toyed with her spoon, making little swirls of ice cream in the bowl.

Donna waited and silently prayed for her daughter.

Carrie Ann finally set the spoon down. "Three weeks ago I went to find one of my English students, a little boy named Juan. His friend said he was in trouble and I had this grandiose idea of rescuing him. I was in an unfamiliar area and … a man dragged me into the alley, and …" As the words trailed off, Carrie Ann began to sob.

Donna shot out of her chair and folded her daughter into her arms. "Oh, Carrie Ann, oh, baby." The rape of a daughter was every mother's worst nightmare. And her precious Carrie Ann had been alone and a thousand miles away.

"Jeremiah and Rose thought I needed to come home now, rather than wait for my furlough this summer. Jeremiah was the one who made all the arrangements and bought my ticket. So, I guess I'm starting my furlough early."

Donna leaned back so she could see Carrie Ann's face, but she continued to hold her hands. "I'm so glad they sent you home. Did you see a doctor?"

"Yes, Rose took me that night. I'm okay physically. We still don't know about … you know … a pregnancy."

"Did you go to the police?"

Carrie Ann frowned and nodded. "Yes, we reported it. But nothing much was done. I'm the foreigner, the blonde American female." She pushed at the hair curving around her face, really more brown than blonde. "They more or less said I asked for it by being on their streets."

"Asked for it?" Donna was horrified. "How could they? You won't go back there, will you? Can't Hope for the Nations assign you somewhere else?"

"Mom, you know better than that. God called me to Bogotá. I'll take the time I need to heal and then I'll go back to work."

Carrie Ann pulled one of her hands from her mother's grasp so she could wipe the tears that were streaming down her cheeks. Donna stood and brought a box of tissues to the table. They both blew their noses.

Carrie Ann stirred her dish of ice cream, mostly melted by now.

"Want me to dish you up another bowl? We can throw that out."

"Nope. This is fine." Carrie Ann licked the drips from her spoon.

Several bites later, she looked up and gave her mother a weak smile. "I'm glad I'm home, Mom."

Much later, Donna put down the book she was reading and rose from her bed to make one last trip to the bathroom. In the hall, she paused to look in at her daughter. She might have been ten years old, instead of thirty-four, sprawled across her bed, covers in a jumble around her feet, arms outstretched, and her hair fanned across the pillow. Donna resisted the urge to kiss her cheek one more time.

Her prayer came as a question: *Why, God? Why is this happening to my family? Why all this hurt?*

CHAPTER 38

Emily arrived at the office with her mocha latte even before the janitor arrived. She sipped coffee while reading emails and checking phone messages. Then she plunged into the payroll. It had to be finished today so she forced herself to concentrate, ignoring the banter of Shirley and Amy in the outer office when they arrived.

"Morning." Amy's smiling face peeked around her door. "Hard at work already?"

"Still behind."

"Bummer. Want to go to lunch today, or did you bring something?"

"Sorry, Amy, I need to work. I put a salad in the refrigerator."

"Awww, I wanted to go to lunch with you. I have *news*." Amy looked like she was about to burst with whatever it was she had to share.

Emily's curiosity was aroused now. "Break at ten?"

"Sure, see you then."

The phone rang and Amy ducked out of the office. Emily answered the phone and cradled it on her shoulder while she attempted to continue her work on the computer. She couldn't avoid the distractions now that the actual workday had started.

At ten, Emily stopped. She wasn't going to miss break time with Amy and the big news. She dug in her purse for change so she could treat herself to a soda.

Amy was drinking water instead of her usual morning Mountain Dew. Emily sat across the table from her with a Diet Pepsi and a small bag of Doritos.

"What's up, girlfriend?"

"I have so much to tell you, I don't even know where to start."

Emily opened the bag of Doritos. "Just start somewhere, the

suspense is killing me."

Amy held up the water. "Notice the lack of caffeine? That's your first clue."

Emily's excitement evaporated. "You're pregnant?" She tried to keep the disappointment from her face.

Amy's grin nearly split her face. "Yep. We didn't intend to have kids this close, but I guess things don't always go the way you plan."

"No, they certainly don't." Emily thought of all the plans she and Nate had made.

"And, since we'll have two little ones," Amy leaned in, her eyes sparkling, "we have decided I can stay home with them for a few years. Justin is due for a promotion at work, and we should be able to make it financially. So, it makes sense. Daycare for two would kill us."

"So you're quitting?" Emily felt a sudden, overwhelming sense of abandonment.

"I told Jim this morning. I'll work until the end of May when school is out and things slow down here. Then ... home with my babies." She leaned back with a smile of pure satisfaction.

"Who will I go to Jen's with for lunch, or commiserate with when the budget is due, or go for ice cream with after work?" Emily almost whined.

Amy reached across the table and put a hand over Emily's. "We'll still be friends. My mom will watch the kids and I'll go to lunch with you, or we'll get together on weekends and go shopping or something."

"Yeah," Emily agreed, thinking it probably wouldn't happen. Then, mustering up all the goodwill she didn't feel, she added, "Congratulations, I'm really happy for you, Amy."

Folding over the top of her chips to eat later, Emily tossed the empty Pepsi bottle in the recycling bin. "I've got to get back to the payroll."

"Yep, keep those checks coming until May."

As Emily settled into her desk chair, her eyes unexpectedly filled with tears. She fought them back and forced her mind to return to work.

Totally focused on the computer, she looked up in surprise when

Jim stepped inside her doorway. "Can you see me in my office, Emily?"

She looked up, hands still poised over the keyboard. "When?" She wondered why he was frowning. She had until five to finish the payroll.

"Right now would be good."

"Okay. Let me close out this data base and I'll be there."

When Emily entered Jim's office, he nodded to the chair beside his desk. "Have a seat, Emily."

She noticed he had copies of the certified enrollment report she'd finished last week.

He cleared his throat and the stern look in his eyes made her uneasy. "This is not easy for me. I understand this has been a tough time for you, and I've tried to be supportive. I didn't say anything about the times you've been late, the missed staff meeting, and the days you took because you injured your foot. But when the quality of your work affects the whole school district, it's time to speak up."

Emily frowned and leaned forward, but Jim held up his hand. He wasn't finished. "This is the certified enrollment report. I don't need to tell you how important this is. Look at the original figures and the figures you reported. In this column, the actual figure is ninety-one, but you keyed it in as nineteen. Emily, this affects our funding. I don't have time to look over your shoulder at everything you do."

Emily looked down at her hands, her hair falling on either side of her face. "Jim, I'm so sorry. What can I do?"

He handed her his copy of the report. "Short term, you can fix this report before we send it out. Long term, I've discussed it with some of the board members. We don't want to take official action at this point. Obviously, I'll oversee your work more closely, and personally check everything you send out. We'll meet two weeks from today. At that point I'll make a decision on whether your work will be taken before the school board in May."

Emily swallowed hard and tried to keep her voice steady. "I love my job here. I know I've been distracted … the accident, my foot …" Nate. "I'll double-check things, I'll stay late, I'll make things right."

The slightest hint of a smile appeared on Jim's face. "I hope you do,

Emily, I hope you do."

Trying not to look at Amy or Shirley as she passed their desks, Emily fled to her office. She closed the door and gave herself permission to cry. Then, wiping tears and smeared mascara with a tissue, she gave herself a mental pep talk.

Straighten up, now. You can do this.

Back to work on the payroll, she meticulously double-checked every number she entered.

CHAPTER 39

Carrie Ann yawned and rolled over. Sunlight streamed in the window as she rose on one elbow to view the clock radio on the night stand. Nine o'clock. She'd slept nearly ten hours without a single nightmare. There was something about sleeping in her old bedroom and under the umbrella of her mother's prayers. She swung her legs over the side of the bed and followed the smell of coffee to the kitchen.

Her mom greeted her with a smile and a steaming, just-poured cup. "I was beginning to wonder if you were going to sleep through your entire furlough."

"Boy, did it feel good." Carrie Ann sniffed the coffee. "Mmmm. Hazelnut?"

"I may be old, but I still remember my daughter's favorite flavor of coffee. And if you give me a few minutes, I can turn out some waffles with strawberries and whipped cream."

"Thanks, Mom, but can we just do toast this morning? I think I have a bad case of jet lag. Too much travel."

"Sure. Wheat bread okay?"

"Fine." Carrie Ann opened the fridge. "Is there juice in here?"

"Behind the milk." Donna dropped bread into the toaster and set butter and jelly on the table. "So, what do we want to do today?"

"See Josh and Stephani?"

Donna set a blue flowered plate and a small juice glass in front of Carrie Ann. "I imagine your brother is working. His firm is doing an addition to Memorial Hospital, and I think it takes a lot of Josh's time."

"Will they be here for Easter dinner on Sunday?"

"I … I don't think so." Donna's voice trembled. "Josh is so angry with me. You may need to go to his place to see him."

Carrie Ann pulled herself out of her own sorrow to consider her brother and his wife. What would she say to him? "Maybe he doesn't want to see me."

"Oh no, sweetie, he needs to see you, to know you care for him. Josh is like a drowning man, and we have to keep throwing lifelines to him. You may be the lifeline he needs right now." Her mom laid two buttered slices of toast on the plate. "Do you want some cinnamon and sugar?"

"No. Plain is fine." Carrie Ann chewed on one piece of toast. "It's so hard to know what to say, Mom."

"I know, sweetie. We have our own hurts and we hurt for each other, but we have to keep reaching out." Donna stood and refilled their coffee cups. "Do you think we should take you to see a doctor here?"

"No, Mom. I'm fine. I went to see a real doctor in Bogotá, not a witch doctor."

"Let me take you shopping, then. I bet you don't have an Easter dress yet."

Carrie Ann brightened. "That's an offer I can't refuse. I don't have a dress period, just my skirts I wear to teach in. But before we go, give me Josh's work number and I'll call him."

★★★★★★★

When the phone rang, Josh started to ignore it, but Jaleen screened his calls and rarely let a call through that wasn't critical. With a sigh, he picked up the receiver. "Josh Nelson."

"Hey, dorkface."

Only one person called him that and got away with it. Josh leaned back in his chair and grinned. In his best executive voice he intoned, "Ma'am, do you know to whom you are speaking? This is Josh Nelson, Maple Valley Community's premier engineer, overseer of projects of international importance."

"Dorkface to me, all the same. When do I get to see you?"

"What does your busy schedule allow? Just name a night and we'll have you over. Tonight? Saturday? What works?"

There was a small pause before Carrie Ann asked, "Why don't you come over to Mom's tonight? Or tomorrow? Sara's coming."

Josh sat up and gripped the edge of his desk. "I think you know why," he said a little more harshly than he intended. "You've talked to Mom. I want to see you in the worst way, but right now, neither Stephani nor I will come to Mom's."

"Okay. Tell me what time and I'll be over tonight."

He relaxed a little and leaned back. "How about six?"

"See you then. Love ya …" Carrie Ann's voice trailed off as if there was more she wanted to say, but couldn't.

Josh willed his breathing to return to normal. He didn't trust his voice, so he sent an email to Stephani letting her know the plans. He rubbed his temples, hoping to rub away the stress.

He'd always prided himself on his self-control, but one little comment from his sister and he was ready to smash and destroy.

It was his mom's fault. He could stay calm if she hadn't taken up with that woman. He stood and paced between his desk and the window.

****

Carrie Ann spotted Josh peering out the window as she pulled up the long drive. She hopped out of her mom's car and the kitchen door swung open.

Josh's voice boomed. "Hey, Sis! Come on in." As she stepped through the door he grabbed her in a tight hug.

When she backed out of his embrace, her eyes filled with tears. "Josh, I'm so sorry. What can I do besides pray?"

"That's the best thing you can do."

Stephani walked into the kitchen carrying a tray. She crossed the room quickly, set the tray down, and hugged Carrie Ann hard. The tears continued to fall. When they parted, they both reached for the box of tissues on the table.

"I'm so glad you could come."

"I wish I could have been here in February."

Stephani sniffed and reached for another tissue.

Carrie Ann looked first at Josh, then Stephani. "How are you two doing, really?"

"Really? We take one day at a time. I don't feel like I'm coping, but somehow I make it to the next day. I'm glad for my job at the library. When I stay busy, I have less time to think … and remember."

"I'll put the meat on the grill." Josh opened the fridge and removed a platter of chicken breasts.

Carrie Ann watched him carry it out to the grill. Stephani shook her head. "I don't know about your brother. He's taking this hard. Nothing seems to comfort him."

"Could I see Isaiah's room?"

After a slight hesitation, Stephani nodded. "Sure. I'll take you." She led the way upstairs. The door was shut and Stephani opened it with what seemed like a huge effort. The large room had slanted ceilings and dormer windows. Late afternoon sunshine shone through the windows, casting bright patterns on the floor. One wall was painted bright blue, the others white with blue stripes. Toys lay scattered where Isaiah had left them: a partially built Lego airplane, a collection of Matchbox cars, and a pile of books about snakes.

Carrie Ann wandered through the room, tenderly touching the bed and the toys as if she were touching their owner. When she had made a full circle, she stood beside Stephani. "I loved your son. I don't know why God allowed this to happen. Isaiah was supposed to be a missionary with me in Bogotá. I know you miss him so much more than I do, but I want you to know I will miss him until I see him again in heaven."

Stephani blinked back tears. "Me too, Carrie Ann, me too."

They both stood gazing at the room that would forever be a little boy's room. There would be no toys boxed up because they were outgrown, no loud rock music shaking the floor, no pictures of pretty girls in prom dresses on the wall. Stephani closed the door and Carrie Ann followed her back downstairs.

Josh moved efficiently back and forth from the deck to the kitchen. He grilled chicken, a vegetable medley, and even put char marks on some juicy pineapple slices. Carrie Ann sat down at the bar to watch him while Stephani removed a salad from the fridge and poured drinks.

Josh carried the platter of grilled foods to the table and held it out proudly. "Let's eat."

After they were all seated at the table, Carrie Ann waited, looking expectantly at him.

Josh met her gaze. "You want me to pray?"

"You haven't stopped talking to God have you?" Carrie Ann asked.

"No," Josh snapped. He prayed, briefly thanking God for their food and their guest.

As they ate, Josh quizzed Carrie Ann on her work in Bogotá. She shared stories about the children, the work of Hope for the Nations, and Jeremiah and Rose, carefully avoiding any discussion of the real reason she was home. They sat at the table long after the food had been consumed.

"How long will you be here?" Stephani asked as she stood to clear the dishes.

"Not sure yet. I'm going to relax, spend time with family. I'll visit the churches that support the mission and the outreach center. For sure, I'll be here through May."

"When will we see you again?" Stephani asked.

"You won't be coming for Easter?"

Stephani paused, her hands full of plates. She looked pointedly at Josh.

Josh growled, "You both know the answer to that. Don't try to manipulate me."

Carrie Ann reached across the table to lay her hand on his arm. "It's not manipulation. I don't understand what's going on, Josh. I know you're hurting, but Mom is too. Seems like family needs to stick together when there's a tragedy, not be angry and divisive."

"She befriended the woman that killed Isaiah. Now who's being divisive? My son was killed. How am I supposed to feel?"

"I don't know, but I don't like to come home and find my family being torn to bits and pieces." Carrie Ann picked up the last of the dishes and took them to Stephani who was stacking them in the dishwasher. "I'll be at Mom's all this week. Call me, and let's get together again." She gave a last hug to each of them and left.

CHAPTER 40

Emily woke to a soft rumble beside her ear. She lay without moving until a soft paw batted her nose. Emily giggled and threw back the covers. "Okay, Minnie, we'll get up."

Minnie led the way down the hall, her grey tail waving like a fuzzy bottle brush. After feeding her, Emily made coffee, wishing she could get up and smell coffee already made. While she ate a small bowl of cereal, she looked through the mail piled on the table, setting aside a couple of bills that needed to be paid. Then she showered, dressed, and hurried out the door.

She was early for work again, but it was taking more of her time to double-check all her figures and reports. Payroll was finished on time and done correctly—she hoped. Never before had she endured such pressure at work.

As she sat at her desk and sipped her coffee, she heard her cell phone's distinctive jingle from the bottom of her purse. She dug it out and answered.

"Hi, Aunt Emily."

"Hi. Is this Brian or Trevor?"

"Ahhh. I'm hurt you don't know. It's your favorite nephew, the talented and handsome one. It's Trevor." His boyish laughter boomed in her ear.

"Well, to what do I owe the honor of this phone call?"

"Mom said I should call you and let you know our youth group is putting on a play, *The Last Week*. We've been asked to give it at a church in Maple Valley. I thought you might want to come see me. I'm Peter."

Who was Peter? Maybe one of Jesus' disciples? "Trevor, that's great. I'd love to see you. When and where? Are your mom and dad coming?"

"Mom can't come. She has a meeting at the school. She and Dad get to come to all three performances here in Kansas City, so I guess they think that's enough. So, can you come?"

"Where? What's the address?"

"It's at the Maple Valley Fellowship Church. I have no idea where that is. But in your dinky town, it shouldn't be hard to find," Trevor teased.

"I can look it up. When is it?"

"Tonight. I was supposed to call you last week. The play's at seven and you can buy tickets at the door."

"Nothing like giving me lots of advance notice. Can I buy you supper beforehand?"

"I don't think so. We're bringing the church van and we have to be there early to get makeup put on. I'll look for you afterwards to say hello, though. Hey, I better get going. I'll be late for homeroom."

"I'll be there, Trevor. Thanks for letting me know."

"Sure. Bye, Aunt Emily."

Emily tucked the phone back into her purse. Finally, something to look forward to. She tried not to wish Nate was going with her.

During her mid-morning break, Emily passed Jim in the hall. "Payroll was fine, Emily. Keep up the good work." She waited for him to add, "Or you'll lose your job," but he didn't.

"I'm double-checking everything."

"You need to." He turned into his office.

Emily stayed focused on her work all afternoon and resisted the impulse to hurry. When five o'clock came, she powered off her computer and left, meeting Amy on the way out.

"You're leaving early today." Amy flung the strap of an oversized purse over her shoulder. A child's sippy cup peeked out from under the flap. She walked out the door with Emily.

"My nephew is in a play tonight at one of the local churches, and I hope to get in a run before dark. I think my foot's had enough rest." Emily held out her foot and wiggled it.

"Are you training for something?"

"I'm not signed up for anything, but there are some charity runs in May. I like to feel that my running is benefiting someone besides me."

Amy shook her head and smiled. "You're always doing good things for others, Emily." She unlocked the door of her car and climbed in. "Have a good night. Say hello to Nate for me. We haven't seen him around the office much lately. He must be selling lots of houses."

A knot of hurt twisted inside Emily. Nate used to drop in often just to say hi or to take her to lunch. "Yeah, he's been busy." She needed to tell her friend that Nate had moved out, but she couldn't talk about it—not yet.

The warmth of the spring day still lingered into the evening. Emily rolled the car window down and enjoyed the fresh air. When she got home, she dropped her jacket and bag on a chair and petted Minnie for a few minutes before she headed to the closet and pulled out her running gear. She slipped into a pair of jogging shorts and a tee, then laced up the shoes.

"I'm only going a short ways, Minnie. It's too nice of a day to come home and sit."

Rather than running her old route of several miles, she opted for a circle around four blocks. Tulips and daffodils poked their heads up from brown flower beds, and most of the lawns had broad stretches of green grass. As she jogged the last few yards back to her house, she noticed a strange silver car in the driveway.

She sped up and sprinted the last few yards. Puffing a little, she called to the well-dressed young man standing at the door, "May I help you?"

"I'm looking for Emily Adams." She watched his eyes take in her running shorts and long legs.

"I'm Emily." She met his eyes with a direct stare.

"This is for you." He held out a thick, official looking envelope. When she didn't reach for it immediately, he thrust it toward her. "Here."

Emily took the envelope and turned it over in her hands. "What's it for?"

"I just deliver. I don't know the contents." He backed toward his car, taking a last look at her legs before getting in and driving off.

The envelope was embossed with the name of an unfamiliar law firm.

Oh, Nate. Not a divorce.

She carried the envelope inside and laid it on the kitchen table. The table where Nate sat to drink coffee and read the newspaper. The table where they played cards until two in the morning. The table where they'd shared countless meals.

Numbly, she walked into the bedroom and stripped off her running clothes. She took a long, hot shower and put on a pair of clean lounging pants and tee shirt. From the cupboard, she took a bottle of red Merlot and poured herself a glass. She took the wine and the letter into the family room, sat down on the couch, and stared at the envelope. Images of the last five years as Nate's wife danced like pages from a scrapbook through her head. If only she could be given another chance. If only she could turn the clock back and change things. She could conquer her fears of failing as a mom. She could give him the children he wanted. But now it was too late.

She took a sip of the wine and set it on the coffee table. Picking up the envelope, she tore it open with her fingernail, withdrew a sheaf of papers, and read:

Dear Mrs. Adams,

This is to inform you that you are being named defendant in a wrongful death suit ...

For a tiny moment, relief flooded through her. Nate wasn't filing for divorce. Their marriage wasn't over. Then the implications of the letter hit her. She was being sued for Isaiah's death. She held the proof that she was guilty, that she had failed to stop the car before it took the life of a child.

Her hands covered her face as the letter dropped to the floor.

CHAPTER 41

Emily wept until there were no more tears. She needed someone to guide her through this. She needed Nate.

When she stood, she nearly tripped over Minnie stretched out at her feet. Emily rubbed the furry head, grateful for the kitten's presence. She glanced at the clock. Six thirty. With a start, she remembered Trevor's play. She'd promised him she would come, but surely he would understand if she wasn't there. No, she would go to the play and sort this out later.

She changed clothes and used the GPS on her phone to find the church. Maple Valley Fellowship ... the name sounded familiar, but she couldn't remember where she'd heard it.

It seemed strange to be going to a church when there wasn't a wedding or a funeral—the only times she had gone to a church growing up. Her parents believed in God, but He just didn't figure into their daily lives.

The sprawling brick building had a large central area, with several wings jutting out in various directions. The only parking spots in the massive lot were at the far end, a long walk from the main entrance. Emily took a deep breath and hurried in, hoping she hadn't missed any of the play. Two young girls were handing out programs at the door. She took one and found a single seat toward the back.

Almost as soon as she sank down onto the cushioned seat, the lights dimmed and the play started. Despite all that was mulling in her mind, she was soon caught up in the story. Trevor did an excellent job as Peter, delivering his lines with energy and passion. When they hung the actor portraying Jesus Christ on the cross, she was amazed to find tears running down her face. *Why? Why did he have to die?* She fumbled in her pocket for a tissue. A gray-haired older man sitting next to her leaned over and handed her a clean, folded handkerchief. She shook her head, not wanting to take someone's handkerchief, but he laid it on her knee. She smiled gratefully and mopped at her streaming eyes.

When Jesus appeared to the disciples, alive again, the play was over. Emily stood and applauded until her hands stung. She held the soggy handkerchief out to its owner.

"Keep it, young lady. I have a feeling the Holy Spirit is tugging on your heart. You may need it again."

Holy Spirit? What was he talking about? Emily stepped out into the foyer and looked for Trevor. Her tall, handsome nephew was making his way toward her, carrying a duffle bag. People crowded around him, congratulating him on his performance.

When he reached her side, he gave her a hug. "What did you think?"

"You were absolutely great. I think you have a career in Hollywood. Don't you dare tell your mom I said that, though."

"Thanks, Aunt Emily. Mom was sorry she couldn't come. She wanted me to say you're invited for Easter dinner if you want to drive up."

"Hmmm. I might do that." Emily frowned, thinking about the play. "Trevor, why did he have to die?"

"Who?"

"Jesus. If he was God's son, why did he have to die?"

Trevor shifted, obviously uncomfortable. "I'm not sure I'm very good at answering questions, Aunt Emily. You want to talk to my youth leader?"

Emily shook her head. "No, I'm sure he's busy tonight."

"Jesus died for us … he, uh, was the atonement … that's the word our pastor used. Do you have a Bible?"

"I don't think so. Nate and I, we just never had much time to read it."

Trevor rummaged around in the bag he had slung over his shoulder. "Here, borrow mine."

Emily looked at it. *Young Men's Study Bible.* "This is for men."

"The Bible part is all the same. Just read it."

"The whole thing?"

Trevor chuckled. "Well, it's all good, but you might want to start with Matthew or something in the New Testament." Someone called his name and Trevor leaned over and gave her a kiss on the cheek. "Gotta go; my fans are waiting." He grinned at her. "Thanks again for coming. It means a lot to me."

"Bye," Emily called as he threaded his way through the crowd. She took the Bible and dropped it in her purse.

When she opened the door to her house, she waited for the thump of Minnie leaping off of wherever she had curled up, and the pad, pad, pad of paws as she came to greet her. But the house was quiet. *She must really be sound asleep.*

Emily flipped on the light switch in the kitchen. "Here, Minnie," she called.

Dropping her purse on the table, she wandered into the family room. The letter from the lawyer lay on the floor, her glass of wine tipped and spilled beside it. Minnie lay on her side, stretched out on the floor. Her legs were twitching and there was a small pool of vomit by her head. When she saw Emily, she attempted to stand, but staggered and fell again.

Emily dropped to her knees beside Minnie and stroked the soft gray fur. "Minnie, Minnie, oh, what have I done?"

She fumbled in her pocket, clutched her cell phone, and found the number for the vet. Emily pushed send and tried to remain calm as she reached his voicemail.

"Please leave a message after the tone."

"I ... I think my cat has alcohol poisoning," Emily stammered, hoping her message was clear. "She spilled a glass of red wine I had sitting on the table. I don't know how much she drank, but she doesn't seem to be able to stand or walk."

She closed the phone and waited. Minnie lay quietly, her breathing fast and shallow. Emily picked up the empty glass and carried it to the kitchen. She would worry about the red stain on the carpet later.

The phone rang and she jumped, flipped it open, and answered.

"This is Dr. Ewing. Bring your cat to the clinic immediately. I'll meet you there."

"Be there in ten minutes," Emily agreed, scooping up Minnie in her arms. The kitten's head lolled over the side of her arm like a worn out stuffed animal. She laid her on the passenger seat of the car and sped the short distance to the clinic.

The vet was waiting outside and rushed them back to a room with shiny steel tables and large medical machines. A faint smell reminded Emily of hospitals.

The vet took Minnie and positioned her on one of the tables. "How much wine was in the glass?"

"I'm not sure. I don't remember taking more than a sip or two. I suppose four ounces or so … is she going to be okay?"

"I'll do what I can." Using a small stethoscope, the vet listened to several spots on Minnie's side and chest. He wound what looked like a large rubber band around Minnie's leg, and inserted a needle to withdraw a small amount of blood. Then another needle went in. Emily felt a little woozy and took a step away from the table.

"You can sit down over there if you need to." The vet tipped his head toward a metal stool.

"I'm okay." Emily took a deep breath and moved back to his side.

Dr. Ewing took a tube and threaded it into Minnie's mouth and down her throat, then poured something through the tube into her stomach. Using the needle in her paw, he started an IV drip. He washed his hands and sat on the stool he'd offered to Emily. "I need you to fill out some paperwork. It may be a long night for your little kitten. I'll stay with her until she has stabilized. If her breathing slows more, she'll need to be put on a respirator. I've given her some charcoal to absorb the alcohol. That should help soon. Do you have any questions?"

"Will she … be okay?"

"If we can get her through the next few hours, she should be fine. Has she been seen here before?"

Emily nodded. "You checked her over when I first got her. I found her in a ditch. And she had some shots that day."

The vet stood and moved toward the office area as he talked. "I'll find her file. That should have a phone number where I can reach you. I'll call you tonight if there's any change. What's your name?"

"Emily Adams. And her name is Minnie."

"Well, I'll do my best to bring little Minnie through this, but," the vet turned and looked gravely at Emily, "you've got to promise you won't leave any more wine around for her to ingest."

"Never again." Emily swallowed, wishing she could swallow the knot of guilt that threatened to choke her.

After she verified the information in Minnie's file, she followed Dr. Ewing back to the surgical room and gave one last pat to Minnie who still lay unmoving and unresponsive on the cold steel table.

CHAPTER 42

Emily didn't think she could bear to enter the dark, empty house. She longed for the sound of her husband's teasing voice and a kitten's yowling. But she had no other place to go.

Using a spot-cleaner, she scrubbed at the carpet as tears streamed down her face and dripped onto the cloth. But no matter how much she rubbed and squirted and rubbed again, the red stain remained. Just like the stains in her heart.

It was late, but she knew going to bed was useless. She would only lie there, waiting for a call from the vet. She slipped into pajamas and started to put her purse away when she noticed the Bible Trevor had loaned her. She took it out, climbed on her bed, and thumbed through the pages. There were a lot of them, but she found the book Trevor had mentioned, Matthew. After reading a story here and there, she found the biblical version of the scenes Trevor and the other actors had portrayed.

Flipping forward she saw a book called Romans. What did that mean? She read some of it but struggled to understand. Just as she was ready to close it in frustration, some verses in the third chapter caught her eye.

There is no difference, for all have sinned and fall short of the glory of God.

Yeah, Emily thought, *but some sin more than others. Some hit children with their cars. That's really falling short.*

She kept reading.

And are justified freely by his grace through the redemption that came by Jesus Christ. God presented him as a sacrifice of atonement through faith in his blood.

Atonement. Emily frowned and laid the Bible in her lap. That's the same word Trevor used. Funny, old fashioned word. She picked up her phone and typed in the word *atonement.* There were two definitions. The first was, *amends for a wrong or injury.* The second, *the reconciliation of God and humankind through Christ's death.*

So, he died to amend the wrong. "Whose wrong?" she wondered aloud.

And then Emily knew. Every wrong she'd ever done—the lie she told her mom in first grade, the test she'd cheated on in high school, lying to her husband, Isaiah's death. Jesus Christ died for her wrongs. She was helpless to right them; only He could. Jesus died for her, Emily Adams.

Tears rolled down her cheeks once again. She pulled out the handkerchief the old man had given her, wiped her face, and blew her nose. She needed to talk to someone. Picking up her phone, she punched in her sister's number.

Her sister's "Hello" sounded sleepy and Emily cast a guilty look at the clock.

"Andrea? My life is a mess. I need to talk to someone."

"I'm listening." The sleepy tones were gone.

"I went to Trevor's play and he loaned me his Bible. Is it true? Did Jesus really die for me? Even when I make such a mess of things? Why didn't you tell me?"

Andrea's voice was gentle. "I tried a couple of times, but you weren't interested in spiritual discussions. And when you were here last month, someone kept interrupting us every time I wanted to talk to you."

"Why? Why did Jesus do that?"

"Love, Em. God loved you enough to send His son to die for you."

Emily chewed her lip as she thought about that. Finally she whispered, "How could He love me after what I did?"

"Oh, Emily, nothing we do is too big for God to forgive. He created us. We're his kids. You think I'd stop loving Trevor or Brian if they did something wrong?"

"No, I guess not." Emily flipped the pages of the Bible in her lap.

"But it's hard to imagine that kind of love. What do I do in return?"

"Just accept His love and His death for you."

"Accept it? How?"

"Salvation—eternal life with God—is a free gift, but we have to accept it. If you know you're a sinner ..."

Emily interrupted with a muttered, "Oh, yes."

"Then ask for forgiveness and tell Him you want to live for Him. It's called by lots of different names: being born again, making Him Lord of your life, getting saved, but it all means the same thing. You're giving up control to God and living for Him. Is that what you want?"

Emily nodded, then realized her sister couldn't hear her nod. "Yes. Can I tell Him right now? While you're on the phone?"

"Sure. Go ahead."

Emily paused. What did you call God? Was He really listening? Whispering into the phone, she began. "God, it's Emily. I've done some terrible things. Please forgive me. I know now that Jesus died for me. So I'd like to, ummm, belong to you. That's it. I mean, amen."

Andrea's voice startled her. "I'm so happy for you, Em! You're a Christian now, and you have God's Holy Spirit living inside of you. When you die, you go to heaven to live with Him. The first thing you should do is look for a church."

Emily wiped at her eyes. It was all a bit much to take in. "Andrea, can God help me with my problems?"

"He's the original problem solver."

"Does he like kittens?"

"Well, yeah, he created them."

"Minnie drank some wine I poured for myself, and now she's really sick."

"Oh, poor kitty. We can pray for her."

"Will you ... please?" Emily asked.

Andrea prayed and Emily listened, feeling like, for the first time since she had hit Isaiah with the car, she was doing something right, something that would help.

"That's not all. I think I have a really big problem."

"Not too big for God."

Emily walked out to the kitchen with the phone. She picked up the letter from the lawyer and read it to her sister.

"Oh, Emily, I'm so sorry." Her sister's voice was drenched with compassion. "Did you call your own lawyer?"

"No, I got the notice right before it was time to go to the play. And when I got home, Minnie was sick. I don't know who to call. I've never needed a lawyer before. How can I even pay for one?" Emily felt that waves of problems were washing over, and she was sinking in the sea. Did God have a lifeline for her?

"Well, I think the first thing is to find a lawyer you can trust. Let me call some people tomorrow and get some referrals." Andi's calm voice steadied her. "You have to let Nate know."

Emily paced the kitchen, stopping to look out the window at the dark night. "I suppose, but it seems he doesn't want anything to do with me. He won't answer texts or anything." She thought about the auburn-haired woman she had seen with him at Jen's.

Andrea's voice was firm. "It doesn't matter. You're still married and this affects him. You need to let him know right away."

For more than an hour, they talked. Then they prayed again, asking God for His help. When they finally said goodnight and Emily closed her phone, she had a plan.

She would call a lawyer as soon as Andrea had some referrals. She would notify Nate right away, and find a church where she could get spiritual support.

Emily turned out the light and pulled the covers up to her chin. Despite so much wrong in her life, she finally felt she could sleep without the overwhelming burden of guilt.

She was roused sometime later by the sound of the telephone. Instantly awake, she stood and grabbed it. "Hello, this is Emily."

"This is Dr. Ewing at the All Paws Animal Clinic. I have some good news. Your kitten is awake and alert. Actually, she's making quite a racket. You can come pick her up anytime."

"Oh, thank you." Emily felt such a surge of relief, her knees went weak and she sat back on the bed. "Can I come get her on my lunch break today?"

"That would be fine. We'll see you then."

Emily laid her phone down. "Thanks, God." Her first answered prayer. Now, for the rest of the list ...

CHAPTER 43

Donna opened the door to two squealing girls. Their hugs were brief as they scooted around her to wrap themselves around Carrie Ann, one girl on each side.

Carrie Ann giggled and tried to steady herself. "Hold on, girls, don't knock me over."

"Aunt Carrie Ann, are you home for forever?" Jocelyn asked.

"Not forever, honey. But I'm home long enough for us to have some fun. Are we going to dye some Easter eggs? And have an Easter egg hunt?"

Tessa jumped up and down, looking like she might burst with excitement. Suddenly she stopped and ran down the hall to Donna's bedroom.

Carrie Ann looked at Sara. "Where'd she go?"

"I have no idea." Sara and Donna looked at each other and shrugged.

They heard her feet stop, then come running back. "Grandma," she demanded, "where's your cat?"

Donna patted Tessa's shoulder. "Minnie wasn't my cat. I was just keeping her for a friend."

Sara finally worked her way into the house with her suitcase and bags and hugged her sister. "It's been too long. I'm so glad you're home. Any reason for the change of plans? Was it Isaiah?"

Carrie Ann shot a glance toward her mom. "That was part of it."

"We'll talk later. This stuff is heavy. Where do you want me, Mom?"

"Why don't you take Josh's old room downstairs? We can put sleeping bags on the floor in the family room for the girls."

Jocelyn and Tessa were tugging on Carrie Ann's hands.

Tessa gazed up at her adoringly. "Aunt Carrie Ann, will you play

Barbies with us? Grandma has lots of girls and they've got clothes and she's got a Barbie car, and ..." Tessa's voice faded as they disappeared into the toy room.

While Sara made two trips carrying suitcases downstairs, Donna went to check on the chili in the crock pot. Her family was home—all but one.

★★★★★★

Easter Sunday dawned warm and sunny. Carrie Ann awoke to whispering in the hallway.

"Do you think she's awake?"

"Maybe. Let's peek in."

"Can she tell us if the Easter Bunny came?"

"Oh, Tessa, you're such a baby. I keep telling you there's no Easter Bunny."

Carrie watched the door fling open and a little girl bounced on her bed. "Aunt Carrie Ann, Aunt Carrie Ann, Jocelyn says there's no Easter Bunny and I want to hunt for candy."

Carrie Ann opened one eye. "Do you guys always get up so early? Where's your mom?"

"See, she *is* awake." Tessa snuggled down for a minute at Carrie Ann's side. "Did the Easter Bunny bring me some candy?"

Carrie Ann untangled the covers from her and Tessa. "Let's go see. I'm hoping the Easter Bunny brought me some coffee."

When they got to the hallway, Sara was coming up the stairs. "Did you girls wake your aunt?"

"It's okay. I want to see what the Easter Bunny brought too."

Donna stood in the kitchen pouring cups of steaming coffee. The girls raced to give her hugs before they scrambled for the baskets on the table. Squeals echoed through the house as they searched for the treats Sara had hidden while they were sleeping.

"I found one!"

"I got a chocolate bunny!"

"Mom, Jocelyn's taking all the good stuff."

Donna had made her famous caramel rolls. After all the chocolate eggs and treats had been discovered and sampled, they ate rolls and scrambled eggs with sausage. The adults lingered over the meal with coffee and a little chocolate. Then Sara ushered the girls downstairs to wash up and put on their new Easter dresses for church.

Carrie Ann went to the bathroom. She still was not feeling well, but with an incredible sense of relief, she saw she'd started her period. No pregnancy. She hoped the crampy, uncomfortable feeling would go away before church so she could enjoy the worship service.

She dressed in her new American dress and admired herself in the mirror. The mango-and-white-striped halter dress had a gathered ruffle, and was much shorter and more revealing than anything she wore in Columbia, but still modest according to American standards.

Her mom had bought a lacey shrug to wear over the dress. "Sometimes it's a little cool on Easter morning," she said, justifying the extra purchase.

When Carrie heard Jocelyn and Tessa tromping up the stairs, she hurried down the hall to see them. "Don't you two look beautiful?"

The girls pirouetted, twirling their skirts for her. Jocelyn's dress was a sophisticated black and white, Tessa's pink and ruffled. Each of them clutched a little pink silk purse. Carrie Ann dropped a handful of jingly coins into each bag so the girls would have something to put in the offering plate.

The sanctuary at Maple Valley Fellowship was filled to capacity. The music was spectacular, especially after worshiping in a small church in Bogotá. But during the sermon Carrie Ann wondered if she squirmed as much as the two little girls. She couldn't find a comfortable position. The cramping that had begun that morning was now twisting through her whole midsection—sharp, rolling bands of pain.

When the service was over, she sighed with relief. Several people stopped to greet her. She was in a hurry to get outside, but pasted on a smile as she returned the greetings. When she and her mom finally reached the car, she sank down in the seat with a moan.

"Are you okay?" her mom asked, eyes filled with concern.

"It's nothing, Mom. I started my period and it's a little rougher than usual. Probably 'cause I haven't had one for a while. You know how irregular I am. I'm just frustrated. I want to enjoy Sara and the girls while they're here. I could have stayed in Columbia to be sick."

"But in Columbia you don't have me to bring you a heating pad and a cup of tea. Let's get you home and you can lie down for a bit while Sara and I finish up dinner."

"Sounds good." Carrie Ann leaned her head back and closed her eyes as the car traveled the short distance.

At the house, Carrie Ann went directly inside, shed her dress and lay on the bed. Her mother brought the heating pad, plugged it in, and Carrie Ann laid it across her abdomen. Through a fog of pain she could hear both Donna and Sara giving the girls strict orders not to bother her. She pulled up the blankets and slept.

Her mom woke her an hour later for a dinner of ham, cheesy potatoes, salad, fresh asparagus, rolls, and the promise of a cake in the shape of a bunny for dessert. Carrie Ann tried to eat, but the pain hadn't lessened while she slept; it had increased. Donna cast worried glances as she fielded Jocelyn and Tessa's questions and visited with Sara.

Carrie Ann finally pushed her half-eaten meal away, trying not to think of the food that would be thrown out, and how it would feed three street children for a day. "Mom, do you mind if I go back and lie down?"

"Of course not, dear. Can I get you something else? Did you take some Tylenol? Do you have the heating pad on?"

"No, I'm fine." Carrie Ann held on to the table as she lurched out of her chair.

"Why is Aunt Carrie Ann sick?" Tessa whined.

"She's not sick, she just has a period." Jocelyn spoke with the air of someone who knows something very important. Her mom shot her a warning glance.

Carrie Ann stumbled back to the bedroom and lay on the bed, but sleep eluded her. She tried to pray, but "Help me" was about all she could get out. She was dimly aware of the girls running up and down the hall. Sometimes they would pause outside her door and whisper. She wished she could get up and play with them, but the pain held her with a heavy hand.

Sometime in the afternoon she felt the urge to use the restroom and tried to rise. With horror, she looked at the spot where she had been lying.

"Mom! Mom! Come here, please. I think something is wrong."

Donna hurried into the bedroom. Her eyes widened when she saw the bed sheet soaked with blood. "Oh, honey. I think we better take a trip to the emergency room."

Carrie Ann held on to the dresser. "I need to go to the bathroom."

Her mom pulled some clean underwear and a pair of jogging pants out of her drawer. "Do you need me to carry you?"

"No, I can make it." Carrie Ann used the furniture and the wall to support herself as she made her way to the bathroom. She sat on the toilet, peeled off the blood-soaked clothes, and threw them in the bathtub. She would rinse them out later. With arms that felt like noodles, she pulled on the clean clothes her mother gave her.

Donna held her arm and guided her to the car. "I told Sara where we were going. She's putting the girls down for a rest. They were up so early. They'll still be here when we get back."

Carrie Ann leaned back in the seat. Trees and houses spun by the window in a frenzied blur. She closed her eyes. The car stopped and almost simultaneously, it seemed, the passenger door flew open. Her mother eased her out, then half carried her to the automatic doors into the emergency room.

"We need a wheelchair." Her mother's voice sounded far away.

Carrie Ann's world faded into blackness.

CHAPTER 44

A young woman in green scrubs responded to Donna's urgent plea and slid Carrie Ann into a wheelchair. She guided it through a set of swinging doors as another nurse met them and rapidly fired questions at Donna. "Name? Age? When did the bleeding start? What was the date of her last period?"

Donna answered the questions the best she could, hating the fact that Carrie Ann had been so far away and she knew so few details of her life. Her daughter remained slumped in the chair, unresponsive.

"Is she pregnant?"

"No," Donna answered quickly. Then, like a punch in the stomach, she remembered the reason for Carrie Ann's visit home. "Umm, maybe … it's a possibility. My daughter was raped."

"When? Was she checked by a physician? Was it reported to the police?"

"She's a missionary in Bogotá, Columbia, and she saw a doctor there after it happened. I'm not sure of the date. Sometime in March. She flew in Friday night and hasn't really felt well since she's been home. We thought it was jet lag and emotional exhaustion from the trauma. I should have brought her in sooner." Tears trickled down her cheeks. Angrily, she brushed them away. She needed to stay strong for Carrie Ann.

While the nurse continued to take information, two others moved Carrie Ann to an examination table and started an IV. A tall woman with dark hair hurried in. She took the chart and skimmed it with a practiced eye. She looked at Donna. "You are …?"

"Her mother." Donna moved forward when she realized this was the physician. "Do you think this might have something to do with the rape?"

The woman's gaze was steady, but kind. "We won't know until we do an examination. I'm Dr. Beth Stanley," she said, extending her hand. "Why don't you have a seat there? We'll find out what's wrong as quickly as possible."

Donna sat on the straight plastic chair at the side of the room. Several people were gathered around the table now, working in a well-practiced synchronization.

"Blood pressure is 100 over 70, pulse is 75 ..."

Two of the nurses covered Carrie Ann with a paper sheet, slid off the jogging pants, and placed them in a bag. Donna held out her hand for the clothes and clutched them on her lap. It had only been a few weeks earlier she waited in this same hospital with Josh and Stephani. Fear gripped her and she wanted to shout, *Fix her up and let us go home!*

When Dr. Stanley finished the exam, she washed her hands in the small sink and turned to Donna. "I want to do an ultrasound. See for sure what's going on."

"Mom?" Carrie Ann's voice was weak, but she was awake. "What are they doing?"

Donna stood and went to her side. "They're going to do an ultrasound, honey, to find out what's wrong. Hang in there. They'll take care of you and you'll be fine. I'm right here."

"I'm sorry I ruined Easter." Her voice was almost a whisper.

"Don't talk that way. I'm glad you're home so I can take care of you. This would be a nightmare if you were in Bogotá."

A nurse shouldered her way in front of Donna. "Mom, can you have a seat over there? We need to bring in the ultrasound machine."

Donna gave Carrie Ann's hand a squeeze and sat down again. She knew she should call Sara and let her know what was going on, but there was nothing to tell her yet. She pushed the fear down and began to pray.

Minutes into the ultrasound, Dr. Stanley nodded as if something had been confirmed. She ran the instrument over Carrie Ann's abdomen a few more times, then handed it to one of the other nurses and leaned close to Carrie Ann's ear.

Donna stood to listen and pushed down the emotion rising in her throat.

"Carrie Ann?"

Carrie Ann's blue eyes opened and she blinked several times.

"You had a tubal pregnancy. Unfortunately, it went undetected and the tube ruptured. We need to take you into surgery immediately to repair it and remove the tissue. Are you able to sign the consent forms?"

"My mom ..." Her head turned to the side and her eyes closed.

Pregnancy. Ruptured. Surgery. Donna struggled to take in all the information. Forms were thrust into her hands to sign. A bustle of activity surrounded them as they prepped her daughter for surgery.

The doctor explained the procedure to Carrie Ann, although she didn't appear to be awake. Donna moved to her daughter's side again. "I'll be right here, honey. You be strong."

When they wheeled Carrie Ann down the hallway and out of sight, Donna yearned to race after her. A young nurse's aide touched her arm.

"Would you like me to take you to the surgical waiting room?"

Donna nodded and followed her through a maze of hallways and swinging doors. The surgical waiting room had comfortable chairs, but no one looked comfortable. An elderly man seemed to be studying the tank of tropical fish. Magazines filled the lap of a young woman, but she wasn't reading. A couple paced near the area where you could help yourself to coffee or soft drinks. Donna sank down into one of the chairs.

The aide stood by her chair. "Can I get you some coffee or juice or soda?"

Donna shook her head. "I'll be fine, thanks. I'm going to make some calls and let the rest of the family know what's going on."

"If you need something, just ask at the desk. We'll keep you informed." The aide turned and her white sneakers squeaked on the waxed floor as she bustled off.

Sara answered on the first ring, probably sitting with it in her hand.

Donna took a deep breath, hoping it would steady her. "Sara, I've got some hard things to tell you."

"What, Mom?" Sara's voice sounded fearful.

"Carrie Ann didn't come home on an impulse. Hope for the Nations sent her. She was raped one night when she went to help one of her students. They sent her home to heal emotionally. She didn't know until just now, but the rape resulted in a tubal pregnancy. The tube ruptured and they've taken her into surgery."

Sara gasped. "Raped? Are you serious? When did this happen? Why didn't she say anything?"

"I don't think she was ready to talk about it. She would have told you eventually, she just needed some time."

"Will she be okay? They're doing surgery now?" Sara's voice trembled over the phone.

"Yes, they took her as soon as they knew what it was. They need to get the bleeding stopped. I had to sign for permission to give her blood if she needs it. What a blessing she was here and not in Columbia when this happened. We might have lost her ..." Donna's voice trailed off and the "too" was left hanging in the air.

"I'm coming to the hospital, Mom. Where are you?"

"No, that isn't necessary. I don't know how long the surgery will take, and then she'll be in recovery for awhile."

"Doesn't matter. I'm coming. I'll get the girls a bite to eat and we'll wait with you. I want to see Carrie Ann as soon as I can."

"Pray, Sara. Pray that she'll be okay."

"I will, Mom. You know I will."

Donna closed the phone and cradled it in her hand for a moment as if it were a touch from her oldest daughter. She needed to call Josh, but didn't know how he would react. As difficult as it was for her to be in the hospital with all the memories, it would be worse for him and Stephani. He'd been so angry the last time she'd seen him; he might not even talk to her. But he had a right to know. She punched in the numbers. The phone rang several times before she got his voicemail.

She took a deep breath and talked fast. "Josh, please listen to me carefully. Carrie Ann is in the hospital, in surgery right now. I thought you'd want to know." She closed the phone.

Within a few minutes, her phone rang and Josh's voice boomed in her ear. "Surgery? For what? What's going on? She was fine Friday night."

"She was raped in Columbia, Josh." Donna swallowed the lump in her throat and continued. "She had a tubal pregnancy and it ruptured. She's in surgery to repair the damage and stop the bleeding."

Josh's voice exploded over the phone. "Raped? Why didn't she tell us?"

"She's hurting, Son. And I don't think she wanted to add anything to the burden you already have."

"She's at Memorial?"

"Yes. I'm in the surgical waiting room. You don't have to come down. I understand."

"I'll be there in ten minutes."

For the second time, Donna closed the phone and held it tightly. Then she bowed her head and poured out her heart to the only one who could make things right.

CHAPTER 45

J osh gripped the phone and resisted the urge to throw it against the wall. The entire Easter Sunday had been a disaster. Stephani had begged him to go with her to church that morning. She'd even offered to attend one of Maple Valley's various other churches so they wouldn't risk seeing his mom. Josh refused, telling her she could go by herself. So she did.

For dinner, Stephani had suggested they roast a ham, but neither of them felt like eating. It was their first holiday without Isaiah and nothing was right. They finally ended up fixing sandwiches, and Josh ate in front of his computer.

Stephani looked up from the Sunday paper as Josh walked into the living room. "Who was on the phone?"

"Mom. Carrie Ann's in the hospital having surgery."

"What?" Stephani dropped the paper.

"I can't believe it. Mom said she was raped in Columbia. She ended up with a tubal pregnancy that ruptured. I've got to go to the hospital, Steph. She's my twin sister. I need to be there for her."

They walked into the kitchen and Stephani stood close by as he covered his half-eaten sandwich with plastic wrap and shoved it into the fridge.

"I'll go with you."

"Let's go now." Josh grabbed his keys from the hook by the door. Stephani slid her feet into her shoes and followed him out the door.

He chose the most direct route to the hospital. He'd avoided this road up until now, driving a longer route to work. Now he had to walk through those same doors that he walked out of two months before— without his son. And he had to face his mom. Anger bubbled within him. Maybe he could wait in a different room and see Carrie Ann without seeing his mother.

He parked the car, stepped out, and started walking toward the hospital before he realized Stephani was still sitting in the car. He swerved back and opened her door. "Are you coming?"

"This is hard for me, Josh."

Remorse washed over him. He wasn't the only one hurting. "It's hard for me too. Do you want to go back home?"

"No, I'll come. Just give me a moment."

Josh waited. He glanced at his wife and realized she was praying. For the briefest of moments, Josh wished he could pray too.

"Okay." Stephani had a look of resolution on her face. When she stood, her back was straight and her chin up. Josh slipped his hand into hers and, together, they walked into the hospital.

When they reached the waiting room, it took a few minutes for Josh to spot his mom. She sat by herself in a chair by the wall, head bowed, eyes closed. Someone else might think she was dozing. Josh knew better.

An image of her kneeling at his bedside flashed before him. Every single night growing up, his mother came in and prayed for him. He never doubted her love or God's love for him—until two months ago. He took a deep breath, straightened his shoulders, and walked across the room, putting his hand on her shoulder. "Mom, I'm here."

She looked up, and the love that flooded her face caused a wrench of guilt in his gut.

"Any word yet?" Josh sat down beside her.

"No. I was hoping someone would come out and talk to me by now. It's been over an hour since they took her to surgery. How are you, Josh?" Her eyes searched his.

Josh looked away. "I'm doing okay. This is all so hard to take in."

Stephani stepped up and Donna stood and gave her a hug. "You didn't have to come, honey. I know this is difficult for you."

"We wanted to be here, Donna. For you and for Carrie Ann."

Stephani sat down in the chair next to his mom, and the three of them settled into an uncomfortable silence. A nearby TV played music from a local production of an Easter play. His mom's foot tapped to the music. Waiting. For the second time that day, Josh wished he could pray. He walked across the room to the window. A flower bed bursting with tulips and daffodils bordered the wall outside. The red and yellow blossoms and green foliage were a cheerful contrast to the dark brick behind them. And the dark sorrow within. As he thought about his sister, his hands knotted into fists inside his pockets. He walked back and sat down.

"Tell me about the rape. How did it happen?"

"Josh, we don't need to know details." Stephani's voice held a hint of scolding.

"I don't want details about the rape itself, I want to know how Hope for the Nations let this happen. Carrie Ann's a young woman. Why wasn't someone with her? Why wasn't she protected?"

His mom wiggled in her chair. Clearly, she didn't want to talk about it.

"Carrie Ann said it happened when she went to look for one of her students. She wasn't following policy when she left the mission in search of the boy, but she felt she needed to find him. She thought he was in danger. Hope for the Nations is in no way at fault. Jeremiah and Rose care a great deal about your sister. They did everything they could to protect her. They were both gone to a meeting when Carrie Ann decided to traipse across Bogotá. After it happened, she went to them first. Rose took her to the doctor, and they all went to the police. Then Jeremiah worked it out so she could come home for her furlough early, so she could heal from the ordeal."

"Did they catch who did it?"

Donna shook her head. "They reported it; that's all they could do."

"They couldn't find a rapist? That's atrocious. I hope she's not planning to go back."

"I understand, Josh. I had the same reaction. But your sister isn't a little girl anymore. It's her decision. She plans on taking her furlough and then resuming her work there."

"How can she do that?"

No one answered Josh's question. When a dark-haired woman entered, a surgical mask dangling at her throat, his mom stood. "That's her doctor."

The woman paused at the desk and the nurse called, "Family of Carrie Ann Nelson." They all trailed over.

His mom spoke up first. "This is my son, Josh, and his wife, Stephani. How's my daughter?"

The doctor's eyes looked weary. "The surgery went well and Carrie Ann is stable for now. Let's go into a conference room where we can visit."

She led them to a tiny room crowded with chairs. His mom sat down, Stephani stood beside her, and Josh hovered at the door.

"The surgery went as planned. We repaired the fallopian tube and stopped the bleeding. We didn't need to give her blood during the surgery, but it may still be necessary. Of course, the one fallopian tube will no longer be functional, so her chances of conceiving in the future are diminished. We'll let her mother see her now, but I'm going to ask the rest of you to wait until she's out of recovery. She'll probably be there another forty-five minutes. After she's taken to her room, you'll be able to see her, but the most important thing now is to let her rest and heal."

Josh stood aside as the doctor led his mom back to see Carrie Ann.

When he and Stephani returned to the waiting room, Sara had arrived. She hurried up to him, slightly out of breath, the two girls trailing behind like some kind of stair-step parade.

"Is she out of surgery yet?"

Josh nodded. "She's in recovery now. Mom went back to see her. I guess the surgery was successful. She said they repaired things and stopped the bleeding."

Tessa tugged at her mom's coat. "Can we get the markers out?"

Sara rummaged around in her bag and pulled out a box of markers and two notebooks. The girls plunked down on the floor and argued over who got the blue marker. Stephani lowered herself to the floor and watched the girls draw.

"You doing okay?" Sara's eyes bore into Josh, her voice soft and level.

"I keep busy at work. My goal is to make it through the days. It was nice seeing Carrie Ann on Friday night. We had a good time."

"You could have seen her all day today too."

"Don't you start on me, Sara," Josh growled.

"Have you filed the lawsuit yet?"

"Yeah." Josh crossed his arms across his chest. "We filed the lawsuit. We're hoping that justice gets served."

Tessa squirmed in between them and peered up. "Uncle Josh, are you still sad?"

Josh knelt down by the little girl and his voice softened. "Yes, honey, I'm still sad."

"I am too." She gave him a motherly pat on his shoulder. "But Jesus will make us feel better." She skipped off to look at the fish tank.

Josh turned to Sara and snorted. "Jesus isn't doing much to make me feel better."

"Healing takes time, Josh."

"What do you know, Sara? You still have your girls."

Josh knew he was being cruel, but he didn't care. He walked over to the window and stared out, wishing he could be anywhere but here, with anyone but his family.

CHAPTER 46

The band played an upbeat melody as a group of energetic song leaders sang a lively, but unfamiliar song. Everyone around her stood, so Emily did too. Although the words appeared on a large screen, she found it hard to sing along. A tiny sprout of guilt made its way to the surface. Maybe she shouldn't be here. Maybe she'd done too much wrong. But then she remembered. Jesus had atoned for her. He'd paid the price. She joined the congregation for the chorus and sang with gusto.

When faced with the dilemma of how to spend Easter Sunday, she'd decided to take her sister's advice and go to the church where Trevor's group had given the play. Walking into the huge auditorium, she fought down the fluttering in her stomach and smiled back at the people who greeted her warmly. She sat not far from the entrance and studied the program she'd been handed. There was a card inserted into the bulletin to fill out with name, address, and phone number. Emily filled it out and checked the box marked *first time visitor.*

When the music ended and everyone sat down, a well-dressed man walked to the center of the stage. Emily listened eagerly to the message on Jesus' resurrection. How could she have missed the truth for so many years? When the pastor prayed, Emily prayed along with him and she felt a connection—with the other people in the church and with God.

After the last song ended, Emily sat for a minute as people around her gathered up bulletins, Bibles, and purses. She felt like she had been starving for many years and now had finished her first meal. She knew she was full, but she still wanted more. She picked up her purse and surveyed the crowd to see if there was anyone she knew. From a distance, she saw Donna with two other women and two little girls, maybe daughters and granddaughters.

How wonderful to be part of a large family sitting down to an Easter dinner, she thought.

She wondered where Nate was, what he was eating, and who he was with. A wave of longing for her husband washed over her. Maybe she would call him tonight. She needed to talk to him about the lawsuit anyway.

Back at home, Emily took vegetables out of the fridge to make a salad. She laid out onions, tomatoes, and mushrooms on a cutting board as Minnie wound back and forth between her legs. She almost tripped over the ball of fur as she stepped between the sink and the refrigerator. Minnie obviously needed her attention, so Emily put the salad aside and sat down. The kitten leaped onto her lap and rubbed her soft gray nose on Emily's chin. She'd recovered completely from her alcohol poisoning and seemed more precious than ever. In the weeks since Emily had rescued her, she'd grown a great deal and was almost an adult, with long, silky gray fur and those wide amber-colored eyes.

"What would I do without you, Minnie?" Emily whispered, burying her face in the kitten's fluffy neck. Minnie's rumbling purr was the only answer.

Later, after she had eaten her salad, she called Andrea. "Happy Easter!" she sang out when her sister answered.

"Happy Easter to you, Little Sis. What are you doing to celebrate?"

"I went to church this morning."

"That's great. Was it a good service?"

Emily paused, looking for words to describe feelings that were still new. "Yes. It's kind of odd. I have more going wrong in my life than ever before, but I feel kind of free, you know?"

"I know exactly." Andrea's voice became muffled for a minute. "Brian, leave those rolls alone." Coming back to Emily she asked, "Have you seen Nate?"

Emily's euphoric mood dampened. "No, not yet."

"And have you called a lawyer?"

"No." Emily felt like a chastened child.

"You need to get that done. This lawsuit will not go away by itself."

Emily leaned on the table and used her free hand to massage her neck. "I know. Work was hectic last week and I didn't want to think about it. I'll call them both tomorrow, first thing."

"Is Jim still on your case at work?"

"Oh, yeah. Some things never change. He hasn't found any more major mistakes, though. I think I'm able to focus a little better. How about you? Still have that belligerent twelve-year-old you were working with?"

Sharing bits and pieces of their lives had always been easy with the two girls and now, Emily realized, it was even sweeter. Andrea prayed with her before they concluded the call and the words washed over her like warm healing oil.

Still holding the phone in her hand, she gazed out the window. It was too nice a day to waste inside. The bright April sunshine beckoned to her. She changed to a pair of shorts and a tank top and laced up her Nikes. With a last pat for Minnie, she left the house. Without really knowing why, she turned south instead of north and followed a route through the residential area. She stopped after three miles and pulled a bottle off her hydration belt and drank, taking a moment to enjoy the newly leafed trees and spring flowers.

Why not just turn east here and run past Stan's house and see Nate? It was only a few blocks further. She could drop in, casually wish him a happy Easter, and tell him about the lawsuit. He might know a good lawyer or have some ideas about what to do. She could even tell him about praying to receive Christ. She turned and jogged east.

As she approached Stan's house, Emily slowed to a walk. The older, two-story home had faded green paint and a front porch that leaned slightly to the left. The shrubbery and lawn looked overgrown and neglected. She paused and took another drink before she turned up the sidewalk.

At that moment, the door opened and a young woman came hurrying out. She glanced in Emily's direction and, with a toss of her curly auburn hair, got into a blue Chevy and drove off.

Emily stood staring after her for a minute, then pivoted and sprinted back the way she came. Nate wouldn't be entertaining a client at his house on Easter Sunday. If she wasn't a client, who was she and why was she coming out of the house where Nate lived? The questions jostled through her brain as she ran, but there were no answers.

CHAPTER 47

Donna watched the nurse wrap a blood pressure cuff around Carrie Ann's slender arm. She appeared to be sleeping, but occasionally her eyelids would flicker. Donna held one limp hand and studied her daughter until her blue eyes opened.

"Mom?" Her lips barely moved, the question softer than a whisper.

Donna squeezed the hand she held. "I'm right here, honey."

"Thanks." Carrie Ann's eyes closed and she slept again.

When two orderlies in dark blue scrubs came to wheel her upstairs, Donna went to the surgery waiting room to let the rest of the family know. The setting sun cast a golden glow on the waiting room floor. Josh stood with his back to everyone, staring out the window. Stephani crouched on the floor with Jocelyn and Tessa, coloring. Sara sat nearby, leaning over to see the pictures. Donna watched them for a moment before she approached.

Jocelyn squealed, "Grandma!" She and Tessa reached her at the same time and wrapped themselves around her as if it had been weeks instead of hours since they had seen her.

"Is Aunt Carrie Ann okay? Can she come home now?" Tessa pulled at Donna's shirt, her little face wrinkled with concern.

By this time all the adults, including Josh, had gathered in a circle around Donna. "She's going to her room—six seventeen. She's doing fine, but she's very sleepy. I'm sure they have her on pain meds. No, she can't come home today, Tessa. She needs rest so she can get better."

"Can we go see her?" Jocelyn asked, her voice wavering just a little.

"Yes." Donna stroked Jocelyn's hair. "Everyone can go up to her room."

Sara scooped up the papers and crayons and took each girl by the hand. "We'll go up for a few minutes, then we'll let Aunt Carrie Ann sleep and the three of us will go back to Grandma's house."

They all crowded into the elevator for the trip to the sixth floor. The private room was across from the nurse's station and the one window overlooked the hospital courtyard, dark now except for the sidewalk lights. Two nurses were busy as they hooked up monitors, hung the IV bag on the stand, and took Carrie Ann's vitals. Sara and the girls crowded in on the far side of the bed. Donna waited near the doorway with Josh and Stephani.

After a few minutes, Sara kissed her sister on the cheek and led her girls from the bedside. Josh and Stephani moved to take their place.

Tessa grumbled, "She didn't wake up to see me."

Donna knelt to hug the girls. "She'll be awake tomorrow." She looked up at Sara and asked, "Are you leaving tonight or tomorrow?"

"I'll wait and leave tomorrow. I've still got a few PTO days I haven't taken. Then I can come by the hospital on my way out of town. What about you? Are you coming home tonight?"

"No, I think I'll stay here. If she wakes up and needs something, I can tend to it."

"Do you want me to get anything for you?"

"No, I'll come home in the morning to shower and change."

"See you tomorrow, then." Sara said her good-byes to Josh and Stephani and walked toward the elevator, the two girls tripping along behind.

Stephani patted Carrie Ann's arm. "We're praying for you."

"She's asleep," Josh muttered.

"Maybe she can hear us. Your mom said she's been awake off and on."

Josh moved away from the bed. "Let's go. Let her rest. We can come back tomorrow."

Stephani looked at Donna. "You're going to stay here by yourself?"

Donna nodded. "You go on. I'll be fine."

Josh and Stephani left, and Donna was once again alone with her daughter and the click and hiss of the machines.

****

Josh pulled the car into the garage and shut it off. He hurried to unlock the kitchen door and followed Stephani inside the house.

Stephani yawned. "I'm going upstairs to read. Coming up?"

Josh shook his head. "I've got some stuff to take care of in the office. You go ahead." He walked into the office and pulled the door shut. After launching the Internet, he read about Bogotá, especially the area where Carrie Ann had been. Photos showed dirty streets and his imagination pictured even filthier people. Images of men with evil desires appeared in his mind and bile rose in his mouth. He went to the kitchen, pulled a Pepsi from the fridge, and gulped some down as his muscles knotted in anger.

I won't let her go back. She needs to stay here where she has family to protect her.

Pacing back and forth, Josh carried on a conversation with his sister in his mind, countering her arguments with the need for protection. Thinking a run might relax his tense muscles and racing mind, he turned on the light in the three-season room. He started the treadmill and listened to the familiar thrummm, thrummm, thrummm of the belt.

A strange sound against the door to the patio distracted him, and he went to investigate. There on the screen was the most incredible insect he'd ever seen. Its delicate double wings spanned at least four inches, the lower two tapering off into an elegant tail. The translucent wings were a soft lime green and each sported a brown spot. Josh held his breath as he opened the inside glass door to get a closer look. Tiny legs clutched the screen as two, long, fuzzy antennae waved at him. Man and insect stared at each other for several long moments, and then the moth released its hold and fluttered away. Josh continued to watch. The outside light spotlighted the insect as he rose higher and higher. Suddenly, from the darkness beyond the garage, an owl swooped into the light, grabbed the moth in its talons, and disappeared into the night.

With a roar, Josh jerked the door open. "Let him go!" he screamed into the dark. There was no answer, only the whisper of a chilly night breeze. The owl was gone, no doubt enjoying the beautiful moth for supper. Rage bubbled as Josh turned inside and grabbed the first thing he saw—a wooden chair Stephani had painted and piled high with pillows. He heaved it toward the door. The chair broke into pieces as it punctured the window. Splintered glass shot forth like a shower of tears and Josh slumped to the floor.

"Josh?" Stephani's slippered feet padded into the room. "What's going on? What happened? Are you okay?"

Josh felt her arms wrap around him and he leaned into her as she rocked him back and forth like a wounded child.

CHAPTER 48

Donna turned to one side, then the other, trying to find a comfortable position. A nurse had showed her how to fold the chair down to make a narrow bed, and she brought her a pillow and blanket. But the soft hums and hisses of the machines, the interruptions from nurses checking on patients, and sounds from Carrie Ann herself, kept Donna awake.

She tried to use the time to pray, but her mind flitted here and there, mostly aching for her family. When she finally drifted off, she dreamed of her husband, David. They were having a picnic somewhere in a grassy meadow. The three children were still small, laughing and running through the field. Then a nurse came in to check Carrie Ann and David was gone again.

"Mom?"

Carrie Ann's voice was a hoarse whisper. Donna swung her legs over the edge of the makeshift bed and took her hand. "I'm here, honey. What do you need?"

"What happened?"

Donna realized her daughter had been so out of it when they rushed her to surgery that, although the procedure had been explained to her, it either hadn't registered, or the pain had washed it away. Donna tried to remember all the medical details as she described the surgery.

Tears trickled down Carrie Ann's cheeks, pale even in the dim light of the hospital room. "Poor little baby."

Donna lowered her head. She hadn't even considered the life that began where it wasn't supposed to be. "You'll have more children, honey. In better circumstances."

Carrie Ann nodded and bit her lower lip. "Mom, will you pray for him?"

Donna's sleep-fuzzy brain tried to grasp Carrie Ann's request. "Pray for Josh? Oh, I am."

"No, Mom. Pray for my ... my attacker. I need to forgive him."

Donna didn't answer. The hums and clicks of the monitoring devices filled the silence.

"Mom?"

Donna squeezed her daughter's hand. Carrie Ann was already at a place she was still making her way towards. Could she submit to obedience? "I'll ask for the strength to do that."

"Okay." A sweet look of peace flooded over her daughter's pale face, and she slept again.

Donna returned to her makeshift bed, but she bowed her head and didn't sleep.

★★★★★★★

Waking was always the worst—slowly becoming conscious and aware that nothing would ever be right again.

Josh looked over at his wife, brown curls framing her face, one hand tucked against her cheek. She looked peaceful. For a second he hated her for that. Remembering the events from the night before, fear rose within him—fear that he could hurt Stephani. The anger within him loomed large and ugly, and he couldn't shake it off.

He scooted out of the bed and went downstairs to start a pot of coffee. He did a quick survey of the destruction in the three-season room. The door looked beyond repair. He picked up a chair leg, but dropped it in disgust. How would he explain this one to the repairman? He got a broom and swept up the broken glass.

Much later, when Stephani came down the stairs, he poured her a glass of juice and held her close for a minute. "Good morning. Did you sleep okay?"

"I guess so. Why?"

"Just asking."

Stephani stepped to the door of the previous night's disaster. "Thanks for cleaning up."

"I'll call someone today to replace that door."

"All right."

"Stephani, I'll get a handle on this anger. Once the trial is over …"

Her steady grey eyes bored into his very soul. "You know, I'm not sure who you're really angry with."

He answered through clenched teeth. "It'll get better. You'll see."

Stephani moved back to the kitchen and set her empty glass on the counter. "Did your mom call?"

"No, Carrie Ann must be doing okay. She would have called if something had gone wrong. I think I'll go to the hospital during lunch. Want to meet me there?"

"Oh, I can't. I'm interviewing someone for the library assistant position at eleven forty-five. Why don't I stop by before I go to the library this morning and then you go at noon? I'll pick up some flowers for her room."

"That's a plan." Josh kissed her cheek, picked up his laptop case, and left.

Jaleen handed him a stack of reports as he walked in. "I added a few things to your calendar." She smiled brightly, but he couldn't bring himself to return the smile. "Meetings Mr. Sturtz set up. And there's another negotiation meeting with the architects at nine-thirty."

Josh's jaw tightened. He didn't need extra things on his calendar. "My sister had emergency surgery on Sunday. I'll be at the hospital over the noon hour."

Jaleen's smile disappeared and her eyes darkened with concern. "What happened? Is she okay?"

Josh didn't want to talk about it, but he tried to be polite. "We think so. We're not going to let her go back to Columbia, though."

"Really? I thought Bogotá was her passion."

Josh scowled and his hands tightened around the reports. "Yeah, but there's lots of ways to do mission work here."

In the office, he pulled the door closed and stacked the mail and reports Jaleen had given him on his desk among the other piles. He pulled up the telephone number of a small home repair service and called.

Josh wished he could avoid the nine-thirty meeting with the architects. Although the entryway window had been resolved, there were some other issues. He felt like every meeting he had gone to, his self-control had slipped a little more. He had lost his temper and shouted at the last meeting. What would he do next?

He waited until the last possible moment before trudging down the hall and sliding into his chair. Paul had already started, going over some changes one of Josh's coworkers felt should be made before they could proceed.

Josh glanced around the table and noticed CJ was absent. Where was he? He pulled himself back to the business at hand, but couldn't focus on the discussion. He kept quiet, his thoughts on his sister.

At the conclusion of the meeting, Josh turned to the architect sitting next to him. "Where's CJ, uh, Curtis?"

"Williamson? I think he's been pulled to work on another project we have going in Kansas City. The three of us," he nodded toward his coworkers, "will wrap up things here in Maple Valley."

"Yeah, okay. The hospital's ready to get going on this." Josh nodded at the architect and walked back toward his office. There was a good possibility he would never see CJ again. And that meant there would never be a resolution to the conflict between them.

The remainder of the morning was spent with emails, phone calls, and attending to small details on a few projects—all unsuccessful distractions from his grief.

****

At noon, Josh plodded across the hospital parking lot. This was even harder without Stephani. But the thought of seeing his twin sister spurred him on. He pushed the button for the elevator and waited.

When he reached Carrie Ann's room, he was relieved to see that no one else was there. She lay sleeping, her brown hair tousled around her. Dark smudges under her eyes made her look like she'd been in a battle. Josh moved a pillow and sat in the squat upholstered chair. He watched his sister as she slept and remembered years ago when he had fought battles for her as they played. She was always the princess and he was the prince, slaying the dragons and giants that threatened her castle.

The picture of the dirty street in Bogotá came again and his hands gripped the arms of the chair. When she needed him most to slay the dragon, he had been two thousand miles away, unable to rescue her. Well, it wouldn't happen again. He had to convince her to stay in Maple Valley where he could protect her.

Carrie Ann's eyelids flickered once, twice, then she fully opened her eyes.

"Josh?"

Her voice was raspy, but a smile spread across her face like morning sunshine spilling over a meadow.

"Hey, Sis. I'm not dorkface today?"

"No, not if you took time to come see me." She propped herself up a bit. "After all, you're the premier engineer of Maple Valley, right?"

"Sure. I guess I should have brought flowers." Josh looked around at the plants and flower arrangements on the night stand.

"Your wife brought me those." She pointed at a bright bouquet in a vase. "Most of those are from people at church. Mom put me on the prayer chain. I think I have enough flowers, but you could bring me chocolate." Carrie Ann moved her head and shoulders, found the remote that controlled the bed, and raised the top portion so she was almost sitting up.

"Need help?" Josh asked.

"Nope, I got it."

"How are you feeling?"

"Like I was hit by three trucks. It even hurts to smile."

"So, don't. Listen, it's probably not the time to talk about it, but you have a degree. I think I can get you a job at Delta Engineering so you can stay in Maple Valley. I know you love Columbia, but there are plenty of opportunities to minister right here. You don't have to be on another continent."

Carrie Ann's mouth tightened into a fierce line and she shook her head. "No, Josh. God called me to Bogotá and I will go back. I'll heal from this surgery, take some time to visit the churches that support me, and go back to do what I was called to do."

Josh felt the anger balling up in his middle again. "It's not safe, Carrie Ann!"

Carrie Ann readjusted her upper body on the pillows and sighed. "You are so angry."

At that point he exploded, using words that stung even his own ears.

Carrie Ann winced. He wasn't sure if it was because of her pain or his language, but at the moment he didn't care.

"First my son is killed right in front of his house. Then my sister is raped. Don't I have a right to be angry? You should be angry too. Look what that man took from you."

"He took nothing from me. He hurt me physically, but I refuse to let him hurt me emotionally. I forgave that man for attacking me, Josh."

Josh sputtered. "Forgave him? How could you? That man violated you and he caused … this." He spit out the last word and gestured toward her bed.

Carrie Ann's eyes darkened to a smoky blue as she leaned toward him. "I had to forgive him. God forgave me. I either accept that He is Lord or I reject Him. If He is Lord of my life, then He is in control. Nothing can happen to me that He doesn't allow."

"He allowed a rape? He allowed Isaiah's death?"

"Josh, your anger's eating you alive. You're angry at Emily Adams, you're angry at Mom, you're angry at my attacker, and now you're angry at me because I'll go back to Columbia and you can't protect me there. But truthfully, you know who you're really mad at? God. You're mad at God."

Josh moved away and stood with his back to her, looking out the window at the courtyard. With muscles tensed and knotted, he felt like a grenade about to detonate. He tried to calm himself with a few deep breaths.

At that moment a nurse bustled in. "Good morning. I see you have another visitor. Is this a boyfriend?"

Carrie Ann gave an exaggerated laugh that ended with a whimper. "That hurt. No, he's my twin brother."

Josh turned and nodded to the short, middle-aged nurse. He watched as she took Carrie Ann's pulse and temperature and asked about her pain level. When she hurried out of the room, he stepped next to the bed.

"I need to get back to work."

"Think on what I said, okay?"

"Yeah, I'll think on it. I'll try to stop by tomorrow to see you."

Josh rushed out of her room and rather than wait for the elevator, ran down six flights of steps.

CHAPTER 49

Nate watched as Nikki almost skipped up the walk.

"Good morning, Nate," she said in a voice bursting with excitement.

"Are you ready to sign the papers to get your house?" Nate asked as he opened the door of the real estate office for her.

"I am so ready. I talked to Kale last night and he has all his toys packed up. Grandma helped him, of course. I've lined up the moving van, and Stan knows he has to help me unload on this end. I'm so glad I chose the blue house. I can't wait to get in and decorate and maybe paint the bedroom beige, with one wall a chocolate brown ..."

Nikki chattered all the way as Nate followed her into the office. He was pleased they were able to close so quickly. The little bungalow would be a perfect home for her and her son.

An hour later, the papers were signed, keys handed over, and the house officially belonged to Nikki. As they walked out of the office, Nate stopped, picked up a newspaper, and tucked it under his arm. Then he turned to Nikki. "Well, what's next for you?"

"Go to the school and get Kale registered. He'll be so excited. He loves his Grandma Cheryl, but we need to be together again. This afternoon I'll head back to Kansas City, pack up, and the moving van will be here on Saturday."

"Good luck, Nikki." Nate held out his hand. "I suppose I'll see you around?"

"Yeah, I'll rope Stan into helping me get furniture arranged. And when Kale and I are settled, we'll invite you over for supper." Nikki unlocked her car doors with the remote, then turned back to him. "It's probably none of my business, but ... you're a real sweet guy, Nate. You need to move back in with your wife. I know what it's like to be without a spouse. You miss her, I can tell."

Nate shrugged his shoulders a little, but didn't answer. How could he tell her that his wife didn't want him anymore?

★★★★★★★

Emily waded through emails and phone messages at her desk. She was determined to be caught up before the end of the day. She'd arrived early and finished balancing the books, carefully checking and rechecking figures. When she finally looked away from her computer, her eyes fell on the picture of Nate. A longing rose, but with it a memory of the auburn-haired woman she'd seen leaving the house where he lived.

I can't do it, Lord. I can't make him love me. Did your death atone for the mess I made of my marriage?

Emily turned back to the computer and closed out the screen. She needed to call a lawyer this morning. Andrea had called on Saturday with several names of lawyers in the Kansas City area she felt were capable and trustworthy. Emily had the list in her purse. She pulled it out and reached for her cell phone.

The first call she made was to Angelina Francisco. Her secretary said Angelina was in court, but she took Emily's name and number and promised she would call back on Tuesday.

Before making another call, Emily picked up her empty coffee cup and headed to the break room for a refill. On the way, she stopped at Shirley's desk to say good morning. As they talked, the front doors swished open and a pretty young woman entered—a woman with curly auburn hair. Emily sucked in her breath and looked for a way to slip out unnoticed.

"Am I in the right place? I need to register my son for school."

"You are." Shirley smiled her best receptionist smile as she reached for the forms. "Did you just move to Maple Valley?"

"I've been here a couple of weeks. I took a job at Memorial Hospital, but my son is still living with his grandparents in Kansas City. I didn't want him to change schools more than once. I just bought a house on Livingston Street, so we're ready to be official residents." She pulled a pen out of her purse and paused, the pen in midair. "My husband was killed in Iraq a year ago. We're still trying to put the pieces of our life back together."

"I'm so sorry." Shirley's smile was replaced by a look of compassion. "Welcome to Maple Valley. I hope it will be a place of healing for you."

"I think it will. My brother lives here, so we'll still have family close."

Emily took in a sharp breath. "Your brother?"

"Yeah. His name's Stan Beyers. Do you know him?"

The woman turned to look at Emily. Did she recognize her as the jogger?

Emily let her breath out. "I think my husband knows Stan." She backed away from the desk and went to the break room to fill her coffee cup. When she returned, the woman was filling out the registration forms and Emily hurried to her office. Nate wasn't involved with the woman; she was Stan's sister. She'd probably been at Stan's house for Easter dinner. And Nate must have sold her the house. Her heart soared. Maybe they still had a chance.

CHAPTER 50

J osh trudged down the path, his shoes making crunching noises on the gravel. He hadn't been to the cemetery since the headstone had been erected. Isaiah wasn't in the cemetery, he knew that. But it seemed like a good place to do some thinking.

One section of the sprawling cemetery was filled with faded white stones leaning in different directions. Simple white crosses marked graves no longer visited. The other section was newer, with shiny granite stones standing over graves still mounded slightly. Isaiah's grave had a simple marker, *Beloved Son*, his name, and the dates of birth and death.

Josh leaned against a tree trunk and slid down until he was sitting on the grass. A gentle breeze carried the fragrance of a honeysuckle vine blooming nearby. Newly emerging leaves on the sturdy shade trees filtered the sunlight, spattering it across the green grass.

Tears trickled down Josh's cheeks. "Oh, Isaiah, my wonderful son, I would give my life, anything, to have you back."

His hand curled around a rock the tree root had pushed from the earth. He threw his arm back and heaved the rock as far as he could.

"God!" he screamed. "Why did you take him? Why did you let it happen? How can I forgive? How can I?"

Josh buried his face in his hands. For a long time he sat, wishing he could escape from the grief and pain that wracked his body. When he finally looked up, his eyes took in row after row of headstones and he wondered how many others had come here looking for answers … looking for solace. But there were no answers … no solace.

He stood and weaved through the headstones to his car. As he drove home, he called the office. "Jaleen, it's Josh. I won't be in for the rest of the day."

"Is it your sister?" Her voice was heavy with concern.

"No, she's doing okay. Something else came up and I need to go home. Take any messages for me. I'll be there in the morning."

Josh pulled in the driveway, parked, and walked behind the garage. There, leaning against the back wall was a ramp—a homemade skateboard ramp that he and Isaiah had built together the weekend before he died—the ramp that Isaiah had used to project himself into the path of Emily's car. A guttural noise escaped his lips as he reached for the wood.

Board by board, he ripped it apart. Splinters stabbed his fingers and a nail ripped through his grey dress pants, but he continued, throwing the pieces in a haphazard pile in the middle of the yard. Then he searched the garage, tossing boxes and garden tools onto the floor. With a swift kick, he knocked a shovel out of the way.

On a shelf behind a bag of charcoal, Josh found some lighter fluid and a dusty propane lighter. He carried the lighter fluid outside and squirted it on the pile in wide swoops, drenching the wood. He tossed the empty container on top of the pile. With a grunt of determination, he touched the propane lighter to a wet section of plywood. It smoldered for a minute before it blazed. The flames rose and licked their way through the pile.

If I threw myself in the flames would I hurt more or less?

Josh heard a car in the driveway and staggered back from the roaring fire, but didn't turn away. A few minutes later his mom was beside him. She stood close, but didn't touch him.

"I went home to shower and change and I'm on my way back to the hospital. I'm not sure why I drove by your house, but I had the feeling I should. I could see smoke from the road."

The heat from the fire was intense, searing his face. *Back away,* he wanted to tell her, but he didn't. He started to tremble and his mother reached for his hand.

"Josh, God forgave you. He forgave you when He went to the cross for you. You have to forgive yourself. You didn't cause Isaiah's accident." His mother's voice carried over the roar of the blaze.

"How? How can I?" The words spilled from the depths of his soul, the pain raw and ugly.

"Accept His atonement."

His mom's words lifted something buried deep within. He collapsed to his knees, head down, and the tears finally came. Her arms went around him, and she held him tightly as he wailed, great gut-wrenching sobs.

CHAPTER 51

Nate unfolded the newspaper. He had thirty minutes before meeting with a new client at the office. The local coffee shop served him a tall cup of coffee and provided a place to catch up on the news. Living at Stan's caused him to miss several things. The daily newspaper was one of them. He read the sports section first, then moved to the local news. He was about to fold up the paper and leave when a small article at the bottom of the page caught his eye:

A wrongful death lawsuit has been filed against the driver of a car that hit and killed a ten-year-old boy in February of this year. The plaintiffs named in the suit, the boy's parents, are Joshua and Stephani Nelson. The defendant, Emily Adams.

The paper dropped to the floor as Nate stood.

Emily ... sued ... she must be devastated.

And he had let her face it alone.

Waves of remorse flooded over him. He glanced at the time on his phone. She would be at work right now. An intense desire to see his wife overrode everything else. He called the real estate office.

"Hi. This is Nate Adams. I have a client coming to meet me in about ten minutes. Is there anyone who can cover for me? I'll give them the list of properties I had in mind for these folks. A family emergency has come up."

"Steve's here. Let me ask."

Nate walked to his car, the phone held to his ear. He slid into the seat and started the engine, but waited to back the car out.

Steve Larson's voice came on the phone. "Hey, Nate. Yeah, I'll take your clients. But you'll owe me big time. What were you going to show them?"

"Just two properties. The two-story on Marsh Road; it's one of our listings. And the split foyer on twenty-second by the high school."

There was a pause and Nate knew Steve was writing the information down. He was a good agent and would take care of the clients well.

"Thanks, Steve, I'll pay you back."

"No problem."

Nate backed out and drove toward the school.

When he got there, he parked his car, but didn't get out. He wasn't sure how Emily would react to him barging in. Since she'd made no effort to contact him in the weeks he'd been gone, maybe she'd tell him to get out. But if he sat any longer, he'd talk himself out of seeing her at all. He stepped out of the car and walked into the office.

Shirley looked up. "Nate, how are you? We haven't seen you for awhile."

"Hi, Shirley. Is Emily in her office?"

"Yeah, back there slaving away, as always."

Nate walked down the hall trying to bolster his courage with each step. Emily's door was closed, but he could see her through the glass. She was on the phone, obviously visiting with someone. She tipped her head back and laughed. A minute later, she hung up and he pushed the door open.

Her eyes widened in surprise. "Nate, what are you doing here?"

He covered the distance between them in two steps. "Emily, I'm so sorry. I just heard about the lawsuit. I want you to know, I'll support you however I can."

Her blue eyes stared up at him. "Oh, Nate, do you really mean that?"

"Absolutely. I didn't want to interrupt your work, but I had to see you. What if … do you want … maybe I could bring dinner over tonight and we can talk?"

Her eyes filled with tears until they spilled down her cheeks and she reached for a tissue. "I'd like that, Nate. I have so many things to tell you."

He resisted the urge to sweep her into his arms and carry her out of the office with him.

"Sandwiches from Jen's okay? Six-ish?"

"That would be great. And … Nate?"

"Yeah?"

"Thanks. I'll see you soon."

Nate's feet barely touched the floor as he made his way out.

****

The afternoon dragged by for Emily. For the first time since her mistake on the enrollment report, she had trouble concentrating on what she was doing, so she shelved the report and busied herself filing some papers and tidying up her desk. When five o'clock arrived, she grabbed her bag from the drawer and hurried through the outer office.

Shirley raised an eyebrow. "Hot date tonight?"

"Maybe." Emily giggled and scooted out the door.

When she pulled into the driveway, Nate's car was already there and her heart leaped.

"I thought you said six," she teased.

Nate grinned sheepishly and wrinkled his nose in that boyish way she loved.

"I did. I was hungry, I guess."

"Watch out for the attack cat." Emily led the way inside, where Minnie met them. The kitten sniffed at Nate in an off-hand, disinterested way, then retreated to her empty dish.

Nate set a Jen's Deli sack on the table and faced his wife. "Emily, I've behaved like a jerk. After the accident, I wanted everything to return to the way it was. You were hurting and I was selfish. Instead of being compassionate and understanding, I moved out. I ran away."

Emily's breath caught. "I waited for you to call."

"I wrote you a note, asking you to call me."

"A note? Where did you leave it?"

Nate tapped the spot. "Right here on the kitchen table."

Emily shook her head and frowned. "I never saw a note, but I did try to call you. I sent you texts and you never responded. Then I went to Stan's house and when I saw Stan's sister coming out, I thought …"

"Nikki? Oh, Em, there's no one but you. Never has been. Even if we never have kids, I want to spend the rest of my life with you."

Emily needed to hang on to something. She grasped the back of a chair and leaned into it. "After the accident I was so scared. I was afraid to be a mom, afraid I'd do something awful to our child. I should have talked to you about it."

Nate reached out to touch her, a fleeting, butterfly touch. "I can live without kids. I just can't live without you."

A teardrop escaped and dropped onto her arm, the very spot Nate had touched. "I won't do that to you. I'm ready now. I want a family— lots of kids—a family the size of yours."

Nate stepped forward, opened his arms, and Emily melted into the warm, protective circle. His lips against her hair, he whispered, "Forgive me for being such a fool. How can I ever make it up to you?"

Emily rested against his chest and held on to him. He was her shelter in a storm. She shook her head and her face rubbed against the familiar fabric of his shirt. "I learned something very important while we were apart. We can't make up for the wrong we do. It's paid for another way. Atonement."

Nate lifted her shoulders a few inches away from him and looked down at her, his brow wrinkled in puzzlement. "Huh?"

Emily gazed up at the dark eyes she'd missed so much. "I'll explain later." She rose up on her tiptoes and her lips tenderly met his.

Minnie yowled her protest. She hadn't been given her supper, Emily hadn't sat down to pet her, and no one was paying any attention to her at all.

Emily ended the kiss, but leaned her head on Nate's chest, unwilling to step out of his embrace.

"Do you need to feed that noisy cat?" Nate peered down at Minnie who had put her soft paws up on one of Emily's long legs.

Emily pulled back and grabbed the sack of cat food from the pantry. As she filled Minnie's bowl, the doorbell rang.

Nate started for the door. "Expecting someone?"

"No," Emily said hesitantly, wondering if it was more bad news. She gave Minnie a quick pat and gathered her courage before she followed Nate to the door. With God's help, and her husband by her side, she felt she could face anything.

A young couple stood on the stoop. They looked vaguely familiar to Emily, but she couldn't quite place them. The man held the woman protectively, one arm around her shoulders. When Nate opened the door, she peered from behind him and watched the man step forward.

"Is Emily here?"

As she recognized the voice, and then the faces, her knees threatened to buckle. She moved beside Nate and clutched his arm, hoping he would steady her. She tried to talk, but at first her voice failed her. Why were they here? Finally she gasped, "I'm … I'm Emily."

The man spoke carefully as though he had memorized a speech. Every word seemed to take great effort.

"I'm Josh Nelson. This is my wife, Stephani. We've … I've … come to ask your forgiveness. I made a terrible mistake. We shouldn't have filed a lawsuit against you. The accident was unavoidable and we want you to know we don't hold you responsible."

Emily realized she was holding her breath. She didn't trust her emotions or her voice.

"Tomorrow," Josh glanced down at Stephani and she nodded at him, "we're calling the lawyers and the suit will be dropped. I apologize for acting out of my grief instead of doing what I know is right."

Tears of relief and joy filled Emily's eyes and her heart sang. *God heard me. God does answer prayers.* But she still couldn't make her voice work.

Josh looked directly into her eyes and she felt like he was looking into her soul. "We're so sorry for what we've put you through, Emily."

Stephani laid her hand on her husband's arm. Turning to Emily, she gave a tiny teary-eyed smile. "Not only are we asking your forgiveness, my husband and I both want you to know we forgive you for what happened. Please don't spend the rest of your life blaming yourself."

Nate reached out to Josh and for a moment they clasped hands. "Thank you. Thank you both. We are so sorry for your loss. I wish there was something we could do."

Still steadying herself with her hand on Nate's arm, Emily took a deep breath and swallowed hard. "I'm sorry too. That doesn't seem like enough, but I've learned a lot about myself and there's nothing I can do on my own strength to make it okay. I also want you to know that through this, I learned who Jesus is and what atonement means. I belong to him now and I pray for both of you every day."

Josh's head was bowed but he nodded. When he looked up, Emily could detect no trace of anger or resentment in his sorrow-filled blue eyes. "That would have pleased our son. He wanted to lead others to Jesus." He looked away for a moment and wiped his arm across his face. "I've learned a lot about myself too—about how anger can consume your life. I've been angry with you, with myself, with the man who attacked my sister, and most of all, with God."

Emily was trembling, and she felt Nate tighten his grip on her.

Josh raked his hand through his hair and blew out a loud breath. He looked as if that confession had taken every ounce of strength he possessed. His wife stepped closer and wrapped her arm around him.

Emotions crashed over Emily like storm-driven waves, and tears continued to stream down her cheeks. She didn't even try to wipe them away. "You'll never know how much this means to me, your forgiveness, your being here. I know it was a huge sacrifice." She let go of Nate and reached out her hand to Josh. He took her hand in both of his, holding it firmly for a long moment.

Stephani offered her hand, but Emily impulsively stepped forward and enveloped her in a hug, their wet cheeks touching. When she stepped back beside her husband, she could not miss the surprised look on his face.

After the two couples said their good-byes, Josh steered his wife to the car.

Nate opened the door for Emily and followed her inside. His arms wrapped tightly around her and held her close. "I love you, Emily."

"I love you too, Nate, and I couldn't be happier."

"There's just one more thing we need to discuss."

"And that is …"

"I think I need to learn more about this Jesus," he whispered in her ear.

EPILOGUE
SIX YEARS LATER

Emily sat at her desk sorting out the figures on the latest special education report. She tapped out an email to one of the teachers who had yet to get her information turned in, and reread the instructions from the State Department of Education regarding the report.

She glanced out the window to see the kindergarten class outside for their afternoon recess. Her eyes hungrily searched through the whirling, shifting, tumble of children. One small, dark-haired boy was playing tag with a half-dozen other children. He sped out of their reach and skidded to a stop by her window. A wide grin spread across his face when he saw Emily, and he waved his whole arm, jumping up and down. Then a little boy with even darker hair joined him and threw an arm around his shoulder. They both waved one more time before racing off.

An hour later, she laid the report on Jim's desk and walked the short distance to the elementary. She made her way through the maze of hallways to the kindergarten rooms. Her spirits lifted as they did every day when she picked up her son from school.

"Mom! Mom!" Ben's high-pitched voice rang out as he hurried toward her. He was obviously trying not to break the no-running-in-the-hall rule. "Mom, we did centers, and read a story about a fireman, and can Ramon come over to play?"

Emily bent down to hug her lively little boy. "It sounds like you had a wonderful day, Ben. We'll have to talk to Ramon's mom and dad before he can come over. Do you know his last name?"

Ben's face, so like Nate's, wrinkled into a frown. "No, but he's my bestest friend. We like dinosaurs and Transformers and we don't like girls that chase us."

"I can see why you would like him." Emily took her son's hand as they walked down the hall. She listened as Ben continued to chatter away.

"He's from Columbia." Ben relayed this bit of information proudly.

"And he likes cats, so he wants to see Minnie."

Emily puzzled as to how she would call the parents of a classmate, knowing only his first name. Suddenly, Ben dropped her hand and tore across the school yard. He joined hands with his friend and they jumped around in a circle, roaring like two baby dinosaurs.

Emily hurried up to them, ready to scold Ben for breaking away from her and running in such a busy place.

"Mom, this is Ramon," Ben shouted.

Emily looked at the couple standing beside Ben's friend, and a shiver of surprise ran over her. Josh and Stephani Nelson stood on either side of the two boys.

Stephani's eyes lit up as Emily approached and she laid her hand on the dark-skinned boy's shoulder. "It's really nice to see you, Emily. This is our son, Ramon. We just adopted him from Bogotá, Columbia. We're so glad he's got a friend already, and especially glad to know you're his mother."

"God is so good," Emily whispered as a tear slid down her cheek.

"All the time," Josh answered, smiling at her—a smile that held complete forgiveness and reconciliation—atonement.

INDIVIDUAL OR GROUP STUDY GUIDE

1. The death of Isaiah changes the main characters' lives forever and sets them on a different path. What events have changed the path of your life?

2. God prompted Donna to pray for Emily. Have you ever found it difficult to pray for someone? How did you respond?

3. When Emily was hurting the most, she seemed to push Nate away. Why do you think she did this?

4. Josh, Stephani, Emily, Nate, Donna, and Carrie Ann all had someone they needed to forgive. Who do you think it was and why?

5. After Emily worked a day with Habitat for Humanity she said, "How could doing something good go so terribly wrong?" Have you ever done a good deed that turned out wrong?

6. After the accident, Emily and Nate seemed unable to communicate. What advice would you have given them?

7. Isaiah had made a poster that contained a quote from Martin Luther King: *We will not be satisfied until justice rolls like waters and righteousness like a mighty stream.* Do we have the right to pursue justice when it hurts others? How can we balance justice with compassion?

8. Emily trained for the race, but never finished. How does this impact her journey to atonement? Have you ever prepared for something you were unable to complete?

9. The accident changed Emily's desire to have a child. What events in your life have put your dreams on hold or even changed them completely?

10. When the Luna moth was taken by the owl, Josh lost control, but was later comforted by Stephani. Who or what has comforted you when you have felt out of control?

11. Emily's nephew, Trevor, invited her to his play. How did this simple act change things for Emily? Have you ever had the opportunity to change someone's life with a few words or an invitation?

12. Minnie the kitten becomes an integral part of the story. How does she aid in Emily's journey to atonement?

13. Both Emily and Josh had to forgive themselves. Can you recall a time when you had to forgive yourself?

14. How did Carrie Ann's ability to forgive her attacker impact Josh? Have others inspired you to forgive?

15. Josh was angry at God. Has this ever happened to you? How did you resolve it?

16. How did God use a terrible tragedy to bring good in the lives of the characters? How has God done this in your life?

To my readers,

My hope and prayer is that *Atonement for Emily Adams* has in some way blessed, encouraged, challenged, or inspired you. By purchasing a copy of the book, you have blessed and encouraged others too. All author's royalties from this book are to be donated to Pour International for the purpose of building a home for abandoned or orphaned babies and children in Swaziland, Africa. For more information about this organization, you may contact me at srlauthor@mchsi.com. You may also contact ScottBorg@yahoo.com or www.info@pourinternational.org.

For I will pour water on the thirsty land,
and streams on the dry ground;
I will pour out my Spirit on your offspring,
and my blessing on your descendants
(Isaiah 44:3).

Made in the USA
San Bernardino, CA
25 April 2014